D0675741

Also By Barbara Freethy

To Dorothy, a wonderful mother-in-law, and my favorite reader!

SO THIS IS LOVE

The Callaways

BARBARA FREETHY

HYDE
STREET
—PRESS—

HYDE STREET PRESS
Published by Hyde Street Press
1819 Polk Street, Suite 113, San Francisco, California 94109

Printed in the United States of America

Cover design by Damonza.com
Interior book design by KLF Publishing

ISBN 978-0-9906951-1-0

One

Emma Callaway walked quickly down the dark street, wishing she'd arrived at her father's party on time so that she could have gotten a better parking spot, instead of having to hike three blocks uphill. As she passed a lone guy smoking a cigarette in front of a twenty-four-hour market, she felt an odd sense of unease. The man's gaze seemed to follow her down the street, and she picked up her pace.

She wasn't normally afraid to walk at night, especially not in the West Portal neighborhood of San Francisco, but the street was filled mostly with retail and commercial buildings, and at nine o'clock on a Sunday night, they were all closed, making her feel isolated and alone.

She took a quick glance over her shoulder. There was no one following her, but the shadowy street did not ease her nerves. She told herself to stop imagining things. She was just on edge. The last few weeks of work had been challenging, and all she wanted to do was relax and spend a few hours with her family as they celebrated her father's recent promotion to Deputy Chief of Operations for the San Francisco Fire Department.

Emma was enormously proud of her father, but Jack Callaway's latest feat had only set the bar of achievement that much higher for herself and the rest of the Callaway clan. Not that the bar hadn't always been high. Firefighting had been a family tradition for at least four generations, including the current one. Three of her brothers were firefighters, and she'd started out as a firefighter as well, eventually becoming a fire investigator a year earlier.

She loved being an investigator, but it was also frustrating work. Determining whether a fire was arson was one thing, finding the perpetrator and getting justice was another. But she wasn't going to think about her open cases tonight. She just wanted to spend time with her family and friends.

Opening the door to Brady's Bar and Grill, she stepped inside and paused, surprised at the huge crowd. Her father was a popular guy, but it seemed as if half the city had come to toast his latest achievement. A long mahogany bar covered the far wall, and there was a line three deep to get cocktails. The dance floor was packed with people drinking, talking, and laughing, and every table in the main dining room appeared to be full. Gazing to the right side of the restaurant, she saw a cluster of people in the hall by the back room where darts and pool were the games of choice.

Brady's would make a killing tonight, she thought with a smile, not that they didn't do a good business most nights. Brady's was a firefighters' bar. The owner, Harry Brady, had a son, Christian, who was also a firefighter, and it wasn't uncommon for shifts to end with a trip to the bar. Wherever she looked, she saw familiar faces. She was a local girl, and Brady's was a local bar—the kind of place where everyone knew each other's name.

The door opened behind her and a blast of chill November air sent a tingle down her spine. Glancing over her shoulder, that cold quickly turned to heat when she met the deeply intense and penetrating green eyes of Max Harrison, an inspector with the San Francisco Police Department.

Max had transferred from Los Angeles three months earlier, and since then their paths had crossed a few too many times. She'd found Max to be a cocky, territorial detective, whose idea of sharing information was her telling him everything she knew, and him giving nothing in return.

While she didn't like Max's attitude, she couldn't help but appreciate the way he filled out a pair of faded jeans and carried off a brown leather jacket over a cream-colored knit shirt. He was tall and athletically built with a mouth-watering physique, light brown hair that shimmered with gold, and a far too sexy mouth. But she knew trouble when she saw it, and the last thing she needed in her life was man trouble. She'd gotten out of a serious relationship a few months earlier, and she didn't need to dive into another one, especially not with someone who could heat up her body with just one look.

"What are you doing here?" she asked shortly.

Their meetings were always tense, the mix of anger and attraction between them making most of their encounters awkward and uncomfortable. It was bad enough they had to occasionally work together; she didn't want to socialize with him, too.

"Your brother Burke invited me. We play basketball together on Wednesday nights."

Of course they did. The police/fire basketball league was hugely popular. As a female firefighter, she'd always felt left out when it came to the basketball games. She could compete in co-ed softball, but the basketball games were all guys, and that was the way they liked it.

Her phone buzzed, and she pulled it out of her bag, hoping it wasn't work calling.

Frowning, she realized she would have preferred a work text than the one she'd just received. "Damn," she muttered.

"Something wrong?" Max asked.

She returned her phone to the outer pocket of her bag. "It's nothing." She'd barely finished speaking when her phone buzzed again.

"Doesn't sound like nothing," he said, a speculative gleam in his eyes. "Aren't you going to answer it?"

"No."

Her phone buzzed again, and she pulled it out of her bag to turn the ring to silent. As she did so, she saw three texts on the screen. Seriously? Jon hadn't talked to her this much when they were sharing an apartment. "I can't believe this," she muttered, then wished she'd kept her mouth shut as Max's interested gaze settled on hers. "Ex-boyfriend," she explained.

"He must want another chance."

"Men always want what they can't have."

He tipped his head in acknowledgement. "The chase can be appealing."

"I'm not good at playing games."

"I doubt that. I've seen your competitive streak."

"Not when it comes to the games of love," she corrected.

Max smiled, and with that smile came sparks, the fluttering of butterflies in her stomach, the sudden dampness on her palms, the tingly feeling of anticipation shooting down her spine. They weren't standing very far apart, only a few inches between them. It wouldn't take more than a step to put her hands on his solid chest, lean in, raise her face to his.

Whoa!

She put the brakes on her runaway thoughts. She was not going to kiss Max Harrison. That would be reckless and stupid. It would probably also be really good, because he looked like the kind of man who knew how to kiss a woman.

But she was not going to test out that theory.

She couldn't let a little lust get in the way of her common sense. They had to work together. She needed to keep things professional.

Clearing her throat, she said, "I should find my father."

"Isn't that him over there?" Max tipped his head toward the center of the room.

As the crowd parted, she could see her parents, grandparents and several of her siblings seated at a table in the center of the room. Her father was the focus of attention, which didn't surprise her. Jack Callaway had a larger-than-life personality, and like his Irish ancestors, there was nothing he enjoyed more than telling a good story and sharing a pint or two.

With dark brown hair that was now peppered with gray, wide-set blue eyes, and a big booming laugh, Jack had charisma and presence, which was probably why he'd done so well in his career; he was a natural born leader. He was also a man of high integrity and deep commitment to his job, which made him a great role model. She'd admired him for a very long time, not just as a father but also as a firefighter. She could see that same respect in the eyes of everyone at the table.

"That's him," she murmured, glancing back at Max. "You haven't met yet?"

"No. Is that your mother next to him, the pretty blonde in the red dress?"

"That's her."

"You look more like your mother than your father."

"I do take after my mom, but Jack isn't my biological father. He's my stepfather."

Surprise flashed in Max's eyes. "I didn't know that. You have his name."

"It all happened a long time ago. My mother, Lynda, married Jack when I was four years old. He legally adopted me as well as my older sister Nicole three years later. Since we rarely saw my biological father, we were both happy to become Callaways."

"So you and Nicole are biological sisters. What about the rest of your siblings? Who belongs to who?"

"Burke, Aiden, Drew and Sean are my stepbrothers. Their real mother died. Jack was a widow when he met my mom. After they got married, the twins, Shayla and Colton, were born. It's a yours, mine and ours kind of situation, but in reality, we're just one big happy, sometimes crazy, family."

"I can see the pride in your eyes," he commented.

"I love my family. Although I have to admit that being a Callaway comes with expectations. Jack and his father are hard acts to follow."

"From what I've seen, you're up for the challenge."

She tilted her head, giving him a thoughtful look. "Is that a compliment, Harrison?"

"Don't let it go to your head, Callaway. Who else is at your dad's table?"

"Next to my mother are Jack's parents, Eleanor and Patrick. Then there is my baby sister, Shayla. She's a girl genius, only twenty-three and almost done with medical school. And lastly there's Colton, Shayla's twin. He's a rookie firefighter. I'm not sure where the rest of my siblings are."

"It sounds like your siblings are all very high achievers."

"Jack told us the Callaways were born to serve and protect, and most of my siblings have followed that tradition: four in firefighting, one in medicine, one in search and rescue, and one in teaching. My brother Sean is the only one who didn't follow the plan. He's a musician, a fantastic singer and songwriter," she added, not wanting Max to think she wasn't proud of Sean. "He couldn't come tonight, because he's touring the Pacific Northwest."

"How does he get along with your father?"

"They have their moments, but Sean has always moved to a different beat. That's my family. Tell me about yours."

"Nowhere near as interesting," he said shortly.

"Let me be the judge."

"Maybe another time. Can I get you a drink? It looks like the line for drinks is thinning out."

She wasn't surprised he dodged her question. He'd been remarkably reticent when it came to his private life. She'd been tempted to do a little research on him more than once, but she'd always stopped herself. The less she knew about him, the better.

"I'll take a sparkling water if you're going to the bar," she said. "I'm on call this weekend."

"Got it."

As Max turned around, he was almost run down by one of her longtime friends, Tony Moretti.

Tony was an attractive thirty-two-year-old of Italian descent. He and his twin brother, Jarod, had grown up around the corner from her.

"Emma," Tony said, opening his arms wide. "I was hoping you'd be here. I was looking for you at Mass today, but I didn't see you." She gave him a quick hug, aware that Max hadn't actually gone to the bar as he'd proposed. Instead, he lingered a few feet away watching them. She wondered why he was so interested.

"I didn't make it to church this morning," she said, turning her attention to Tony. "I've been really busy at work."

"I couldn't believe someone torched the school at St. Andrew's. Do you have any suspects?"

"Not yet. But I haven't given up."

"Speaking of not giving up, you owe me a date," Tony said. "Remember? I helped you move out of your ex-boyfriend's apartment, and you offered to buy me dinner."

"I do remember. I'm sorry I've been busy."

"So let's make a date."

She saw the determination in Tony's eyes and wondered where it came from. She'd known him since she was six years old, and while they'd been a part of the same social group for years, they'd never gone out alone together, and she wasn't sure she wanted to change that. She liked Tony a lot, but he was a flirt, and she didn't want them to end up in an awkward situation. Their families were friends.

"I'll take a look at my calendar tomorrow, and we'll find a day that works," she said.

"Good."

"What's good?" another man asked.

She smiled at Tony's brother Jarod. The Morettis were fraternal twins but looked almost identical with their dark hair and dark eyes.

"Is my brother hitting on you again, Emma?" Jarod asked.

"We're just talking," she said. "How are you doing? How's the construction business?"

"It's picking up." He cocked his head to the right, giving her a thoughtful look. "I don't think I've seen you since you became an arson investigator. How's that going? Are you working the fire at St. Andrew's?"

"Yes, I am." She paused. "I need to say hello to my dad. I'll talk to you guys later, all right?"

"Don't forget to call me," Tony said as she walked away.

As she moved through the crowd, her gaze drifted across the room. Max had gone to the bar, and she felt relieved that he was no longer watching her. She didn't need any more tension in her life, and that's what Max brought with him every time he came around. Hopefully, he wouldn't stay at the party long.

———➤➤◄◄—

As he waited for their drinks, Max felt restless and irritated. Emma Callaway always got under his skin, and tonight was no exception. Usually, he could keep the attraction between them at bay. Usually, he saw her in uniform or in firefighting gear, her blonde hair covered by a helmet, her slender body in thick, shapeless overalls, but tonight, in a short turquoise dress, her sexy legs bare, her feet encased in high heels, her blonde hair styled, and her blue eyes sparkling under thick black lashes, she'd stolen the breath right out of his chest.

Damn! He really shouldn't have followed up on Burke's invitation. But he'd been tired of his own company, and he'd wanted to see Emma outside of work. Now that they'd seen each other, now that his pulse was racing and his entire body was on edge, he realized his mistake. It was too late to retreat, but he could make this a short night. He'd buy her a drink and then he'd head home. She wouldn't miss him. She had her huge family to keep her company, not to mention all the single guys in the bar.

It would actually be easier if she were dating someone. He didn't poach other men's women. But she was single and so was he. And as much as she annoyed him with her stubbornness and independence, she also impressed him. Besides being beautiful and sexy, she was strong, courageous and smart.

He needed to stay away from her. They couldn't hook up; they had to work together. And they couldn't have a deeper relationship because he wasn't a relationship guy. So the only option was to take a hands-off approach, which would be a lot of easier if he didn't want to touch her so badly. For a second earlier, he'd had the strangest feeling that she wanted to kiss him. He'd probably imagined it.

Max glanced across the room. Emma had made her way to her father's table and was giving her dad a hug. There was a lot of love in the warm smile they exchanged, and for some reason, that shared look tugged at Max's heart, reminding him of a connection he'd lost a long time ago.

The bartender set down his drinks. He was grateful for the interruption. He handed over cash and then headed across the room feeling oddly nervous. He'd never been good at meeting the parents, and even though this wasn't that kind of moment, he still felt tense.

Emma accepted her drink with a cautious smile. "Thanks."

"No problem." He could see various members of the Callaways giving him curious looks. He had a feeling Emma's family was as protective of her as she was of them.

"Let me introduce you," she said. "Dad, this is Max Harrison. He's an inspector with the SFPD. My father, Jack Callaway."

Jack got to his feet to shake Max's hand. His gaze was sharp and direct. "Nice to meet you. Hank Crowley speaks very highly of you."

"I have the utmost respect for Captain Crowley," he replied, at the same time wondering why his mentor had been talking to Jack Callaway about him. Hank knew he preferred to stay under the radar, and if there was ever a man who wasn't under the radar, it was Jack Callaway.

"How do you know Emma?" Jack asked.

"We worked on an arson/homicide case last month."

"Max is a recent transfer from Los Angeles," Emma added. "But maybe you already knew that if you've been talking to Captain Crowley." Emma shot her father a speculative look.

"Hank mentioned that. How does it feel to be home?"

"Home?" Emma interrupted, glancing from her dad to Max. "You're from San Francisco? You never told me that."

"You never asked," he replied.

"Where did you live?"

"On Noriega Street in the Sunset District."

"I had a place on Noriega Street once," Emma's grandmother said.

Max looked across the table at Eleanor Callaway. She had white hair and blue eyes that seemed a little hazy, dreamy almost, as if she wasn't quite present.

"When did you live on Noriega, Grandma?" Emma asked.

"A long time ago," she said. "When your father was in high school. It was such a pretty house." She turned to her husband. "You painted the wall behind our bed blue, remember?"

"Just like your eyes," Patrick said, his loving gaze on his wife.

There was clearly a strong connection between the two, Max thought, wondering what it would be like to be in love and married to someone for fifty years. He couldn't even imagine it.

Eleanor smiled at her husband. "We had so much fun in that house, big dinners with all the kids around the table. I was happy." She paused, her smile fading. "But then we had to leave. We had to move after that bad, bad day."

"No one wants to hear about that," Patrick told his wife, his tone sharp and purposeful.

"It's going to be okay, isn't it?" she asked, worry in her eyes as she gazed at her husband. "You said it would. You promised."

"It's fine," he assured her. "It was a long time ago."

"What was a long time ago?" Emma asked.

"Don't add to the confusion with questions," Patrick said, giving Emma a harsh look.

Emma quickly apologized. "I'm sorry."

"I'm Patrick Callaway," her grandfather said, his attention turning to Max. "And this is my wife Eleanor."

"I'm very happy to meet you both." He wondered how he could extricate himself from a situation that seemed to be turning more awkward by the moment. He had no idea what Emma's grandmother was talking about, but her odd comments seemed to have left everyone at the table speechless.

Eleanor suddenly stiffened, confusion in her expression as she pointed her finger at Max. "You're not Emma's boyfriend. You're not Jon."

"No. I'm Max."

"I like Jon." She gave Emma an annoyed and bewildered look. "Why aren't you with Jon? He always brings me those hard candies."

"Jon and I broke up, Grandma."

"But he loved you. You loved him. You were going to get married and have babies."

Emma cleared her throat. "We decided it wasn't right."

"So this man is your new boyfriend?" Eleanor demanded, not looking at all happy about it.

"No, he's a colleague. We work together sometimes. That's all." She looked relieved when Burke arrived at the table, interrupting their conversation. "Burke," she said with relief. "You're here. And Max is here."

"So I see," Burke said, shaking his hand. "Did you meet everyone?"

"Emma was just introducing me," he replied.

Emma waved her hand toward the other members of her family. "My mom, Lynda, sister, Shayla, brother, Colton."

Her mother and siblings said hello. Colton appeared more interested in whatever he was reading on his phone than the conversation at hand. Shayla gave him a very curious look. Fortunately he did not have to talk to anyone, as a group of people approached the table to offer Jack congratulations.

To give the newcomers more room, Max moved a few steps away. Emma did the same.

"Sorry about that," she said. "My grandmother is in the early stages of Alzheimer's, and we never know what is going to come out of her mouth."

"I'm sorry to hear that she's ill."

"It's hard to watch her deteriorate. She was a very sharp woman when I was younger. I couldn't get anything past her." Emma frowned. "I can't believe she remembered Jon. He hasn't been around the family in months."

"Apparently, the candies he brought her stuck in her head."

"I brought the candies for her birthday. He just took the credit." Emma's gaze drifted back to her grandmother. "I don't know what she was referring to when she alluded to some bad, bad day. It was such an odd thing to say."

"It sounded like your grandfather knew what it was about. He was quick to cut her off."

Her gaze swung back to him, her eyes questioning. "I thought so, too. It's the second time in the last few weeks that Grandma has mentioned a secret, and the second time Grandpa has changed the subject. But I can't imagine what secret she would be keeping.

"Have you asked your grandfather about it?"

"No. You don't ask my grandfather things like that. To be honest, I've always been a little scared of him. He's the only one in the family who ever made me feel like a stepchild."

Her comment surprised him. Emma seemed so confident, so sure of her place in the world, but in this moment he could see uncertainty in her eyes, and he wondered if she had to be good, had to be right, in order to prove herself to her family because she wasn't a Callaway by blood. It might explain why she was so determined to win, to succeed, to be the best at everything.

"Anyway," she said, turning her focus back to him. "How come you never told me you grew up here, and don't say it's because I didn't ask. I spoke to you about Los Angeles and your reason for transferring, and you never said anything about the fact that you were actually coming home."

"I haven't thought of this city as home in a very long time. I left when I was eighteen. That was fourteen years ago."

"Is your family still here?"

"Some of them."

"Why did you leave and why did you come back?" she asked, as she took a sip of her water.

"I left to go to college, and I came back because it was time."

"That's deliberately vague, Harrison."

"Maybe you should take a hint and drop the subject, Callaway."

She gave a dramatic sigh. "Another person with a secret. I seem to be surrounded by them tonight."

He smiled. "I don't know about that. Your Italian boys seemed up front and outgoing."

"The Moretti twins? I've known them forever. They're

not to be taken seriously."

Her dismissive words made him feel oddly better about the interaction he'd witnessed earlier. "Are you sure about that? The first one looked really into you."

"Tony is a huge flirt. He's that way with everyone."

"If you say so."

"I do say so," she said firmly. "What about you? No date tonight?"

"Not tonight."

"You do like to be the man of mystery, don't you?"

"I've heard it adds to my charm."

"Charm? You think you have charm?" she asked doubtfully.

He couldn't help but grin at her disgruntled expression. "Apparently, you don't think so."

"Tonight is the first time I've ever seen you smile. So maybe there's more to you than I thought."

"Maybe there is."

She stared at him, then said, "Well, I don't have time for mystery men. I have my hands full at the moment."

He should be relieved by her answer, but he found himself oddly disappointed.

"I should go and mingle," she added.

"You should," he said, downing his drink. "I have to take off."

"So soon?"

"I have an early morning. Have a good night."

"You, too."

He set his empty glass down on a nearby table and moved quickly through the crowded restaurant. When he stepped outside, he was surprised to see a guy peering into the windows of the bar. He wore jeans and a big sweatshirt with the hood pulled up over his head. The man jerked when he realized Max was looking at him. He turned quickly and walked away.

Uneasiness ran down Max's spine. His car was in the opposite direction, but something made him follow the guy down the street. The man picked up his pace when he reached the corner. Max did the same, but when he jogged around the block, the guy was gone.

Max stopped, frustrated that he'd lost him, even though he didn't really know why he was in pursuit. But he'd trusted his instincts for a very long time, and most of the time his gut did not steer him wrong. Maybe this time, however, his instincts were off. He was on edge. His life was about to change in a big way, and he didn't know if he was ready.

Turning, he walked back the way he'd come. When he reached his car, his phone rang. He pulled it out and saw his mother's number. His stomach muscles clenched.

"Mom? What's up?"

"I just want to make sure you're going to pick me up at eight o'clock tomorrow," she said.

"I promised I would," he replied.

"Don't be late. Your brother has waited long enough for this day."

"I won't be late," he promised. He slipped his phone back into his pocket and then opened his car door and slid behind the wheel, his heart racing a little too fast as he thought about the next morning—about the sixty-mile drive north to the prison where he would pick up his brother.

Two

The fire call came in at three o'clock in the morning on Monday, three hours after the Callaway party ended. Emma had been asleep, lost in a crazy dream that involved her ex-boyfriend Jon, the annoying Inspector Harrison and her grandmother when she'd been awoken by the sound of her cell phone.

It had taken a minute for the bad news to sink in. This wasn't just any fire, it was a fire at Brady's Bar and Grill, and first responders on the scene had determined the fire to be suspicious.

She threw on her clothes and drove back to the bar. She had to park a block away; there was a line of fire engines and police cars blocking the street. As she walked toward the fire, she saw flames shooting out of the roof and through the broken windows. She felt sick to her stomach. The warm, cozy neighborhood bar where she'd spent so many hours was totally engulfed with fire. It seemed a bitter irony that a place so special to the firefighting community was now going up in smoke. A few hours ago there had been dozens of firefighters celebrating her father's promotion. Now there were dozens fighting the blaze.

Was that the point? Had someone wanted to make a statement in a place where firefighters gathered?

Her mind whirled with questions as she drew closer to the scene. She scanned the gathering crowd for anyone who looked out of place or appeared a little too interested or too happy about the fire. It wasn't uncommon for arsonists to stay and watch their handiwork. It was part of the thrill. Some even called the fires in so they could watch the fire trucks come roaring down the street and see the terrified residents pouring out of their homes.

Fortunately, this city block was made up of commercial buildings, with only a few second- and third-floor apartments mixed in, so they didn't have many people to worry about. There were a dozen or so individuals wearing pajamas and robes standing across the street. The adjacent buildings had obviously been evacuated. Fighting fires in San Francisco was always a challenge, as many of the structures shared common walls. A fire could spread through an entire block if it wasn't caught early.

As soon as she arrived on scene, she checked in with Incident Commander Grant Holmes, whom she'd worked under in her firefighting days.

He gave her a tense nod. "Callaway. You got here fast."

"I couldn't believe it was Brady's. We were just here celebrating my father's promotion."

"Looks like it will be the last party here for a while."

"How did it start?"

"We found gasoline cans inside the front and back door. The rear portion of the roof collapsed seconds after the first guys in reported a deceased female. We haven't been able to get her out yet.

Emma's stomach turned over. She knew several of the female servers at Brady's. "Do you have an I.D.?"

"No."

"Has the owner been contacted?" she asked, looking

around for Harry Brady.

"He was here with his son, Christian, but Harry started having chest pains, so the paramedics took him to the hospital."

She was sorry to hear that. "I hope he's okay. This bar is his whole life."

"Let's hope he wasn't the one who burned it down," he said cynically.

She couldn't believe Harry would destroy his livelihood, but as the owner, he would be at the top of her interview list.

As Grant moved away to talk to one of the crew captains, she saw Max walking toward her. He wore the same clothes he'd had on earlier, but his hair was tousled, and there was a shadow of beard on his jaw. He looked even sexier, if that was possible.

"What do you know?" he asked abruptly.

"Not much. There's apparently a female victim. I guess that's why you're here. They haven't been able to retrieve her body." She glanced at the building. "I feel like I'm dreaming. We were just here a few hours ago. Everyone was having a great time. Now, this raging blaze..."

"An interesting irony," Max said. "Firefighters' bar goes up in flames."

He'd jumped to the same suspicion she'd had, that someone had wanted to make a statement to the firefighting community. "It could be a coincidence," she felt compelled to say. "But I will find whoever decided to torch this place. This one isn't just business; it's personal."

Max tilted his head, giving her a thoughtful look.

"What?" she challenged.

"Just thinking that the last two fires were also personal to you—the high school and St. Andrew's Elementary School."

"I grew up in this neighborhood, and all three fires have

been at buildings important to the community, but that's hardly personal to me. It's a matter of geography. It's not unusual for firebugs to work close to home. It adds to the secret thrill that they know something no one else does."

"A logical point. But you have to admit that you're a common denominator."

"So are a lot of people. Thousands of children have gone through St. Andrew's and the high school in the last twenty years." She paused. "Speaking of St. Andrew's, has there been any progress in locating Sister Margaret?"

Margaret Flannery, one of the teaching nuns at St. Andrew's, had disappeared a little over a week ago, right before the fire at the school that had destroyed two classrooms. Sister Margaret had also been a teacher at the high school a decade earlier, a fact that Max had used to link her as an arson suspect. But Emma didn't believe for a second that Sister Margaret was their firebug.

"Unfortunately, no," Max replied. "What about your fire investigation?"

She hated to admit that she was no further ahead on her case, but there were no witnesses to the school fire and no forensic evidence. Her investigation was basically stalled. "Nothing new. I need to focus on this fire. I'm going to talk to the neighbors."

"I'll go with you," he said.

"If you must," she said unenthusiastically.

Her words brought a small smile to his lips. "I can be helpful, Callaway."

"You can also get in the way," she retorted.

"So can you, but don't forget we're on the same side."

Somehow, it never quite seemed that way. Most of the time they were butting heads and challenging each other's results. They needed to find a better way to work together;

she just hadn't come up with one yet.

It didn't take long to speak to the small group of people huddled together. They were shaken up and worried about their apartments. No one had seen anything. They all reported having been woken up by firefighters or cops ordering them to evacuate. By the time they'd gotten outside, the fire was blazing.

Emma jotted down names, addresses and phone numbers. After her first few questions, Max disappeared, and she couldn't help wondering where he'd gone. He usually liked to be right in the middle of the action.

When she'd finished her interviews, she saw Max coming out of an alley between two buildings across the street. She walked over to him. "Where did you go?" she asked suspiciously.

"Just looking around."

"For what?"

He shrugged. "It's probably nothing," he muttered.

"Tell me."

"When I left your father's party, I saw a guy outside of Brady's. He was staring through the windows, and he jumped when I came out, as if he'd been caught doing something he wasn't supposed to be doing. He ran off before I could get a good look at him. He was probably in his twenties. He wore jeans and a gray sweatshirt with a hood up over his head."

She doubted Max would have mentioned the man if he didn't think he was a possible suspect. She didn't like the way Max took over their cases, but she did respect his instincts.

"There's our victim," Max said, moving quickly across the street as two firefighters brought out a body. They set her down on a stretcher.

Emma stepped up next to Max to take a look. The woman's features were shockingly familiar. She gasped, putting a hand to her mouth as waves of nausea ran through her. "It's Sister Margaret," she said.

Max's eyes widened. "Shit!"

It was hard to look at the lifeless body of a woman who had been a mentor to her, but she forced herself to do just that. Every detail was important.

Sister Margaret had very short, white, thin hair. Her face had not burned, but her skin was very white with tints of blue. She wore black loose-fitting slacks that hung in shreds over her burned, blistering legs. What had once been a white button-down shirt was blackened from smoke and dirt. The long sleeves had also been burned away, and her hands and fingers showed only remnants of flesh over the bones.

Emma had to breathe through the urge to vomit. She saw burn victims a lot, but she never got used to it.

"Her hands are burned," Max commented, as he, too, took a good look at her body.

She wanted to say that there was no way Sister Margaret had set the fire, but she couldn't. Had the woman had a secret fascination with fire? Had she gotten caught up in her own work?

There were no other visible wounds from a knife or a gun or any other type of weapon. Had she died from smoke inhalation, or had something else happened?

"The medical examiner should be able to tell us more," Max said, motioning for the paramedics to take the body away.

"I can't believe this," she muttered, watching them load the body into the ambulance. Her mind ran through the clues they'd already accumulated. "Whoever set this fire killed Sister Margaret."

"That's one theory."

"Stop trying to make Sister Margaret the villain," she

said sharply, taking out her anger and pain on Max. "She didn't do this."

"I'm keeping an open mind. Maybe you should do the same instead of letting your personal feelings cloud your judgment."

"My judgment is not clouded," she snapped. "You do your job, and I'll do mine."

"We need to work together."

"Not tonight we don't. You're not cleared to enter the building until the fire is out, but I can get in now."

"Emma, wait," he said, as she turned to leave.

"What?"

His lips tightened. "Be careful."

She didn't know how to take his words, because it almost sounded like he was worried about her.

"I always am," she said, then strode away. She was relieved when the commander gave her clearance to enter the building. Sister Margaret's death had raised the stakes, and she wanted to find the bastard who'd killed her favorite teacher and torched Brady's Bar.

→ ⇒ ⇐ ←

Max watched Emma enter the still-burning building. He couldn't help but admire her courage. The fire was under control, but it wasn't out, and part of the roof had already collapsed, but there was no hesitation in her step. She was a woman on a mission. He wished he could have gone inside with her, but he would have to wait, and he hated to wait. He also hated the fact that Emma would get first crack at the crime scene, but she knew what she was doing, and her goal was to preserve as much evidence as she possibly could. Hopefully, that evidence would take them both in the right direction.

Glancing down at his watch, he realized it was four-thirty in the morning. There was nothing more for him to do at the moment. He would wait until the medical examiner gave him official identification before notifying Sister Margaret's family. That wouldn't happen before tomorrow. He also wouldn't be able to get inside Brady's for a few more hours. He might as well go home and grab a couple of hours' sleep. He had a big day ahead, and he was nowhere near ready for it.

After returning to his apartment, he tumbled into bed. Unfortunately, his mind was too worked up to let him rest. Whenever he caught a new case, he had a rush of adrenaline, and Sister Margaret's death had sent a million questions racing through his brain. He'd originally taken on the case as a favor to his mentor, Captain Hank Crowley. Hank had known Sister Margaret for years, and he hadn't wanted to dump the case onto an already overloaded missing persons detail, so he'd asked Max to investigate.

He'd spent a lot of time interviewing the nun's friends and family since her disappearance, and he'd been hoping for a different outcome. Now that the worst had come true, his investigation would continue in a new direction. Hopefully they would find some DNA or some clue as to who had killed her if, in fact, someone had killed her.

While he appreciated Emma's staunch defense of her former teacher, he couldn't overlook the fact that she'd disappeared right before a fire at her place of employment and now had turned up dead in yet another suspicious fire. If she wasn't the arsonist, she was tied to him or her in some significant way. He just had to figure out the connection.

After three hours of tossing and turning, he took a shower, grabbed some coffee and headed to his mother's house. He arrived at exactly eight a.m. as promised. The front door was open, and as soon as he pulled up, his mom was out of the house and locking the door behind her. She was eager to get on the road. He didn't feel nearly as enthusiastic.

As she walked down the stairs, he couldn't help thinking that she looked more energetic and put together than she had in a long time. She'd lightened her brown hair with blonde highlights and exchanged her usual jeans and sweaters for black slacks and a gray blazer. As she got into the car there was a sparkle in her brown eyes, making her look younger than her fifty-six years. Susan Harrison had been reborn into someone with optimism and energy. He barely recognized her from the tired, weepy, depressed woman she'd been for most of the last two decades.

"I didn't think this day would ever come," she said, as she fastened her seatbelt. "It feels like a lifetime."

It could have been an actual lifetime, he thought, as he put the car back into drive, but fortunately for his brother, the murder charge had been dropped to manslaughter.

"I bought all your brother's favorite foods," his mom continued. "Dinner tonight will be roast beef, mashed potatoes and mixed vegetables, followed by apple pie and ice cream. I haven't cooked like this in years. It felt strange to go to the supermarket and buy for more than one person."

"I'm sure Spencer will love whatever you put on the table."

"You'll come to dinner, too," she said.

"I don't know if I can."

She shot him a dark look. "Don't be ridiculous, Max. This is the first night in forever that we'll be able to eat as a family again. Of course you're coming to dinner. We have a lot to talk about." She drew in a deep breath and let it out. "I hope Spencer is all right. I hate to think of what he's had to go through in that terrible place. I hope prison hasn't damaged him forever."

He hoped the same thing, but he had his doubts.

"I wish we were there already," his mom said. "I can't wait to get my boy home."

He didn't bother to reply, knowing his mother was lost in anticipation of a happy family reunion. His older brother had always been her favorite. Spencer had been twelve when their father took off, and his mom had turned her oldest son into the man of the family. At eight, he hadn't been able to offer her the kind of support she needed. But Spencer had stepped up to the challenge.

Max had looked up to his older brother, too. Later on, as an adult, he'd come to realize that his hero had a few flaws, but he doubted his mother had ever come to that realization. She'd always seen the best in Spencer.

"You're not saying much, Max." His mother gave him a warning look. "I don't want anything to mar this day, so if you've got something negative to say, say it now, before we pick up Spencer."

"I don't have anything negative to say."

"Good. I know things have been complicated and awkward between us all. But we're family, and we're going to be together again, and that's all that matters."

"You're right." He just hoped Spencer would be able to let go of his anger and move on.

Three

——→→→←←←——

Emma entered the kitchen Monday morning, bleary-eyed and exhausted after spending the night digging through the ashes of Brady's Bar and Grill. Her mom and dad were seated at the table along with her older brother Drew.

Her mother immediately rose and pulled out a chair at the table. "Sit," she said. "You look exhausted."

Emma didn't have to be asked twice. She sank into a chair and glanced across the table at her father. "I guess you heard about Brady's?"

Jack nodded, his expression somber. "I spoke to Harry about an hour ago. He's devastated. He could barely speak. His voice was shaking with emotion. I haven't heard him like that since his wife left, and that was twenty years ago."

"Is he all right? I heard he might have had a heart attack."

"Fortunately, he didn't. It was just the stress of the moment. He's home now, resting. Christian is with him. Robert is on his way. We need to find the person who did this, Emma. This was a full out assault on one of our own."

"I know." She suddenly realized how much added pressure would be coming her way.

"Let me know if you need more resources. The investigative unit is short-staffed right now."

"I can handle it."

"If you change your mind—"

"I'll let my boss know, and he'll let you know. First things first. I need to speak to Harry. When I called the house, Christian told me he was sleeping."

"Harry told me he doesn't know anything. He can't imagine who would want to burn down the bar. He said he was the last person to leave, and he didn't see anyone on his way out."

"There was no forced entry, so I need to know who else has access to the building." She paused. "But first I need to take a shower and maybe get some food." She gave her mom a hopeful look.

"I'll make you some eggs," Lynda said with a smile. "Scrambled okay?"

"Perfect."

"I have to get to work," her father said, as he got to his feet. "Drew—we'll talk later?"

Her brother nodded. "Sure."

As Jack left the room, she glanced across the table at her brother. Drew had brown hair like the rest of the males in the family but his eyes were brown, not blue, and today his gaze was filled with dark shadows. She wondered what had brought him home. He didn't spend much time at the house. He lived across the bay and worked long hours flying helicopters for the Coast Guard.

"What were you and Dad talking about?" she asked.

Drew picked up a mug of coffee and took a sip. "None of your business."

"You know that when you tell me that it only makes me more curious."

Her mother set down a tall glass of orange juice in front of her. "Do you want bacon and toast, too, honey?"

"That would be awesome, Mom."

"Spoiled brat," Drew muttered with a smile that belied his harsh words.

"One of the benefits of living at home."

"Aren't you a little old to be living with your parents?"

"Don't tease her," Lynda interjected. "Emma can stay as long as she wants."

"How long will that be?" Drew asked.

"Not too much longer," she said, surprising both him and her mother.

"Really?" her mother asked, as she broke some eggs into a bowl. "I didn't realize you were thinking of leaving, Emma."

"I saw some apartments on Saturday that looked good. I put in an application on one. I should hear today."

"I'll miss having you around," her mother said. "It's been nice."

"It has been nice." She'd been emotionally shaken by her breakup with Jon, and being able to live at home for a few months had helped her heal. But she needed to make a life for herself.

"Well, you don't have to rush," her mom added. "Find something that's right for you."

"I plan on it."

"Where are you looking?" Drew asked.

"Hayes Valley, maybe the Marina if I can afford it. So what are you doing here, Drew?"

Drew ran a hand through his short hair, and there was an odd, strained expression on his face.

"Just checking in with the family," he said.

"Really?" she asked doubtfully.

Before he could reply, her mother set down her breakfast. "I need to run over to Nicole's house. She found Brandon a new doctor, and she wants me to go with her."

"Another new doctor?" Drew asked. "How many has she been to?"

"Your sister is determined to find the right physician for Brandon," Lynda said. "I'll see you both later."

"Thanks for breakfast, Mom," Emma said.

"Anytime, honey. You look tired. I hope you can nap for a few hours before you go back to work."

"I'm going to try." As her mother left the room, she turned back to her brother. "We missed you at Dad's party last night. Where were you?"

"I had things to do."

"Why are you being so vague today?"

"Why are you being so nosy?"

"Because I'm always nosy. You know that."

He grinned. "I'd forgotten."

"So, talk."

He hesitated. "Have you ever had one of those weird moments where you think you recognize someone but you don't know for sure?"

His question was not what she'd expected. "Who did you see?"

"Someone I thought I knew."

She took a bite of her scrambled eggs. Her mom had added onions, avocado and cheese into the scramble. "This is so good. I'd offer you some, but I'm starving."

"I already ate."

"So, this person you thought you saw—what's the mystery? And don't try to tell me there isn't one."

A long silence followed her words, which didn't surprise her. Drew had always been one to keep his own counsel.

"I believed she was dead," he said finally. "In fact, I *know* she was dead. There was a death certificate, an obituary, a funeral." He shook his head. "It had to be someone who just looked like her. Or my mind is playing tricks on me."

"Who was she, Drew? A girlfriend?"

"No," he said quickly. "She was…"

"What?" she prodded when his voice drifted away.

"Just someone I knew for a very short time."

"She obviously made an impression on you, though."

"Because I didn't save her. It was my fault she died." His eyes filled with remembered pain.

She didn't know how to respond. Drew had worked in search and rescue, first for the Navy and then for the Coast Guard. And he'd never shared his work with her, or anyone really. That wasn't his style.

"Forget it," he said. "I don't know why I told you."

"Because you needed to tell someone. They say everyone has a twin. Maybe the person you saw was a relative."

"Yeah, maybe." He took another sip of his coffee and then set it down.

"I can help," she offered. "What was her name?"

"Thanks, but I don't need your help."

"I'm a good investigator, Drew."

"I know that. But you have enough on your plate."

"I can juggle more than one investigation."

"Leave it alone, Emma. I need to figure this out for myself."

"Fine." She took another bite and then said. "Do you remember Sister Margaret?"

"Of course. I spent a lot of hours with her in detention."

She put down her fork. "You did?"

"Sure. Not as many as Aiden, though. I think he had his own seat, along with the Morettis. Tony loved playing jokes on the nuns. Why are you asking about Sister Margaret?"

She hesitated. "It's not official yet, so I shouldn't say anything, but her body was found in the rubble of Brady's Bar."

"Are you serious?"

"Yes. She disappeared about ten days ago, right before the fire at St. Andrew's."

"You don't think she was the arsonist, do you?"

"No, but I'd like to be able to rule it out. Once the medical examiner determines cause of death, that should help."

Drew's eyes narrowed. "You need to be careful, Emma."

"Why does everyone keep telling me that?" she asked with annoyance. "I'm always careful, and I know what I'm doing."

"You don't usually have to deal with murder."

"It's actually not all that uncommon, although the fact that the victim is Sister Margaret is more personally disturbing. But it also motivates me. She was such a kind and sweet woman."

Drew rolled his eyes. "Maybe to you."

"What does that mean?"

"She loved the girls, but she was not nice to the boys."

"I don't remember that."

"That's because you were never in detention."

"Because I never did anything wrong. You and Aiden, on the other hand…"

"It wasn't just us," he said, shaking his head. "She hated all boys. We figured it was because she got dumped at the altar and that's why she became a nun."

Emma frowned. "I never heard that story."

"I'm surprised. It was all over the school."

Perhaps she needed to look at Sister Margaret in a different light.

Drew stood up. "I'm going to take off."

"If you need my help on your missing woman, let me know."

"She's not missing; she's dead," he said firmly, as if needing to convince himself as well as her.

"You've always had good instincts, Drew. You should trust them."

—➤◄—

Max felt restless, impatient, unsettled... They'd been waiting for his brother's release for over an hour, and he wanted to get on with it. His mother was getting more worried by the moment, fearful that something bad might happen at this very late hour and that somehow Spencer would not be released. He had to admit to sharing some of her concern, but he told himself that was just fear talking.

Adrenaline made him pace back and forth in front of the prison gate. As a cop, he'd sent more than a few people to prison, and as a detective, he'd conducted many prison interviews, but today was different. He wasn't here as a police detective, but as a son and a brother, two roles that he'd failed in the last several years.

"Why isn't Spencer coming out?" his mother asked.

"It's just red tape," he reassured her.

"He has to come home now. It's long past time for him to be free. He should have been out years ago. In fact, he never should have gone to prison in the first place."

He could see the accusation in his mother's eyes. She'd always believed he could have done more to free his brother. And Spencer believed the same thing.

"He'll be out soon. We're early. It hasn't been that long."

"You're always calm. I don't understand how you can be so patient."

He'd had to be calm growing up in his family. It was the only way he'd been able to survive the drama of his childhood, his father's affairs and subsequent departure, his mother's hysteria and then depression, his brother's short fuse and ability to find trouble wherever he went.

"I'm confident that he'll be free," he said evenly.

"You were wrong before. You told me he'd never go to prison at all."

"Actually, I told you that he could have avoided prison if he'd followed my advice in the first place, which was to go to the police," he corrected.

"He didn't have a chance to do that. Things were escalating too quickly."

"We don't need to get into this again."

"It's easy to look back and say what he should have done, but Spencer was afraid for his girlfriend, and he acted to protect her. I don't understand why the jury didn't believe him. He'd never done anything wrong in his life. But they sent him to jail. That's how your beautiful justice system worked."

"Stephanie's testimony was damaging. She didn't back up Spencer's story, and the evidence didn't, either."

"But he didn't intend to kill that man. He acted in self-defense." She paused. "Are you working with those detectives now? I wanted you to come back to San Francisco, but I never wanted to see you in the same police department that destroyed your brother's life."

Max drew in a deep breath. "They've both retired." He couldn't have accepted Hank's offer if it had meant working with the two men who had sent his brother to jail. While he didn't hold them completely responsible, their sloppy investigation had hurt Spencer's case.

"Well, at least they can't send any more innocent people

to jail." She stopped abruptly, her gaze on the prison doors.

Max felt a wave of relief when Spencer appeared. At six foot three inches, Spencer was two inches taller than him, but he probably weighed thirty pounds less. His blue jeans and gray t-shirt hung loosely on his long, lean, lanky frame. Spencer's skin seemed extremely pale against his dark hair. The hours he'd spent outdoors in the last seven years had been minimal.

As the guard opened the gate, Spencer hesitated, as if he couldn't believe he was about to return to the outside world. Then he straightened his shoulders and moved forward. There were a dozen emotions running through Spencer's eyes, but there wasn't enough time to decipher them before his mother hurled herself into Spencer's arms, hugging him with a tight desperation.

Max watched the two of them cling together and felt oddly left out by their embrace.

Finally, his mother let go, gazing at her oldest son with tears streaming down her face. "You're free," she said. "I can hardly believe it."

Spencer's jaw was tight with emotion. "Let's get the hell out of here."

His mom got into the back of the car, urging Spencer to take the front seat. As Max watched his brother buckle up, he couldn't remember the last time they'd been in a vehicle together.

"What are you waiting for, Max?" Spencer asked impatiently. "Drive."

He started the engine and pulled away from the curb. No one spoke for several miles. Spencer's tension was palpable, and it wasn't until he got on the freeway that his brother let out a relieved breath.

His mother must have sensed the opening, because she

jumped into the silence. "I'm making all your favorites for dinner tonight, Spencer," she said. "I'm sure you're hungry for a home-cooked meal."

"You don't know how much," Spencer said.

"It's all going to be good now," his mom added, a fierce note in her voice as if she were daring anyone to disagree with her. "Our family is back together. And we're going to help you get on your feet, Spencer."

Max glanced over at Spencer, feeling the heat of his brother's gaze.

"Now you want to help?" Spencer asked, with a cold, bitter note in his voice.

"I'll do whatever I can." The last thing he wanted was to get in a fight with his brother. He'd barely had any sleep the night before, and they were both on edge.

"It's a little late," Spencer said.

"Let's not talk about the past," his mom interjected. "It's time to move forward."

Spencer didn't comment, and Max didn't either.

He hoped the past was behind them. That would be up to Spencer.

Four

$\rightarrowtail \mathord{>}\!\!\!>\!\!\!\ll\!\!\!\mathord{<}\!\!-$

After a sixty-minute power nap, Emma showered, dressed and returned to work just after one o'clock. She had a brief meeting with her boss, Scott McAvoy, then spent the rest of the afternoon inputting data into the computer and following up with witnesses. When that was done, she returned to the crime scene.

She knocked on doors and spoke to the owners of businesses in the area to see if they'd noticed any suspicious people in the neighborhood in the days prior to the fire. Unfortunately, no one had seen anything out of the ordinary.

Her last stop was the bar. There was yellow tape across the entrance, but she ducked under it and stepped inside. She wasn't surprised to find Max poking around the main dining room, although there was not much to see in the blackened, burned out room. The only good thing about the blown-out windows was that much of the thick smoke had dissipated.

Max wore black slacks and a dress shirt, a tie hanging loosely around his neck, as if he'd spent some time tugging on it. He'd ditched his jacket, and his shirtsleeves were rolled up to the elbows.

He gave her a tired nod. "Callaway."

"Why do you look worse than I do? You went home before I did last night."

"I didn't sleep at all."

"Thinking about the case?"

"Among other things."

"Any word from the medical examiner's office on cause of death?" she asked.

"Unofficially, it looks like Sister Margaret died of a heart attack."

His words surprised her. She didn't know what she'd been expecting, but it hadn't been that. "A heart attack? Are you saying that she died of natural causes?"

If that were the case, then Sister Margaret would return to the suspect category, and Emma really didn't want to put her there.

"I didn't say that," he replied. "The ME found traces of duct tape around her mouth and wrists. She'd obviously been bound and gagged, but there was no evidence of physical or sexual assault."

"What about time of death?"

"Fifteen to twenty hours before her body was discovered."

Emma blew out a breath. "Then she definitely didn't set the fire."

"What did you find here?" Max asked.

"Gasoline cans, rags, same as at St. Andrew's. There were forensic teams from both your department and mine bagging up evidence earlier, so hopefully they'll find something. In the meantime, we continue investigating. We should work together."

"I agree." He sounded no more enthusiastic about the idea than she felt, but they were both professionals.

"Okay, then. Do you want to get out of here? Go somewhere with clean air where we can go over the case?"

"Sure. But I'm going to need to get some coffee."

"I know just the place. I'll drive."

"You really hate to give up control, don't you?" he said, as he followed her out the door.

"I'm a great driver. And since there's a good chance you'd fall asleep at the wheel, I think we'd both be safer in my car."

"Lead the way."

———⟫⟪———

"So where is this mysterious coffee place?" Max asked, as Emma headed west toward the beach.

"It's near the Cliff House. It's called Water's Edge. Do you know it?"

"I know the Cliff House but not Water's Edge. I don't remember a coffee house along the beach."

"It's about ten years old." She gave him a sideways glance. "I keep forgetting that you grew up here. I'm still curious as to why that never came up before now."

"You're curious about a lot of things," he commented.

"So are you," she retorted.

"Must be why we both went into investigation."

"You're definitely better at asking questions than answering them."

"That's true." He let out a sigh that turned into a yawn.

"We need to get you some caffeine fast," Emma said with a laugh.

"Yes," he agreed. "The long night is catching up with me. It doesn't seem to have affected you, though."

"I took a nap this morning. It gave me a second wind."

She fell silent as she maneuvered through the late afternoon traffic with confidence and purpose. She was a good driver. She was also a fast driver, which didn't surprise him. Emma definitely had a wild side. He couldn't help wondering what she'd be like in bed. That thought woke him up from his afternoon daze.

He deliberately forced his gaze out the window, idly watching the traffic and the streets of San Francisco passing by. He'd been back in the city a little over three months, but most of that time had been spent at work or in his barely furnished apartment. He'd left a lot of his furniture in a storage unit in Los Angeles, not sure he was ready to commit to a permanent move.

However, he had to admit that the charm of the city was beginning to take hold. He liked the constantly changing neighborhoods, the steep, narrow hills followed by surprisingly startling vistas of blue water, whether it be the ocean or the bay. He liked the food and the mix of cultures, but was he ready to call the city home again?

With the exception of his family and his boss, Hank Crowley, Max hadn't reconnected with anyone from his past. Not that there was anyone he was dying to see. The last thing he wanted to do was answer questions about Spencer, and with old friends, those questions would undoubtedly come up.

Another sigh escaped his lips, drawing Emma's attention.

"Still awake?" she asked.

"Barely."

"We're here." She drove down a steep hill that gave them a spectacular view of the Pacific Ocean.

It was a beautiful afternoon, a bright sun in a royal blue sky and a sea that went on forever. A large restaurant sat at the bottom of the hill perched on the edge of a cliff, hence the name Cliff House. Above the restaurant was a smaller café called the Water's Edge.

Emma pulled into a spot out front. "This place is crazy busy on the weekends, but not too bad during the week."

He was happy to see the empty parking spots. He was a

little too close to his old neighborhood for comfort.

He got out of the car and drew in a deep breath of cool, salty air. It felt good to be outside. He needed a moment to regroup after the chaotic events of the last twelve hours.

"I love this place at sunset," Emma added, as she joined him on the sidewalk. "That's my favorite time of day. What about you?"

"I like mornings—dawn, the first sunrise, the potential of the day ahead. Nothing bad has happened yet."

She nodded. "I can see that about you. A new day, a new adventure."

He smiled. "Now that sounds more like you. I'm not the one who runs into burning buildings."

"But you do chase down bad guys, and that's just as dangerous."

As they started down the hill, Emma walked in front of him. Her blonde hair blew in the wind, and she drew her black windbreaker more closely around her shoulders. She wore the field uniform of her office—black slacks, black knit shirt, black jacket—but she was still pretty, still feminine. Whether she was wearing a sexy short dress like she'd worn to Brady's, or bulky firefighter's gear as she had last night, or pants and a jacket, she always looked exactly right, which was a huge problem for him, especially when he was tired. His muddled brain was happy to suggest that having a professional relationship and a personal one could work out just fine.

But it wouldn't work out, and the last thing he wanted to do was put his job in jeopardy. It was the only thing in his life right now that was actually working. He didn't need to screw it up.

Emma opened the door to the café, and he followed her inside, his senses assailed with the fragrant smell of coffee beans and sweet pastries. They paused in front of a glass display case filled with mouthwatering sweets.

"Those look good," Emma said, pointing to a chocolate pastry. "Do you want one?"

"No, but you go ahead. I'll just take a coffee." He gave his order to the cashier, then grabbed a table by the window.

The waves were big today, crashing against the shoreline with a white shimmering spray. He could see a large freighter in the distance, making its way toward the Golden Gate Bridge. It was a view that he'd seen many, many times in his life, and he hadn't realized until just this second how much he had missed it.

Emma sat down across from him with her pastry. "I wish I could say that I felt guilty for eating this, but I don't." She took a bite and smiled happily. "I love chocolate."

He smiled back at her. For the moment they were not competing or battling, and it was a nice respite from their usually tense conversations.

"Do you want a bite?" she offered.

"You mean you'd actually share?"

"I feel compelled to be polite."

"But hoping I'll say no. Thanks, but I'm good."

"Your loss." Her unbridled enthusiasm and the way she attacked the gooey chocolate pastry sent all kinds of unwanted images through Max's head.

Emma never did anything halfway, and he couldn't imagine that she'd be any different in bed. But he was not taking her to bed, he reminded himself. Having coffee with her was bad enough.

The server called their order, and he jumped to his feet, thrilled with the interruption. "I'll get it. You eat."

He returned to the table a moment later and set down their drinks. He took a sip of his coffee and liked the immediate kick the extra shot of espresso gave him. He needed to wake up, pay attention, and stop daydreaming about Emma naked in bed with her sexy mouth just ripe for the taking.

"I love the view from here," Emma said, oblivious to his thoughts.

"It's very nice," he muttered.

"I don't think I could ever live too far from the ocean. Whenever I feel like the world is closing in on me, I go to the beach. It opens up my perspective."

He gazed back at her, and his heart tightened as their eyes met—her beautiful, sparkling blue eyes. Emma was such an intriguing mix of hard and soft. Her hair was cut in sharp angles, but the strands were silky smooth. Her voice could be sharp and demanding, but her lips were full and sweet. She had an incredibly kissable mouth. But if he tried kissing her, he'd probably see the hard side of her fist.

"What are you thinking, Max?" she asked, her gaze curious.

"Nothing," he said quickly.

"It doesn't look like nothing."

"Trust me, you don't want to know." He looked out the window and decided to change the subject. "I used to surf those waves," he said.

"Really? I would not have taken you for a surfer dude."

"Why not?"

"Because you're always tense. I can't quite picture you waiting patiently for a wave to take you to shore."

"When I was out on the water, I could be very patient. The perfect wave would deliver the ultimate ride, and I didn't want anything less."

Her thoughtful gaze met his. "That makes sense. Do you still surf?"

"I haven't been out in at least ten years."

"Why not? They have beaches in L.A."

"Surfing was part of another life."

"A life you've come back to," she pointed out. "Maybe you could take it up again."

"Maybe." He didn't know if he could go back to that place in time. "What about you? Have you ever surfed?"

"I tried it a few times with my brothers, but they liked to go out early in the morning, and I'm not really a morning person."

"The mornings are the best. The water is calm, the sun is just coming up, and everyone else is still asleep. It's just you and the ocean. The day's problems are hours away."

She tilted her head, studying him with a thoughtful gaze. "It sounds like the sea was your escape, too."

He'd forgotten how good she was at reading between the lines. "It was," he admitted. "My parents fought a lot when I was young. They eventually divorced, but that didn't end the fights or the drama. My mother was an emotional person, so even when my father was gone, she was often a mess. When I was on my surfboard, all that seemed very far away."

Emma nodded, understanding in her gaze. "I used to hide in my closet. My parents didn't fight in front of us, but late at night, I could hear their voices. I was too little to understand what they were talking about, but I could hear my dad's low angry voice, and then my mom would cry. Her sobs always made me feel afraid. So I'd get out of bed and take my dolls and my blanket into the closet. One morning, my mom found me in there. I usually got back into bed before they woke up and came into my room. But that night, I didn't. She told me later that she took one look at me curled up like a ball and knew that she couldn't stay married to my dad."

He'd forgotten for a moment that she wasn't talking about

her mother and Jack Callaway but about her biological father. "Did their split make you feel guilty?"

"Very much. How did you know?"

"Because I'm starting to know you, and you feel responsible for people, especially people you care about."

"That's true. I worried for a long time that I was the reason for the divorce. I remember my name coming up quite frequently in their arguments. I have a feeling that my father didn't really want a second child. But as I got older, and I saw my father for who he really was, I was better able to accept the fact that they would have divorced eventually."

"How's the relationship between your mother and Jack?"

"It's great," she said with a smile. "They'll be married twenty-five years next year. I'm sure they have their problems, but they always seem very happy and connected to each other. My mom got lucky the second time around."

"Do you still see your biological father?"

"The last time was probably seven or eight years ago. We ran into each other while we were both shopping at Union Square at Christmas. He was with his second wife. It was awkward, and we both tried to get away from each other as quickly as possible." She paused. "What about you? How old were you when your parents divorced?"

"I was eight." He realized how quickly she'd turned the tables on him. He preferred to be the one asking the questions.

"Did your parents remain friends after the divorce?"

"God, no," he said forcefully. "I'm not sure they were ever friends. But I do know they became bitter enemies."

"I'm sorry. I touched a nerve, didn't I?"

"It happened a long time ago," he said with a dismissive shrug.

She gave him a speculative look. "It doesn't seem that

way."

"Why don't we talk about the case?" he suggested. "What did you do today?"

"I touched base with the witnesses I spoke to last night to see if they remembered anything new. I also spoke with the woman who called in the fire. She's a nurse at San Francisco General, and she was driving home after her shift when she saw the fire. I don't believe she had anything to do with setting it. I also spoke to the bartender at Brady's. He said he left before Harry did. He didn't notice anyone hanging around the bar, nor was he aware of anyone who might have had a grudge against Harry or one of the other employees."

"What about Harry?"

"I called twice, but his son Christian told me that Harry took a sleeping pill. I'm hoping to talk to him later tonight or tomorrow."

"A little convenient," Max said dryly. He could see she was itching to defend Harry, who was apparently a longtime friend of the Callaways, but she refrained. "Anything else?"

"I checked with the insurance company. Brady's had a standard policy. Premiums were paid on time. No changes were made in the last five years. I checked Harry's credit report and didn't see any problems with debt that might give him motivation to burn down the bar for the insurance payout."

He wasn't surprised by her findings. The fire at the bar had to be connected to the fire at St. Andrew's. Sister Margaret's body made that connection. "I don't think the fire had anything to do with money."

She met his gaze. "I don't, either. So what's the motivation—attention, revenge, a thrill?"

"Maybe all of the above. The fact that Brady's was a firefighters' bar also makes me wonder if that was a factor."

"But the school fires had nothing to do with firefighters, so maybe that link doesn't work. Which brings us back to Sister Margaret," Emma said. "I thought she was an amazing teacher, but my brother Drew told me earlier today that Sister Margaret was much nicer to the girls than the boys. Drew, apparently, spent a lot of time in detention with Sister Margaret, along with some of the other boys in the neighborhood. I don't know what to make of that information. It probably means nothing, but I thought you should hear another perspective." She paused. "I feel a little guilty even saying it, because I'm sure that the boys probably deserved to be in detention, and she was just doing her job."

"It's good to look at all facets of her personality."

"Oh, and there's one more thing. Drew said that he heard Sister Margaret was once engaged to be married, and her groom ran out on her the day of the wedding. That, according to my brother, is why she disliked the boys and why she became a nun."

"That must have been a long time ago. I've gone through her relationships and history over the past ten years, and that didn't come up."

"I think she was in her twenties. And, as I said, it could have just been a rumor."

"I have run into a few people who were not big fans of Sister Margaret," he commented, thinking about some of his interviews. "The new principal at St. Andrew's said she thought Margaret was stuck in her ways and not open to change. They were not on the same page. That's why the principal put another teacher in charge of the choir that Sister Margaret had run for twenty years. She wanted to freshen things up."

"I'm sure Sister Margaret didn't take that too well."

"The principal said Margaret was unhappy and

mentioned she might have to rethink her employment." He paused. "But none of this information gives us a suspect. All we have is a possibly unhappy nun who disappeared after school one day. She had no financial problems. She had no known enemies. She lived a relatively quiet life of devotion to her job and her church. Very few people knew her well. Even her roommate, Ruth Harbough, said that Margaret was an extremely private person. Ruth claimed she had no idea Margaret was considering leaving St. Andrew's."

Emma stared back at him with a contemplative expression. "Where does that leave us?"

"I'm not sure. Let's look at the circumstances surrounding Margaret's death. She disappears the night before a fire. Her car was in her parking spot in the garage of her apartment building. Some trace amount of blood was found nearby, but not enough to warrant a suspicion of foul play. It's believed Margaret walked to work. She was in her classroom all day, and the last time anyone saw her was four o'clock. She dies a week later of a heart attack. There's evidence she was being held against her will. But no one actually killed her."

"I think that hesitation to kill her might have to do with the fact that Sister Margaret knew her kidnapper, or possibly because she was a nun."

"I agree. There's a good chance it was someone who went to the church or the school."

"So let's say the arsonist is a former student." Emma rested her forearms on the table. "How can we narrow that down?"

"We could start with the detention records."

"How far back would we go?" she asked. "Ten years? Twenty years?"

"I'd start at least ten years ago. The arsonist is most likely in his twenties."

"I would agree. Maybe even older based on the pattern of the fires," Emma added. She picked up her coffee and took a sip. "After I spoke to Drew, I tried to remember which boys in my class had been in trouble or what some of my brothers and their friends had done in school."

"Are you saying the Callaway boys weren't all saints?" he asked with a raise of his eyebrow.

"Not by a long shot. Only Burke was perfect. I don't know if that came from being the oldest, or if it was always his personality, but he never did one damn thing wrong. Aiden came next in the lineup, and he was a terror. Drew was also rebellious but not as bad as Aiden. Sean just didn't care about school. All he wanted to do was play music. And Colton was another Aiden, just ten years later. I think it's safe to say that St. Andrew's was relieved to see the last of the Callaway boys. Although they loved having me, Nicole and Shayla," she said with a smile.

"I'm sure you were perfect."

"Actually, I did get into trouble for talking too much in class, and one teacher hated that I asked questions. He used to roll his eyes every time I raised my hand. I really annoyed him."

"I can imagine how he felt," he said dryly.

She made a face at him. "My questions are always good ones. Anyway, as I was saying, I was thinking back to problems at St. Andrew's, and I have this vague recollection of a fire in the school dumpster when I was in the fifth or sixth grade. I remember standing out on the playground and hearing that some boys had been playing with matches." She frowned. "I just wish I could remember who did it. A lot of arsonists start with smaller fires in their juvenile years."

"St. Andrew's may have a record of that fire, although it was a long time ago. I'll check with Mrs. Harbough."

"Were you the one to tell her that Sister Margaret is dead?" Emma asked, a somber note in her voice now.

He nodded. "Yes, I spoke to her earlier. She was devastated. She said Margaret didn't have any blood relatives. She considered the church community her family."

"I wonder when the funeral will be," Emma mused. "I'm sure the church will be packed with mourners."

"And maybe suspects," he said.

"Maybe."

He could see the sparkle in her eyes as she worked the puzzle in her mind, and he found himself smiling.

"What?" she asked suspiciously.

"You're in your element."

"This is my job," she said.

"And you love it."

"I do. Probably more than I should. It already cost me one relationship. My ex-boyfriend thought I put more energy into my work than into him. And he wasn't completely wrong," she added with honesty. "I've always felt like I had a lot to prove, both to get this job, and now to do it well. I figured there was time for everything else later. Turns out I was wrong."

"If he couldn't support you, you're better off."

"To be fair, he thought I was the one who wasn't supporting him. But in reality, we were both too focused on ourselves to give the other person what they needed. And in the end Jon got what he needed from someone else."

"There's no excuse for cheating," he said. He'd never had any tolerance for infidelity. If someone didn't want to be in a relationship, then they should get out of it.

"I don't think there is, either. Wow, we just agreed on something. Miracles can happen."

He grinned. "Don't get too excited. It may never happen

again."

"I'm sorry I brought my personal life into our conversation. The chocolate must have gone to my head."

"Good thing I didn't have any."

"Why? So you can continue to be the man of mystery?"

He shrugged. Seeing the determined look in her eye, he had a feeling he wouldn't be getting out of this conversation without giving her some personal information.

"What are you hiding?" she pressed.

"If I were hiding something, why would I tell you?" he countered.

"Because if you don't tell me, I'll start digging, and I'll probably learn far more than you want me to know."

"Why would you go to the trouble?"

"I like to know who I'm working with. Why did you come back to San Francisco after being away for so long?"

"Maybe I missed the sourdough bread," he said lightly. "Or the clam chowder."

"Fine, I'll figure it out myself."

He sighed. "You're like a dog with a bone."

"I've been called worse things."

"My life is complicated."

"Tell me something simple."

He drank his coffee as he thought about what he wanted to say. She would be able to find out just about everything with a simple Internet search. And with her resources, she could probably get every last dirty detail. He might as well give her his side of the story.

"Seven years ago, my older brother Spencer was convicted of manslaughter and sent to prison. Today, he was released."

Her eyes widened. "I—I had no idea."

"My mother asked me to move back to San Francisco so

that I could help Spencer get his life back together. When Captain Crowley offered me a job a few months ago, I decided to take it. Tonight will be the first family dinner we've had in a decade, and I think it's probably going to be incredibly awkward and uncomfortable."

"Why? I would think everyone would be happy."

"My brother blames me for not getting him out of prison. And my mother feels much the same way," he said flatly.

"That's rough."

The compassion in her eyes undid him. This was exactly why he didn't talk about his family. He'd been holding in his emotions for a decade, and he had no intention of putting them on display now, but his stomach was in knots, and his heart was beating way too fast. He needed to move. He needed to breathe.

"I've got to get out of here," he muttered, jumping to his feet.

He was out the door before she took her next breath.

He raced down the hill, trying to burn off some of the adrenaline rushing through his veins. When he got to the bottom, he hit the beach, enjoying the hard work of walking through the shifting sand, the ocean breeze blowing in his face, the watery spray of the waves cooling off his heated body.

Finally, he stopped and sank down on the sand, staring out at the ocean that had gotten him through a lot of bad moments. He needed the sea to work its magic.

A few minutes later, Emma sat down next to him. "Are you all right, Max?"

"No," he said, his voice clipped.

"Can I help?"

"It's my problem, not yours."

"That's not exactly true. We're partners. What affects you

affects me."

"You don't have to worry. I don't let my personal life impact my job."

"I'm not worried about the case. I'm concerned about you. You're hurting, and I don't like to see people in pain."

"Then you should get the hell away from me."

"Max—"

"No, I mean it," he said forcefully, giving her a hard look. "You should walk back up that hill, get in your car, and drive away."

"And how will you get back?"

"I don't know. I'll take a cab. I'll walk. It doesn't matter. Just go, Emma."

"Why?"

"Because I feel in the mood to do something I shouldn't do."

Her blue eyes sparkled in the sunlight. "Then you shouldn't be alone."

"Emma, you have about two seconds..."

"Or what?" she asked recklessly, her sweet lips so tempting.

"Or this."

He put his hand on the back of her neck, pulled her close, and covered her mouth with his.

Five

She tasted like coffee and chocolate—warm, sexy, irresistible, and he couldn't get enough of her. He threaded one hand through her hair, holding her head so he could explore her mouth, slip his tongue through those soft lips, and completely lose himself in her. Everything faded away, all the worries, all the problems. It was just Emma—her scent, her touch, the give and take of her mouth.

One kiss turned into two, then three. He should stop, but he couldn't. Every breath made him want another taste, a deeper connection. He nibbled on her bottom lip and then slipped his tongue inside her mouth. Her breath quickened, but she didn't pull away. Instead her arms crept around him, and her breasts grazed his chest.

The tantalizing touch made him want so much more.

He pressed her back against the sand, loving the feel of her body beneath him. He wanted her clothes off. He wanted her skin bare. He wanted to bury himself inside of her.

But Emma's arms were no longer holding him close. She was pushing him away.

He rolled over onto his side as she sat up and stared at him, her eyes blazing with desire, her hair tangled from his fingers, her lips red and full.

She stared at him for a long moment.

He didn't know what to say, and for once she seemed to have no words.

Slowly, reality seeped into his brain. They were on a public beach. There were kids throwing a ball to a dog not thirty feet away, and he'd been making out like a teenager.

"What was that?" she said finally.

"That was—what I've been thinking about the past three months," he admitted.

"Really?" she asked, a note of wonder in her voice. "I thought you didn't like me."

"I didn't like what you made me feel. There's been attraction between us from the start. You know that." He paused. "And you feel the same way, don't you? Because I'm pretty sure you kissed me back, Emma."

"You took me by surprise."

"Did I? I distinctly remember telling you to go. You didn't move."

"I don't like to be told what to do."

"Yeah, I know. I should have said stay and then you would have left," he said dryly.

She frowned. "Max, that can't happen again."

"I know," he agreed. There were a lot of reasons why he shouldn't kiss her again, and they weren't all because of their professional relationship.

Emma tucked her hair behind her ears as the wind blew the silky strands across her face. "We should go back to work."

Despite her words, she made no effort to get up.

He rolled onto his back and stared up at the sky.

"What are you thinking about?" she asked a moment later.

"Nothing and everything."

"That covers a lot of territory."

"I feel…" He searched for the right words. "Like I'm at a crossroads. And I don't know which path to take."

"What are the choices?"

"One involves trying to salvage the relationship with my brother and my mom. The other takes me back to a world where I don't have to worry about anyone but myself."

"You didn't worry about your family when you were in Los Angeles?" she questioned.

"It was easier not to think about them when I was farther away."

"Can you tell me what happened with your brother, Max?"

"You can go online and learn everything you want to know."

"Why don't you save me the trouble and just tell me?"

"I already told you the short version. The long one will have to wait."

He sat up and brushed the sand off his sleeves and pants. Then he got to his feet, and held his hand out to her. After a moment, she took it.

He pulled her to her feet and held onto her hand longer than he should have. The heat between them still smoldered. Looking into her eyes, he saw the same awareness, and the same worry.

She pulled free and then dug her hands into her pockets as she started walking away. They didn't say anything on the way back to the car, or even on the drive back to Brady's. The destruction of the bar reminded him that the brief respite from work was over. He had a murderer to find, and she had an arson case to solve.

"We'll talk soon, right?" Emma asked, as she pulled up behind his car.

"Sure."

"I don't want what happened to jeopardize this case."

"It won't."

"Good. I'm going to chalk that kiss up to temporary insanity."

He smiled. "Insanity? That sounds about right." He opened the door and then paused, glancing back at her. "I won't kiss you again, unless you ask me."

"That's not going to happen."

Emma's protest was cut off by the slamming of the door. Max had shown her a different side earlier in the day, but that last comment reminded her how arrogant he could be. She was not going to kiss him again—for many reasons. She'd worked too hard to get taken seriously at her job to jeopardize her reputation by having a fling with the cop on her case. Max might be able to get away with it. The guys in his department would probably all give him a high-five if they found out. But the fire guys would lose respect for her. It was a double standard, but one she had to deal with.

She just wished Max hadn't been such a good kisser. She put her fingers to her mouth, her lips still tingling from the intensity and force of his kiss. That hadn't been some brief, tender caress but an all-out assault on her senses. She didn't think she'd ever been kissed quite like that, with so much intensity and need, as if she alone could drive away whatever demons were plaguing him. Which reminded her that that kiss had not been solely driven by desire but also by emotions inside of Max, emotions that she didn't completely understand. It was obvious he was in some sort of turmoil. She'd never seen him so rattled. In the three months that she'd known him, he'd always been in control. But he'd been out of control on that beach, and she'd liked him even more.

Blowing out a breath, she pulled back into traffic and headed home. It was after five and dusk was settling over the city. Despite the coffee and chocolate, she was feeling the effects of having been up most of the night. She needed to give her mind a rest.

Ten minutes later, she pulled into the driveway of her parents' house. To her surprise and delight, she saw Sara Davidson leaving the house next door.

Sara had been her best friend in middle school and high school. They'd spent a zillion hours together, but after Sara's mother died and Sara went off to college, they'd lost contact. That had changed two weeks ago when Sara had come home for her father's birthday. Her surprise visit had triggered a series of events, including a house fire at her father's house and a reunion with Aiden, Emma's older brother.

As a teenager, Sara had had a crazy crush on Aiden. Back then the three-year age difference between them had been too great. Not to mention the fact that Aiden was a reckless, rebellious bad boy, and Sara was a really smart good girl. But somehow the two of them had found their way to each other after ten years apart, and Emma couldn't be happier.

She threw the car into park and got out. Sara came across the grass with a smile on her face. She looked relaxed and happy, her big brown eyes filled with joy, her long brown hair falling in soft waves around her shoulders. She wore cute black boots over skinny jeans and a soft pink sweater.

"I didn't think you'd be back so soon. It hasn't even been a week," Emma said. "What happened with your job?"

"I gave them two weeks' notice, and they told me to leave that day. It's basically what happens to anyone when they quit," Sara replied. "Aiden helped me pack up my apartment, and here we are."

"Big change," she said, a little surprised that Sara had thrown away her high-paying attorney position in New York so quickly.

"I know," Sara said, a guilty smile on her face. "My boss thought I was crazy to leave when I was on the fast track to partner. But in truth I'd been thinking about leaving that job for the last few years. Being back in San Francisco reminded me of how much I missed the city. It was time to come home."

"You're leaving out Aiden," Emma reminded her.

Sara's cheeks turned pink, and her eyes sparkled. "He's been amazing, Em. I never thought I could be this happy. Aiden was the star of all my teenage fantasies, but I never imagined those dreams could come true."

"You weren't ready for each other before; you are now."

"I really love him, Emma."

Emma felt moisture gather in her eyes at Sara's words. "I'm glad. I always wanted you to be my sister, and now you will be."

"Well, he hasn't proposed yet."

"He will," Emma said confidently. "Are you going to live at your dad's house, or will you and Aiden get a place together?"

"We're headed in that direction, but we have some decisions to make about work first, so we're taking our time. I need to spend this week getting my dad's house ready for his return."

"How's his leg?"

"Healing. It was broken in two places, and there was also damage to the cartilage, but he's doing better than expected at the rehab facility. I know he's anxious to get home. Your Uncle Kevin has already started the kitchen remodel, so I'm hoping the house will be ready when he comes home next week." Sara paused. "What's new around here?"

"Well, Brady's Bar burned to the ground last night, and it was not an accident."

Sara's gaze filled with dismay. "That's terrible."

"It gets worse. Sister Margaret's body was found in the ashes."

Sara's jaw dropped. "Sister Margaret is dead? Are you serious?"

"Yes, so now we have arson and homicide. It looks like the fire at St. Andrew's might also be connected to this one."

"And you're right in the middle of it."

"Along with Max Harrison," she said, a small sigh escaping her lips.

A gleam came into Sara's eyes. "Wait, isn't that the hot cop you were trying to avoid last week?"

"I can't believe you remember that," she grumbled.

"I have an excellent memory."

"Too good." Emma was happy to see Aiden coming down the driveway. She didn't want to talk about Max yet. She was still unsettled by how quickly they'd gotten carried away on the beach.

Aiden wore jeans and a t-shirt, his usual choice of dress, and his thick brown hair looked like it hadn't seen a comb all day. The second oldest Callaway, Aiden had always had a reckless streak. She wondered if Sara would be able to tame him. Probably not. It looked like Aiden was having more of an impact on Sara than the other way around. But she suspected that in the long run, they'd be really good together.

"Hey, Em," he said, giving her a quick hug.

Then Aiden put his arm around Sara and kissed her on the lips.

"Well, aren't you two sickeningly sweet," Emma said.

Aiden grinned, and the happy twinkle in his eyes matched Sara's. "Get used to it."

"Will I have to get used to it? Does this mean you're going to stay in San Francisco? No more smokejumping, Aiden?"

Her brother had spent the last several years working as a smokejumper in Redding, about four hours north of San Francisco. The tragic loss of his best friend had made Aiden question whether or not he wanted to go back when the season started again in the spring.

"For the next week I'm going to help Uncle Kevin at Sara's house. After that—I'm not sure," Aiden said. "I'm weighing my options."

Sara looked at Aiden. "I need to run to the store and get some food in the house. Your uncle hooked up a new refrigerator, so at least I can stock a few essentials. Do you want me to get you anything?"

"No, I'm good."

Sara smiled at Emma. "We'll catch up at dinner. Your mother already insisted we come over. I hope you'll be there."

"I will."

As Sara walked to her car, Aiden's gaze followed her. Emma punched her brother lightly in the arm. "You have it bad," she said. "Goofy grin and all."

Aiden gave an unrepentant shrug. "Sara is great, what can I say?"

"Nothing. She *is* great. It took you long enough to see that. I knew it a long time ago," she pointed out.

"Well, I had to wait for her to grow up."

She laughed. "Maybe Sara had to wait for *you* to grow up."

He grinned. "Possibly."

"How was New York?"

"Crowded, energized. I wouldn't want to live there full-time. Fortunately, Sara wanted to come back here."

"Would you have considered moving to New York if she hadn't wanted to leave?"

"Absolutely."

"Really, Aiden?" she asked doubtfully. "You love nature. You're more comfortable in the woods than anywhere else."

"I want to be where Sara is," he said simply.

She was impressed and amazed that her usually obstinate brother had fallen so hard for Sara that he was willing to change his entire life around. It reminded her of how little Jon had been willing to change for her. And she supposed, the opposite had been true as well, which was exactly why they hadn't been right for each other.

"I heard about Brady's," Aiden said, changing the subject. "How's the investigation going?"

"Slowly. I need to talk to Harry, but every time I call, Christian tells me his father is asleep."

"You have a suspicious note in your voice," Aiden said, giving her a questioning look. "Why?"

"I don't like being given the runaround, especially from people who have known me most of my life. Not that Christian has ever been particularly friendly towards me."

"That's just Christian. He has always been in a bad mood."

"But he likes me even less since I became a firefighter. He told me once that chicks belong in the henhouse, not the firehouse," she added, quoting Christian's exact words.

"Did you punch him?" Aiden asked.

"I was tempted, but he was so drunk at the time, he fell over all by himself."

"Christian can be an asshole, but he's got a good heart. He's very protective of his brother and his friends. And he's always been devoted to his father and to the bar. I think he owns part of it. I know he bartends there between his shifts. He must want to find the person who burned it down and killed Sister Margaret."

"I'd think so, too. I'm going to go over there in the morning."

Aiden shook his head. "I can't believe that cranky old nun is dead."

Her gaze narrowed at his words. His attitude was very similar to Drew's. "I thought Sister Margaret was sweet and kind."

"The only thing sweet about her were those gelatos she used to eat every day in detention."

His words rang a distant bell. Sister Margaret had loved walking around the corner to the Sugar Shack to get a gelato and sometimes bags of black licorice. Had she gone to get gelato the day she disappeared? Even if she had, what would that mean? She doubted there were security cameras at the Sugar Shack. Still, it might help Max pin down the timeline on the day of her disappearance.

"Emma?" Aiden asked. "Where did you go?"

"Just thinking. Drew told me that Sister Margaret didn't like the boys."

"You got that right. She was mean as hell to us."

"Obviously, Sister Margaret had two sides. I need to understand both of them."

"I thought you were working on the arson case."

"They're tied together."

"I don't like the idea of you getting involved in a murder," he said with a frown.

"I can handle it. Don't go all *big brother* on me."

"I can't help it. You'll always be my little sister."

She smiled. "I get it, but I'm a big girl now." She decided

to change the subject. "Are you really going to give up smokejumping, Aiden?"

"I'm not sure. I know what it's like for the wives of the smokejumpers, and I don't know that I want to put Sara through that."

"Are you already thinking marriage? That's big news."

"Not that big. There's no ring yet. So don't get too excited."

"When you do pick out a ring, you should take me with you. I know Sara's taste."

"I'll think about it."

"So much thinking," she teased. "You usually jump, then consider the consequences."

He grinned. "You know me too well."

"I'm glad you're taking it slow. I thought I was in love with Jon, but I was wrong. I'm just glad he never asked me to marry him. I might have said yes. I might have had kids with him, and then we'd be in the middle of a horrible divorce right now. The last thing I ever want to do is put my children through a divorce. Even though I was really young when it happened to my mom and dad, I've never forgotten that horrible feeling when I saw my dad move out."

"I didn't realize you remembered that," Aiden said.

"Some things never leave your memory. Do you remember when your mom died?"

He nodded. "Worst day of my life. But I got a second mom who is wonderful."

"And I got a second dad, who is also great," she said, meeting his gaze. "I wasn't so sure about all the brothers that came with him, but you grew on me."

He smiled. "And you and Nicole grew on us. I can't imagine our family without everyone in it."

"Neither can I."

"I have to run an errand. I'll see you at dinner, Em."

"Okay." As she headed inside the house, she thought how lucky she was to be a Callaway. No matter what happened in her life, she could always count on her family to be there for her, the whole crazy bunch of them.

Six

–⟫⟪⟪–

Family dinner was excruciating, Max thought. They were sitting in the dining room of his childhood home. The house was the one thing his mother had gotten in the divorce, and it had taken all she had to hang onto it all these years. But after his dad moved out, they'd rarely eaten in the dining room. In fact, his mom had refused to set this table for at least a decade, saying it reminded her too much of his father, Steve.

Why she'd decided to hold this family reunion in the formal dining room, he did not understand. There weren't any good memories in this room, and he didn't think tonight's meal was going to change that.

His mom had cooked up a feast fit for a king, but he didn't think any of them were really enjoying it. The few words of casual conversation they'd exchanged hadn't made it past the salad. Since then the silence had grown tense and uncomfortable.

His appetite gone, Max set down his fork and looked across the table at his brother. His mom had obviously picked up new clothes for Spencer, as he now wore a crisp button-down shirt and a pair of gray slacks. He looked more like the old Spencer, the one who'd gone to college and then gotten a job as a commodities trader, the one who'd been on the fast track to wealth and importance. But that life was gone. Spencer had destroyed it, and he was going to have to start over. It wouldn't be easy now that he was an ex-convict.

Spencer met his gaze, but whatever he was thinking was impossible to read. Prison had taught Spencer the value of hiding his thoughts and emotions.

After a moment, Spencer looked down at his plate and forked the last piece of roast beef. Dinner might be awkward, but Spencer had obviously enjoyed having a home-cooked meal for a change.

Max glanced across the table at his mother, who seemed intent on sending him some sort of silent message. She wanted him to break the tension; he just wasn't sure how to do that. His mother and Spencer were far closer to each other than he was to either of them.

But he had to try something. He pulled a piece of paper out of his pocket and slid it across the table. "I looked through some online employment sites earlier, and I wrote down a couple of possibilities."

Spencer didn't bother to pick up the paper. "I can find my own job," he said flatly.

"I'd like to help."

"So you can stop feeling guilty?" Spencer's gaze filled with anger. Apparently, his brother was done hiding his feelings.

He knew Spencer was baiting him, itching for some kind of fight, although he didn't know why. Spencer should be happy to be free, but instead he was extremely pissed off. Obviously, he found some comfort in anger, but Max was tired of being the focus of his brother's rage.

Actually, he was just tired, another reason he should bite his tongue.

"Nothing to say?" Spencer persisted.

"You obviously have a lot to say, so say it."

"Let's not do this now," his mother interjected, giving them both a worried look. "Can't we enjoy the fact that we're finally together again?"

"I don't think Spencer can," he said, staring at his brother.

"No, I can't." Spencer looked him directly in the eye. "You let me go to prison. You let me rot in that hellhole for seven years."

"I tried to help you. There was nothing I could do."

"You were thinking like a cop and not like a brother."

That was so untrue, it was almost laughable. He'd almost lost his job for interfering with the investigation. But Spencer had never understood the difficult position he had been placed in. No amount of explanation would ever make Spencer see things differently, so Max was done trying.

Spencer threw down his napkin and stood up. "I've had enough."

As Spencer strode out of the dining room, his mother gave him a disappointed look. "I was hoping you two could make peace, Max."

"I'm not the one you should be talking to."

"I know Spencer is angry and bitter, but who can blame him? He tried to save the life of the woman he loved, and he went to prison for it. You have to find a way to reach your brother, Max. It can't be on him. He has enough to deal with. He needs your support whether or not he asks for it or wants it."

He hadn't heard his mom so passionate about anything or anyone in a very long time.

"Please, Max," she said, desperation in her eyes. "He's so angry. I'm worried what he'll do. I'm afraid I could lose him all over again."

"I'll talk to him," he said, getting to his feet. It probably wouldn't help, but he'd give it a shot.

He found Spencer out on the back deck. He was sitting in a deck chair, staring out at the night.

Max took the chair opposite him and for a few minutes there was nothing but the quiet of the night, and in the distance, the sound of the waves crashing on the shore.

"Do you want to talk?" he asked after a moment. "Fight some more? We might as well clear the air."

"I don't feel like fighting anymore."

He was surprised but also relieved. "All right."

A few minutes passed, and then Spencer added, "The flowers smell so strong. It's been a long time since I smelled anything so—pretty. I'd forgotten that the world could smell this way, that the stars could be so bright, that the air could feel so crisp against my face. I can taste the salt in the air, and it's both familiar and very odd."

There was less anger in his tone now, more of a dreamy quality, as if he was experiencing some surreal moment.

"I feel like a stranger in a strange land," Spencer continued. "I don't know how I'll fit in here."

It was the most his brother had said to him in years and revealed some of the vulnerability that Spencer had been hiding behind his anger.

"You have to give yourself some time, Spencer."

"Time has passed so slowly the last seven years. I don't want to waste any more of it." He glanced at Max. "I can't imagine anyone will want to hire me with my record."

"It won't be easy," Max agreed. "But you'll find something. You're smart and well-educated."

"And a murderer. Who's going to trust me? People will probably cross the street when they see me coming."

"You can't think of yourself that way. The worst is behind you, Spence. You're a free man, and you're starting a new chapter in your life."

"A new chapter?" he asked, doubt in his eyes. "I'm a thirty-six-year-old man living in his mother's house. I have no money, no car, and no job prospects."

"That's all temporary." He hated to see Spencer getting bogged down in the negative, but he doubted there was anything he could say to change that. Spencer would have to find his own way forward.

"Where do you live?" Spencer asked.

"An apartment a couple of miles from here. It's a one-bedroom," he added.

"Don't worry. I wasn't going to ask if I could move in."

He was happy to hear that. "Mom isn't around that much. She works nine to five at the insurance company. You'll have time to yourself during the day."

"Yeah." Silence fell between them for a few moments, then Spencer said, "Do you know what happened to her?"

His body stiffened at the question he'd hoped he'd never hear. "Are you talking about Stephanie?"

"Who else would I be asking about?"

"Does it matter what happened to her? She let you down at the trial, Spencer. Her testimony was halfhearted and vague. She couldn't remember things she'd told you. She had text messages she couldn't explain. She's the reason the jury didn't believe you."

"I didn't ask for a rehash; I asked if you knew what happened to her," Spencer said, an edge to his voice now.

"You have to forget about her. You can never see her again. This is your second chance, and you cannot let her mess it up for you."

"Is she married?"

He let out a sigh, knowing that he was only postponing the inevitable. If he didn't give Spencer answers, his brother would go looking for them, and that would be even worse. "Yes, she's married. And she has a kid."

"How old?"

"Around two, I think."

"You kept tabs on her."

He had kept an eye on Stephanie because he'd always believed she'd been hiding something, and during the course of appeals, he'd hoped she'd reveal the truth. But she never had.

"Is it a boy or a girl?" Spencer asked.

"Boy."

"She had a son," Spencer said, drawing a shaky breath. "We talked about having a child together."

"How can you have an ounce of feeling for her?" he asked harshly.

Spencer looked at him with agony in his eyes. "I loved her more than I've ever loved anyone in my life."

He knew he was being harsh and not at all understanding, but he couldn't support this part of Spencer's re-entry into the world. "You paid for your love. She's moved on, and you need to do the same."

Spencer stood up. "Don't worry about me, Max. I know exactly what I need to do."

After the Callaway family dinner, Emma went upstairs to her bedroom, grabbed her laptop computer and sat down on her bed. She'd been thinking about Max all evening, wondering how his reunion was going with his mother and brother. While he'd told her the basics, she wanted to know the whole story.

She opened her search engine and typed in Spencer

Harrison, then waited for the results. It didn't take long to find a series of news articles about his trial. The first one was from the *San Francisco Chronicle* and gave the basics of the case.

Spencer Harrison, age twenty-nine, a rising commodities trader at Harrington and Stowe, was arrested after a fight outside his girlfriend's apartment building that resulted in the death of Kurt Halstead, age twenty-seven. Harrison claimed that Halstead was stalking his girlfriend, Stephanie Porter. But Halstead's attorneys stated that Harrison had a jealous temper and had mistaken a friendship between the two for something more.

Emma pulled up another article, this one discussing the deceased Kurt Halstead, who was also the son of a former San Francisco Supervisor. That couldn't have helped Spencer's case. She could only imagine the kind of influence the Halstead family might have had on the investigation.

Further searching led Emma to a video shot outside the courthouse the day of Spencer's conviction. A tearful Susan Harrison, Max's mother, spoke about her wonderful son and the miscarriage of justice. Susan wore her brown hair pulled back in a knot and had on a navy blue suit. She was very thin and quite distraught. Her voice shook with every word, and tears streamed down her face as she looked into the camera and pleaded for someone to help her right a terrible wrong.

Emma's stomach clenched at the raw pain in her voice. It was obvious she believed completely in Spencer's innocence.

What had Max thought?

There was no sign of Max in the video. And he'd told her enough to know that there had been some break in his family. Had that break come with Spencer's arrest? Had Max doubted his brother's story?

He would have been a young cop at the time of Spencer's arrest, and Max had told her that he'd started at the LAPD, so he'd been a long way from the scene of the crime. But he must have gotten involved. It wasn't his personality to stay on the sidelines. He would have contacted the detectives in San Francisco. He would have used whatever connections he had to make sure that his brother got justice.

She really wanted to talk to Max, to ask him what had happened and how he'd felt about it all, but she doubted he'd be interested in answering her questions.

Her fingers hovered over the keyboard and then she gave into an impulse and typed Max's name into the search box. The Internet might reveal some secrets about the man of mystery. Maybe if she knew more about him, she'd find new energy to dislike him, because at some point in the last two days she'd found herself softening towards him. She'd seen another side to the cocky cop, a side she liked way too much.

Unfortunately, when his picture appeared on the screen, she liked him even more. Even in a formal police department headshot, he looked handsome, with his brown hair, penetrating green eyes, and very sexy mouth. She felt a tingle run down her spine. How could one man's kiss be so good?

Shaking that question out of her head, she skimmed through several news articles. Max had made a name for himself in the Los Angeles Police Department. He'd put away a lot of criminals and he'd also saved the life of his partner during a drug bust. As she read about his exploits, she realized how courageous and brave he was. She'd seen him mostly in a suit, working an investigation, not throwing himself in front of a bullet, but it was clear he was comfortable doing that, too.

So her Internet research experiment was a dismal failure. Now Max was not only sexy but also a real live hero.

"Emma?"

The voice made her jump. Startled she looked to the

door, meeting Sara's questioning gaze.

"Did I scare you?" Sara asked.

"I didn't hear you come down the hall."

Sara moved over to the bed. "You were pretty engrossed in what you were doing." She glanced at the screen. "Ah, so now I know why you were lost in thought."

Emma quickly closed the computer. "I was doing some research."

"On the cop who has you hot and bothered," Sara said with a knowing glint in her eyes.

"I was actually doing some research on Max's brother," Emma said. "Max told me earlier that his brother got out of prison today, and that was all he would say."

"Which, of course, made you curious."

"How could I not be? I like to know who I'm working with."

"So what did you find out?" Sara asked, as she sat down on the bed.

"There were conflicting reports, but it appears that Spencer, Max's brother, got into a fight with a guy Spencer thought was stalking his girlfriend. As a result of that fight, the other man died, and Spencer was eventually convicted of manslaughter."

"Was Max involved in the case?"

"Not officially. He was living in Los Angeles at the time, and the investigation was here in San Francisco. Obviously he couldn't impact the case enough to get his brother off. I'm sure there must have been appeals over the years."

Sara nodded. "At least one. Which means the evidence was strong against Max's brother."

"It must have been. I can see where the intent of that fight could be cloudy, though."

"That's why he was charged with manslaughter and not

murder."

"It must have been hard on Max to see his brother go through that, especially since he was a police officer."

"Interesting to have two brothers in a family—one is a cop and one is a criminal."

"And how far do you go to protect or defend your brother?" Emma asked. "I have more than one hotheaded brother, Aiden included, and I could see any one of them getting into trouble, especially if they were defending someone."

"Aiden would not kill someone," Sara said quickly.

"Don't get all protective," Emma said with a smile. "I was just using Aiden as an example. But we both know that my brother would fight to protect someone he loved. He wouldn't be able to stop himself."

"But Max's brother was convicted, so the jury didn't believe he was acting in self-defense or protecting someone else."

"Evidence can be manipulated. You know that; you're a lawyer."

"True. So what are you going to do with all this information?"

"Nothing. It's not my business."

"It sounds like you're making it your business."

"Max and I have to work together, and I want to know where his head is at."

Sara nodded, a knowing gleam in her eyes. "Sure, but you also can't help yourself. You sense a mystery, and you have to solve it. You've been this way your entire life. I remember the time you were convinced that Shayla was stealing your hairbands. We set up a stakeout here in this very room, as I recall," she added with a laugh. "We put all the bands on the floor, and then I hid in the closet, and you were behind the curtains."

Emma groaned. "I cannot believe you remember that."

"Oh, I do. And after an agonizingly boring thirty minutes in the closet, someone came in to swipe the hairbands—your cat Muffy."

"Well, you can't say we didn't find the guilty party."

"True, but you had the wrong suspect in mind."

"My investigative techniques have actually improved since then," Emma said.

"Well, I would hope so, but my point is—once you get your mind stuck on something, you don't let go."

"True." She paused. "Let's talk about you. What are you going to do for a job now that you've quit the fast track? Are you going to work for a firm out here, open your own practice, or quit law and grow vegetables?"

"I would like to grow vegetables and herbs, too. How wonderful would it be to have a beautiful, organic garden?"

"In my mind, not so wonderful, but I'm not a gardener like you."

"I've missed digging in the dirt, planting a seed, watching it grow," Sara said, a wistful smile on her lips. "I haven't done any gardening since my mom died. It was something we shared together. I couldn't bear to do it without her. And where would I have done it anyway? I've been living in a crowded city for most of the last decade."

"But that's changed now." Emma thought about her earlier conversation with Aiden, about how he was open to changing his life for Sara. "Can I ask you something?"

"Of course."

"Are you really willing to give up your career for Aiden? You've worked so hard for a long time. I understand making a change and coming home, but I can't see you following Aiden to the mountains and living in a small town while he spends half the year jumping into fires and is gone for days at a time. Won't you feel like you're giving up too much for him?"

"Aiden hasn't asked me to give up anything," Sara said quietly.

"Maybe he hasn't had to, because you've already offered."

"No, he wants me to be happy, and I want him to be happy. We haven't figured out how we're going to make that work yet. I've thought about moving north. I could open my own small law firm. I'm sure there's business there."

"Not big business."

"I'm ready to move beyond corporate law. It's dry and impersonal. I'd like to know the people I'm working for. I always wanted to help people, not just find loopholes in contracts."

"I guess I can see that."

Sara gave her a long look. "I didn't grow up like you, Emma. I had my mom's love, but my father treated me with cold disdain most of my life. When I lost my mother, I lost my family. And while my dad and I are trying to make a new connection now, I've been alone a long time. I'm not saying that I leapt into Aiden's arms because I was lonely. We both know I've loved him since I was fifteen years old. Now that he loves me back, I feel like my world is suddenly filled with warmth and color and opportunity. I'm happy. I'm free. Whatever happens next will be part of a new adventure."

Emma smiled, seeing the joy in Sara's eyes. "With Aiden involved, your life will definitely be an adventure."

"I'm ready."

"I can see that."

"I'm sorry," Sara apologized. "I'm not being very sensitive, talking to you about love when you're still getting over your breakup."

"Don't be silly. When I listen to you and Aiden talk about your relationship, I'm amazed by how open you both are to changing your lives for the other person. Jon and I weren't willing to do that."

"Then you're better off."

Emma smiled. "It is good to have you back, Sara. I've missed you."

"And I've missed you. You were always on my side, Emma. I was such an awkward, nerdy outcast in school. If I hadn't met you, I wouldn't have had any kind of life back then. You saved me from being bullied. No one would go against a Callaway."

"There is some power in our name," Emma admitted. "Speaking of family, let's get back to yours. Have you told your father about your new relationship with Aiden?"

"No. There's been so much else to discuss."

"Has your dad told you any more about the big family secret?"

"Only that he doesn't regret not telling me about my brother, because Stephen Jr.'s death was too painful for him to handle," Sara said, referring to the fact that she'd recently discovered her parents had had another child before she was born, a child that died at the age of four from a tragic car accident.

"My father didn't want another baby," Sara continued. "When my mom got pregnant with me, he was furious. He'd told her he couldn't love another child, but she'd been desperately lonely, and she'd hoped he'd change his mind when I was born. Unfortunately, she couldn't sway him, and he treated me harshly just so he wouldn't accidentally start to love me and put his heart in jeopardy." Sara paused. "I understand so much more now. Not that it makes it all better or excuses the way he treated me, but at least I know he had a reason for his coldness."

"Do you think the two of you will become closer now that everything is out in the open?"

"Too early to tell. I want to be optimistic, but we'll see." She got to her feet. "I should go. I still have to put my bed together."

"*Your* bed?" Emma asked mischievously.

"I am not going to answer that question," Sara said.

"Hey, you used to tell me the good stuff."

"Not true. Back then there wasn't any *good* stuff. I was a very dull girl."

Emma laughed. "Well, your life will not be boring with Aiden. Where is he tonight anyway? He disappeared after dinner. Is he still trying to avoid Jack?"

"No, they spoke earlier. Aiden said your father was surprisingly understanding about his not having a job at the moment. He was expecting more pressure to make decisions and plans."

"Jack is happy that Aiden and you are together. He loves you and he thinks you're a good influence on my brother."

"I don't know about that. Anyway, Aiden went out to meet Burke and Drew—some kind of brotherly powwow." She paused. "Don't work too hard tonight, or spend too much time gazing and daydreaming about your hot cop."

"My research is strictly business," she lied.

"I don't believe you for a second."

Emma grabbed a throw pillow and tossed it at Sara as her friend ran through the door. Then she opened her computer and looked straight into Max's questioning gaze.

"Tomorrow, we start over," she said firmly. "Professional, not personal. That's going to be our relationship—got it?" She closed the computer before his eyes could call her a liar.

Seven

--->>><<<---

Aiden walked into Shanghai Kelly's, a bar on Polk Street, not far from his brother Burke's condo. With Brady's out of commission, they'd had to pick another place to meet. He was happy to be across town and not surrounded by firefighters. Although he'd been cleared in the incidence of his friend's death, there were still some men who thought he'd just found a way to get out of taking the blame for Kyle's death. He'd built a reputation for being reckless and daring in his twenties, and now in his early thirties, he was still paying for playing fast and loose with the rules.

He'd always been the black sheep in the family. Second in line, he'd had to follow Burke, who was the definition of perfect. Burke had been a fantastic student in school, a talented athlete, and a natural-born leader. He never did anything wrong, and despite having a squeaky clean image, he was still very well-liked, mostly because he was good at so many things.

Growing up, Aiden had heard teacher after teacher proclaim in disgust, "Why can't you be more like your brother Burke?"

Because it just wasn't in his DNA. He didn't like rules

and he had little patience for those he didn't respect. But as much as Burke's perfect behavior irritated the hell out of him, he did respect his brother. And he had been grateful for Burke's defense during the recent events in his life. He hoped that as time went by, they'd become closer. He'd never made the effort before, but he was starting tonight.

He looked around the bar, spotting his two brothers seated at a back table. He walked across the room and took the chair next to Drew.

"You're late," Burke said, with his usual scowl.

Some things never changed. "It's not my fault this time. Dad cornered me after dinner. And you know how many questions he always has."

"We do know," Burke said, motioning for the waitress. "Let's get you a drink."

Aiden ordered a beer and then looked at his brothers, realizing that he'd actually started to miss them the last few years. The three of them had shared a room together when they were really young. At one time they had known everything about each other. But sometime after the age of eighteen, they'd lost that connection. Drew had joined the Navy, and while Aiden and Burke had gone into firefighting, those early days had pitted him against Burke in yet another competition. When he'd decided to go into smokejumping, he'd been relieved to take a path that no one in his family had taken before him. He could make his own way in the world.

"So what did you tell Dad?" Burke asked. "I assume he asked you about your career plans."

"I told him that I'm considering my options."

"He must have loved that vague answer," Drew said, taking a sip of what appeared to be a vodka tonic.

"He was over the moon," Aiden said dryly. "But I told him the truth."

"Are you really done with smokejumping?" Drew asked.

"Maybe."

"It's difficult to believe," Burke commented.

He saw that same disbelief in Drew's eyes. "Why?"

"Because you live for thrills," Burke said. "You're addicted to the adrenaline rush that comes from jumping out of an airplane, or flying down a mountain road on a dirt bike."

"Or climbing a sheer rock wall with a pick and a rope," Drew added.

He grinned. "All true. But I have a new addiction."

Drew smiled back at him. "And her name is Sara."

He nodded. "Oh, yeah." He paused for a moment as the waitress set down his beer.

"I can't believe you two hooked up after all these years," Drew said. "Actually, I thought she used to have a crush on Burke."

"I thought so, too," Aiden admitted. "But she told me it was always me."

"And you believe her?" Drew challenged.

"Why wouldn't I?"

Drew laughed. "You cannot stop smiling."

"I know," he admitted. "I have no idea what I'm going to do for a living, where I'm going to live, but none of it matters because tonight I'll go home to Sara. And I never thought a woman could make that much difference in my life."

As he finished speaking, he saw a shadow in Burke's eyes and realized he'd probably touched an old nerve. Burke had been engaged several years earlier and had lost his girlfriend in a tragic car accident. His brother never ever talked about the loss, but it obviously was still with him.

"So what's up with you two?" he asked, changing the subject.

"Just working," Burke said, finishing his drink and motioning for the waitress to bring him another.

"It's a two-drink night?" he asked, raising an eyebrow. He couldn't remember a time when Burke had had more than one drink, especially during the week.

"Feels that way," Burke said, not bothering to explain what was on his mind.

That was Burke. He kept everything inside.

"I'm with you," Drew added, draining his glass.

Aiden turned to his younger brother, noting the shadows under his eyes. "What's going on with you?"

"I'm having nightmares about a woman." Drew tried to infuse a note of humor into his voice, but he fell short of the mark.

"I didn't realize you were seeing anyone," Aiden replied.

"Not that kind of woman." Drew let out a sigh that seemed to come from the depth of his soul. "She was part of a rescue mission I was on about five years ago. We saved three people, but we didn't save her."

Aiden understood exactly what Drew was going through, and Burke did as well. As firefighters, they rescued a lot of people, but not everyone.

"You can't torture yourself," Burke said. "You have to know you did your best. And that's all you could do."

"I'm not sure I did. But it's not a dead woman that's haunting me. It's a live one. I saw her last week. I was at Fisherman's Wharf with friends, and she was right there in the crowd. She turned, and she looked right at me, and I knew. She knew, too. I could see the recognition in her eyes. But we were fifty yards away from each other. There were tons of people. I lost her in the crowd."

"It wasn't her," Burke said flatly, no doubt in his voice.

"How do you know?" Drew asked.

"Because you saw her die."

"Maybe—"

"Don't go there," Burke put in forcefully, resting his forearms on the table. "I know what it's like to be haunted by a ghost. But that's all this woman is—a memory. You saw someone that looked like her, that's all. You want to believe it was her, because she died during your watch, and maybe you blame yourself for her death, but you can't bring her back, no matter how much you want to."

Silence followed Burke's words.

Aiden cast a quick glance at Drew and saw understanding in his younger brother's eyes. Burke might think he was talking about Drew's lost woman, but he was really talking about his own.

"Do you still see Leanne?" Aiden asked quietly, referring to his brother's fiancée.

Burke paled. "I don't want to talk about her."

"It might be helpful," Drew suggested.

"No, it wouldn't be helpful," Burke replied. "And I didn't invite either of you here to play shrink."

"So why are we here?" Aiden asked.

"I wanted to catch up with you both, but I also wanted to talk about Emma. I spoke to Max Harrison, the police inspector investigating the murder of Sister Margaret, and he thinks the perpetrator might be tied to the fire department."

"Because of the fire at the bar," Drew put in.

Burke nodded. "And the schools. Let's face it—a lot of guys in the department went through St. Andrew's."

"What do you propose we do?" Aiden asked. "I can tell you right now that Emma is not going to back down from doing her job."

"Agreed," Drew said. "Emma is one stubborn woman."

"We still need to keep an eye on her. She has a lot on her

plate right now, and Max also told me that Emma has been getting harassing texts from her ex-boyfriend."

"Now that we can handle," Aiden said. "I'd be happy to have a talk with Jon."

"So would I," Drew said. "I never liked him. I can't believe he's harassing her, though. I heard he cheated on her."

"Where did you hear that?" Aiden asked.

"From Nicole, but she wasn't positive. Emma doesn't share as much as she used to."

"I can't believe he cheated on Em," Aiden said with an angry shake of his head. "Now, I really want to talk to him."

"Calm down," Burke said. "I'm not suggesting you go break his kneecaps, just be aware. Especially you, Aiden. Now that you're back at the house, you can keep a closer eye on her."

"I will," Aiden said. They'd always been protective of their sisters, but Emma was the one who had a tendency to get into trouble more easily and more often.

"I'd still like to talk to Jon," Drew put in.

"Let me speak to Emma first," Aiden interjected. "I want to hear from her exactly what's going on."

"Keep us in the loop," Burke said.

Aiden smiled. "So I'm not just back in the loop, I'm actually leading it?" he joked.

Burke shot him a pointed look. "Don't screw it up."

"You know every time you say that, all I want to do is screw something up."

Drew laughed. "This takes me back to all the times I watched the two of you fight. All I need is some popcorn."

"We're not fighting," Burke said.

Aiden laughed. "Not yet anyway." He shoved back his chair. "I'm going to take off. I'll talk to Emma tomorrow."

—»»««—

Emma was back in work mode early Tuesday morning. On her way to her office, she stopped at Harry Brady's house. The owner of the bar had had twenty-four hours to recover. Hopefully, he'd be available for an interview.

She rang the bell and Christian Brady opened the door with an unhappy expression on his face. Christian was three years older than her and had been in Aiden's grade growing up. He was a stocky man with a square face, receding hairline and a few extra pounds around his middle. She knew that he'd recently left his wife, which was why he was back with his father. His life was obviously not going well at the moment. She would try to remember that and have some compassion.

"I told you my father would call you when he was ready to talk," he said.

"I need to speak to him now, Christian."

"He's upset, and he almost had a heart attack. The doctor told him to avoid stress, and you're stress."

"I'll make it as quick and painless as possible." She wasn't going away until she spoke to Harry. "I know you want to find out who did this to the bar. So help me out here, Christian."

"My dad doesn't know anything," he said, but he stepped back and waved her inside.

As he shut the door behind her, she said, "Where's Robert?"

"I'm right here," Robert said, coming down the stairs.

Christian's younger brother Robert was the same age as Emma. He wore black sweat pants and a gray t-shirt. He was thinner than Christian, had far more hair, and looked a lot happier to see her than Christian had.

"Emma Lou," he drawled, using his old nickname for

her. Louise was her middle name, and one of her teachers had insisted on calling her Emma Louise, which the kids in her class had shortened to Emma Lou.

"Hi, Robert. How have you been?"

"Good. Christian said you're investigating the fire. Any leads?"

"Not yet, but I'm working on it. Were you out of town this weekend?"

"Yeah, I was in Santa Barbara."

"Business or pleasure?"

"Business. It was a job interview." Robert's gaze didn't waver. "If you need more information, I'm happy to provide it. Although I'm surprised you're looking to the family for suspects."

"Because she doesn't know where else to look," Christian said sourly. "You sure do make a hell of an investigator, Emma. You think we burned down the bar? I own part of that building, and don't try to make it about insurance, because there isn't much."

"There's no need to be so defensive. These are standard questions, part of every arson investigation," she said. "Where were you when the fire broke out, Christian? I checked the duty roster, and you weren't on it."

"I was here, asleep, when my father got the call. He woke me up. I drove him over there."

"All right," she said, refusing to be intimidated by his angry gaze.

"Give her a break," Robert told his brother. He sent Emma an apologetic look. "It's been stressful around here. Seeing Dad like he is—it's rough."

"I understand. Where is Harry?"

"He's in the kitchen," Robert said.

She followed Robert down the hall. When she entered

the kitchen, she saw Harry seated at the table, a cup of coffee in front of him, and a full plate of eggs that looked like they'd been sitting there for a while.

Emma sat down at the table while Christian stood behind his father, and Robert leaned against a nearby counter.

Harry gave her a bleak look. "Emma," he said heavily. "These are terrible times."

"I know. I'm sorry, Harry." She gave him a compassionate smile. She could hardly believe this was the same man she had seen at her father's party. On Sunday night he'd been laughing and talking, serving up drinks, telling jokes. Now he was pale and fragile, and she could better understand Christian's protective attitude. "I'd like to go over what you did Sunday night before you left the bar."

He gave a nod. "I locked up the way I usually do. Normally, on Sundays we close by eleven, but we stayed open until almost one o'clock. Everyone was having a good time, celebrating your dad's promotion. No one wanted to go home."

"It was a great party," she agreed. "Were you the last person to leave?"

He nodded. "Yes. Mark left about ten minutes before me," he said referring to the bartender.

"Did you notice anyone hanging around the bar, the street, the parking lot?"

"No. It was quiet. I locked the door, got in my car and drove home—the way I've done a million times."

"Who has a key to your bar?"

"Mark has a key. He closes up for me sometimes, but he's completely trustworthy. His wife recently had a baby. He wouldn't want to put himself out of a job."

"Anyone else?"

"Christian and Robert both have keys," he said. "And the

janitorial service—J.P. Cleaners. I can get you their number."

Her heart sank at that piece of information. A janitorial service widened the circle considerably. Any number of people might have had access to the key or the ability to make a copy of the key. "What time do they usually come in?"

"Seven a.m., depending on the day." He paused. "Oh, and Mitchell has a key—my cook," he added. "He has worked for me for ten years."

She jotted down the names on her tablet. "Is that it?"

"Yes."

"Do you know if any of your employees are in any kind of trouble—financial or personal? Anyone have a grudge? Have you fired anyone who got angry about being terminated?"

"I haven't fired anyone in years. My employees are great people. If they have problems in their personal lives, I haven't heard about them." He let out a long sigh. "You're going to have a difficult time finding out who did this, aren't you?"

"I won't quit until I do."

He gave her a weak smile. "You sound like your father, now—confident, determined—a true Callaway."

"I'm going to need a list of employees, Harry."

"I have the list here," Christian said, as he picked up a file folder from the counter. "I anticipated your request."

"Thank you."

"Emma," Harry said. "I heard on the news that there was a body in the bar."

"I told you not to watch the news," Christian interjected.

"I'm a grown man. I can do what I want," Harry said with some bite in his tone. "Did the police identify her?"

"They did," she said slowly, not sure she wanted to tell him the bad news.

"And?"

He'd find out soon enough; she might as well tell him. "It was Sister Margaret Flannery from St. Andrew's."

Harry's pale skin turned white, the blood draining from his face.

Christian put his hand on his father's shoulder and Robert also moved across the room, giving his father a worried look.

"Dad?" Robert said. "Are you all right?"

"It's okay. I'm okay," Harry said, drawing in a deep breath. "How did Sister Margaret get into my bar?"

"We don't know yet."

"I can't believe she's dead. She taught both Christian and Robert. And I saw her a few weeks ago at Mass. She was organizing a fundraiser of some sort. She was always working for the school. She cared a lot about the community." He shook his head in confusion. "I feel like I'm in a nightmare and I need to wake up."

"Emma," Christian cut in. "I think my father should rest now."

She actually agreed with Christian. Harry's hand shook as he reached for his glass of water. His life had been shattered with the lighting of a match, and someone he cared about had died. Sometimes she got so caught up in the science of her cases that she forgot about the personal aspect.

"You take care of yourself, Harry," she said. "Don't scare us with any more trips to the hospital."

"I'll try not to," he said weakly.

Robert stayed with his father while Christian walked her to the front door. As he opened it for her, she asked one last question. "Do you know of anyone who might have wanted to hurt your father by burning down the bar?"

Christian shook his head. "I don't. My father has no enemies. A stranger is just a friend he hasn't met yet."

"Let me know if anyone comes to mind."

"I will," he said shortly. "I hope you're as good at your job as you think you are. My father and I both lost a lot, and I want someone to pay."

"So do I," she said. She didn't like Christian, but she had every intention of getting justice for Harry and all the others who had suffered at the arsonist's hands.

Eight

Emma stopped by the Hall of Justice on her way back to the office. The homicide detail of the police department was located on the fourth floor. As she stepped off the elevator, she felt a little nervous at the thought of seeing Max again. The last time they'd been together he'd kissed her senseless on the beach.

She hoped that she'd just built up that kiss in her mind over the last twelve hours, but when she saw Max at his desk, there was no denying the sudden flutter of butterflies in her stomach or her racing pulse. She fought the urge to flee. She was here on business, and she wasn't going to let an inconvenient attraction run her off.

She sat down in the chair next to his desk. Max turned away from his computer to look at her. His green eyes darkened. There was a memory in his gaze. He was reliving their kiss, too.

She cleared her throat. "I spoke to Harry Brady a few minutes ago as well as his sons, Christian and Robert. I thought you might want an update."

"I should have gone with you," Max said, annoyance in his voice. "We agreed to work together."

"I'm sure we'll talk to them again. They gave me their employee information as well as the names of those individuals with keys to the bar. It's a long list."

"Great."

"Christian, Harry's oldest son, was antagonistic. I don't know if it was personal against me, or if he was angry about the fire and trying to protect his father."

"Why would it be against you? I thought your families were friends."

"They are, but Christian doesn't like female firefighters. He's made no secret of that. He doesn't want to put his life in the hands of a woman. Apparently, he's not that interested in putting this investigation into my hands, either."

"What about his brother?"

"Robert has always been easier to get along with, but he didn't have much to say. Harry was very upset to learn about Sister Margaret's death. He's been in the St. Andrew's Parish for forty years, and both Christian and Robert had Sister Margaret for a teacher."

He stared at her. "What's your point?"

"I'm just telling you what I learned." She frowned, irritated with his short, clipped questions. "Why are you in such a bad mood?"

"I'm not in a bad mood. I'm busy."

"Busy working on our case?"

"How convenient of you to remember that it's *our* case," he said sarcastically.

"Okay, you are definitely in a mood." He did not want to talk to her, and maybe that was for the best. This arrogant, angry side of Max was much easier to handle than the charming, sexy side. She got to her feet. "I'm going back to my office. Let me know when you want to work together."

"Yeah, you, too," he shot back.

He was itching for a fight. "Look, I don't know who has pissed you off, but it's not me, and I won't be anyone's punching bag. So whatever you're going through, get over it before we talk again."

Max blew out a frustrated breath as Emma walked away. He'd thought he'd put her out of his head, that he'd gotten his priorities straightened out, but one look into her intelligent blue eyes, and he'd been filled with desire, wanting to touch her soft skin, feel the heat of her kiss, lose himself in her arms.

The irresistible pull to Emma made him angry. He didn't bring his personal life to work. But Emma was different. He'd never been attracted to anyone he worked with. Fortunately, his behavior just now had probably turned her off, which was a good thing. One of them had to back away, and since he seemed incapable of doing that, it might as well be her.

Although she'd seen right through him, and he had to admit that he liked the way she'd called him out. She could read people really well, a fact that also scared him. He was used to keeping his thoughts to himself. But Emma slipped past his guard every chance she got.

With another sigh, he ran a hand through his hair, stared at his computer screen and tried to remember what he'd been doing before Emma had walked in. While he was pondering his next move, he got a text from the medical examiner's office. Hopefully, they were about to get a break.

Several minutes later, he entered the medical examiner's office and checked in with Maya Kyoto, an Asian woman in her mid-thirties, who'd been very thorough and detail-oriented on the two cases they'd worked on previously.

"What did you find?" he asked.

She held up a plastic bag that appeared to contain dirt. We found this in the victim's clothes."

"Tell me it's more than just dirt."

"See the little yellow buds."

"Barely."

"I believe they come from a plant called Tahoe Yellow Cress, which can only be found on the shores of Lake Tahoe. I still need to confirm it, but that's where I am right now."

His heart sped up. If he could figure out where Sister Margaret had been in the time period between her disappearance and her death, he'd be a step closer to finding her kidnapper. "You're a genius, Maya."

She smiled. "This isn't definitive yet, but I wanted to let you know in case it helps with the investigation."

"It just might do that." Lake Tahoe was about four hours east of San Francisco and was a popular vacation destination. If he could find the plant Maya was talking about, maybe he could find someone who'd seen Sister Margaret. "Is there anything else?"

"We're still waiting on pathology and toxicology reports. I tried to get a fingerprint off the rosary we found in her pocket, but no luck. She didn't have anything else on her, no jewelry, no identification, nothing."

He nodded, wondering where her personal items were. According to her roommate, when Sister Margaret had gone to work that day, she'd taken with her a large black handbag. It had never been found.

"Thanks," he said. "You made my day."

She smiled. "Remember that the next time I tell you to be patient."

"I'll try." As he walked back to his office, he felt re-energized. He needed to get Sister Margaret's picture up to the sheriff's office in Tahoe and also the local media. Maybe someone had seen her. He finally had a clue. Hopefully, it wouldn't lead to another dead end.

→➤◄◄←

By lunchtime, Emma had worked her way down the employee list at Brady's. None of her phone calls had turned up any pertinent information. Everyone loved working at the bar, and they were very concerned about whether or not Harry would reopen. No one had noticed any strangers hanging around, and no one seemed to be having trouble with a spouse or lover.

Sighing, she told herself to be patient. Arson investigation was a slow process. Clues did not usually come quickly unless there was an eyewitness. So far, she had yet to find one.

Deciding to take a break, she headed outside at one o'clock and walked around the corner to the Second Street Deli. The street was bustling with people. There were some tourists, but her office was located near the San Francisco Civic Center, and most of the people who frequented the deli were local government workers.

The deli was run by Gus Halsey, a big, burly, scary-looking guy with tattoos all over his arms and a jagged scar that ran from his right eye to his ear. Gus intimidated a lot of people, but no one could deny that he made the best sandwiches in the area. Today there was a line out the door.

When she got to the front, Gus's stern expression softened. "Emma. Haven't seen you in a couple of days."

"I've been busy, but your most loyal customer is back."

"The usual?"

"Sounds good," she said, her mouth already watering at the thought of biting into Gus's delicious French Dip sandwich.

"You want cheese?"

"Always."

"Are you eating here or taking it back to your office?"

"I'll eat here." There were a couple of empty tables by the window, and she was tired of grabbing meals at her desk. Maybe a change of scenery would also open up her mind to new possibilities.

As Gus made her sandwich, she grabbed a soda out of the glass case and took it to the register. Gus's sister, Mary, gave her a smile. Mary had a sweet, round face that looked nothing like her brother's. Her normally cheerful eyes were fatigued today, probably due to the extra thirty pounds she was carrying around. Mary was very, very pregnant.

"It's almost your due date, isn't it?" Emma asked.

"One week late," Mary said, as she rang up Emma's order. "It's turned out to be a good thing, because my cousin was supposed to help out and he bailed on us. The next person we found said yes, then called in the next day and said no, she'd changed her mind. So we're still looking for a temporary cashier if you know anyone."

"I'll think about it."

"Here you go," Gus said, handing over her order.

"Thanks. It looks delicious." She took her tray to a table and sat down. A newspaper had been left behind, and her gaze immediately caught on Sister Margaret's photo. The accompanying article was short and to the point. Hopefully, the news coverage would bring forward someone who knew something.

She took a bite of her sandwich and skimmed through another article while she was eating. A long shadow fell over her table, and she looked up, surprised to see Max.

"What are you doing here?" she asked.

"Looking for you," he said. "I went by your office. Your assistant said you were probably here."

"So you do have investigative skills. I was beginning to wonder."

A half-smile curved his lips.

"And I see your mood has improved," she added.

"Can I sit down?"

"Are you going to be nice?"

"Yes."

"Then sit." She wondered what had changed in the past few hours, because this Max was not the one she had left earlier.

"I have a lead," he said.

"Now I understand the sparkle in your eyes." She sat up straighter in her chair. "Don't leave me hanging."

"An assistant medical examiner found some dirt and leaves in Sister Margaret's clothes and believes they may come from a rare plant that's native to the Lake Tahoe region."

"Really?" she asked, as a surge of excitement ran through her. "That could be a huge break."

"I've forwarded Sister Margaret's photo to the sheriff's office in Lake Tahoe, and I also spoke to one of their detectives. He'll get the word out to the press and local law enforcement. Hopefully we'll find someone who saw her in the area and/or we'll be able to pinpoint the region of the lake where she might have been staying. It's still a long shot," he warned.

"At least it's a shot. It's more than we had before."

"I am feeling more optimistic."

"I can see that. Do you want to tell me what the hell was wrong with you earlier?"

"I'm sorry I snapped at you. I had a lot of things on my mind." He glanced around the deli. "I'm hungry. What's good here?"

"Everything."

"I like the looks of your sandwich."

"Then get your own," she said, taking another bite.

He smiled. "You don't even like to share your food, do you?"

"I grew up with seven siblings. If you didn't protect your food, you might go hungry."

"Somehow I doubt your parents would have allowed that. I'll be right back."

As Max went to order his meal, Emma thought about what he'd told her. Tahoe was a four-hour car ride away, and during that trip Sister Margaret could have been spotted by any number of people. Max had checked the neighborhood around St. Andrew's for witnesses, but maybe he'd been looking in the wrong place.

As Max returned to the table, she said, "A lot of people who live in San Francisco have cabins in Lake Tahoe."

"A lot being the problem," he said, popping open his can of soda.

"Maybe we could narrow it down to people who have a connection to St. Andrew's—students or teachers."

"Or parishioners," he reminded her. The school is connected to the church."

"Yes, but the fire was started in the school. I want to stick with that focus."

"I think that's a good idea." He sat back in his seat as Mary brought over his order. He'd also gotten the French Dip. He dug into it with enthusiasm, obviously happy to put their conversation on hold while he ate.

"This is good," he said as he downed the first half in a few bites. "I have to admit I'm a little surprised. This place is a hole in the wall."

"True, but Gus takes pride in his food."

He tipped his head toward the counter. "That's Gus? He doesn't look like your typical deli owner."

She smiled. "He's lived a couple of different lives."

"Well, in this one he's a good sandwich maker."

As Max ate, Emma sipped her soda and thought about the investigation. But as she watched Max wipe a dab of juice off his lip, she got distracted and a little hot. She forced herself to look away, to think about something else besides his sexy mouth.

"So how did your family dinner go last night?" she asked.

"It was all right. Maybe a little better than I expected. It started out awkward, but I had a conversation with my brother that for a moment felt almost normal."

"I looked your brother up online," she confessed.

There was no surprise in his eyes. "I figured you would."

"I know the basics. Your brother got into a fight and a man died. But obviously there's more. Can you tell me what happened?"

"You already know, Emma."

"Only the basics. Your brother claimed that the person he fought was stalking or harassing his girlfriend. Was that true?"

"Spencer believed it was true."

"What about you?"

"In the beginning I had no doubts. But his girlfriend's testimony didn't support Spencer's statements. I don't know if she got scared, if she was pressured by the victim's family, or if she really hadn't seen things the way Spencer had seen them, but her words sent Spencer to jail." He paused. "I thought she screwed him over big time, but Spencer doesn't hold her accountable. I think, crazy as it is, that he's still in love with her."

"Really? I can't imagine having fond feelings for someone who sent me to jail."

"It doesn't make sense to me either, but I didn't know Stephanie. I was living in Los Angeles. I never met her until Spencer was arrested."

"You must have tried to keep him out of jail."

"I did try. I just didn't succeed. Captain Crowley also helped, but in the end the jury believed the prosecutor's story. After watching the way the attorney put together the facts, I almost thought Spencer was guilty."

"Almost?"

"My brother is reckless and impulsive, and he was not one to walk away from a fight, but he was never the instigator. He never hit anyone unless he was defending himself or someone else."

She thought about his words. "If this guy was stalking Spencer's girlfriend, why wouldn't she confirm that fact?"

"She did in the beginning, but the prosecutor picked her story apart, and she crumbled."

"What was her story?"

He frowned. "You really want to hear all this?"

"I'm curious."

"Are you ever not curious?" he countered.

"Rarely," she admitted. "Did Stephanie date Kurt Halstead?"

"No, she worked with him at his grandfather's investment company. They were friends, and he asked her out a few times, but Stephanie had started dating Spencer so she said no. She'd find flowers on her desk at work. She'd get text messages from Kurt asking her to meet up for drinks or lunch, some of those implying that he could help her get ahead at her job if she came to talk to him. She felt like Kurt was always watching her. On the weekends, he'd show up wherever she was. On a couple of occasions, she thought he followed her home. She didn't want to say anything to anyone, because she was afraid she'd lose her job."

"That sounds a little ambiguous."

"It got worse. More phone calls, some hang-ups, footsteps showing up in the mud outside of their first-floor window. Spencer called me about it, and I told him to go to the police. But he said Stephanie didn't want him to do that. She was very focused on her career. She didn't think they had enough proof. But then proof arrived. Stephanie received an envelope at work with three photos inside. They were all of her—one as she unlocked her apartment door, another at the gym where she worked out and a third taken outside a restaurant where she was having drinks with girlfriends. There were words written on each photograph, all adjectives: *beautiful, gorgeous, hot.* That's when she realized that someone was watching her every move."

"What happened next?" Emma asked, caught up in the story.

"Stephanie showed Spencer the photos. He was livid. He wanted to go after Kurt, but Stephanie said she would take the pictures to the police. She left the apartment, but she didn't go to the police that night; she went to her boss's apartment. She wanted to get his advice on what to do."

"Didn't he tell her to go to the police?"

"No. He told her she'd better make sure it was Kurt before she accused him of anything, or her career could be ruined."

Emma frowned. "That's terrible advice."

"Unfortunately, while Stephanie was at her boss's house, Kurt showed up outside her apartment building. He was leaving a floral arrangement by her front door. He didn't realize Spencer was there. I think he thought they were out together. Spencer saw him and came outside. He confronted him on the steps. They started to argue. Spencer pushed Kurt.

Kurt pushed back, and the fight was on. It ended two punches later when Kurt hit his head on the pavement. Neighbors called the police, and Spencer was arrested. Kurt died later that night without ever regaining consciousness." Max blew out a breath as he finished the story.

Emma considered his words for a long moment. "It doesn't really sound like Spencer did anything that wrong."

"That's because I'm telling you his side of the story. The prosecutor twisted everything. He produced witnesses who said that Kurt was afraid of Spencer, that Kurt and Stephanie were just friends but Spencer was insanely jealous. It went on and on. And the one person who could have really made a difference was Stephanie, but she fell apart."

Emma shook her head, unable to understand the other woman's actions. "Why?"

"I think it was all based on her fear of losing her job."

"Why would she want to continue working for the grandfather of the guy who'd been stalking her?"

"Spencer told me that Stephanie grew up in foster care. She was dirt poor, homeless at one point. She was obsessed with money and security. She finally had it, and she didn't want to lose it."

"But she was willing to send her boyfriend to jail?"

He shrugged. "I don't think she thought it would go down that way. None of us did."

"She didn't continue to work at the company after Spencer went to jail, did she?"

"Yes, she did," he said.

Emma stared at him in disbelief. "Oh, come on. Seriously?"

"The Halsteads didn't blame her. After all, her testimony got Spencer convicted."

"And this is the woman your brother harbors no ill will

towards?"

"I don't know what he's thinking."

"Is Stephanie still in San Francisco?"

He nodded. "Yes."

She saw the worry in his eyes. "Your brother wouldn't try to see her again?"

"I hope not. She's married and has a child. I told Spencer that. But he didn't promise me he wouldn't look her up. And she's obviously still on his mind."

"He's probably still asking himself why she did that to him. Did they stay together after Spencer went to prison?"

"No. Spencer says he broke it off. He couldn't handle the look on her face when she came to visit." He took a breath. "I'm not entirely sure it was all him, though. He might be saving face. It's quite possible she dumped him. I just want him to stay away from her now. He doesn't need more trouble. And she is trouble." He ran a hand through his hair. "But will Spencer listen to me? I highly doubt it."

Emma understood his frustration. She'd felt powerless when it came to her siblings, especially her brothers. "It's going to be his choice," she said.

"I know."

"Were you and Spencer close when you were young?"

He shook his head. "Not really. There was a gap of four years between us. After my father took off, Spencer wasn't my brother anymore; he was a pseudo father figure. He told me what to do and expected me to do it. Occasionally, we broke out of those roles, usually when we were surfing. That's when I thought Spencer was incredibly cool."

She smiled. "Is he like you—patient enough to wait for the right wave?"

"No. Spencer would have ten rides in before I had one. We approached life very differently."

"Maybe you should go surfing with him again, bring back some good memories."

"It's November," he protested. "It's cold."

She smiled. "With family, there's always a price. You can wear a wet suit."

"I'll think about it. I'd probably make more of a difference in his life if I helped him get a job. It won't be easy. He killed someone. Very few people want to work with a murderer."

"It was a fight that got out of control. I don't think I'd call your brother a murderer."

"Because I told you his story, but if you were looking at a resume…"

"I get it. But surely someone will give him a break." As she thought about whether or not she had any connections, her gaze came to rest on Mary, who was sitting on a high stool behind the cash register, absentmindedly stroking her pregnant belly. "Why not here?" she said. "They're looking for a part-time clerk to cover while Mary is on maternity leave. It would be three months, probably minimum wage, but it would get your brother on the road to something."

Max frowned. "You don't need to get involved in helping my brother find a job."

"Why not?"

"Because we're already a little too involved." His gaze met hers. "I think we both know that."

"I'm just making a suggestion that could help your brother. It's not a big deal."

"Do you think Gus would hire an ex-con?"

She nodded. "Gus *is* an ex-con. He ran with gangs when he was young, and he got into trouble stealing cars. But he got his life together. I think he'd be the perfect person to consider giving your brother a second chance. I can ask him if you want."

"You do like to be in the middle of things, don't you?"

"I was born in the middle. Well, actually, that's not true. I started out as the baby, but after my mother married and had more children, I ended up in the fourth position out of eight. So I'm pretty comfortable being in the middle and getting into everyone's business. But in this case, it's a matter of practicality. I know Gus. You don't. My recommendation will go further."

"You don't know Spencer."

"Then maybe I should meet him."

She could see in his gaze that that's the last thing he wanted to have happen.

"Let's put the idea on hold. Gus has a line, and I want to head over to St. Andrew's to speak to Ruth Harbough."

"She's working today?"

"She said Sister Margaret would want life to go on and responsibilities to be met."

"I can't remember a day in school when Mrs. Harbough wasn't at the front desk when I arrived. I'll go with you."

"All right," he said slowly.

"Trying to think of a reason to say no?" she challenged.

He tipped his head and a smile spread across his face. That smile made her catch her breath and doubt the wisdom of her latest decision, but Max was already getting to his feet. And she did want to talk to Mrs. Harbough.

As they walked out of the deli, Emma was stunned to see her ex-boyfriend approaching. This was no chance meeting. There was purpose in Jon's walk and in his gaze. He'd obviously come looking for her. She really needed to let her assistant know that giving out her lunch whereabouts was a bad idea. Not that Jon couldn't have figured it out on his own; she'd been eating at the Second Street Deli three times a week for the last year.

"Who's that?" Max asked, giving her a quizzical look.

"Jon," she ground out.

"That's your ex? The one who has been texting you nonstop?"

"Yes."

She hadn't seen Jon in several weeks, and she waited for some kind of feeling to hit her—sadness, anger, or relief. But oddly she felt nothing. She felt neutral. His expensive suit, his golden blond hair and hazel-colored eyes didn't ignite any lingering sparks. She felt like she was looking at a stranger, not someone she'd shared an apartment with. The heavy feeling left her chest. She was over him.

Apparently, he wasn't over her.

Nine

> ➤➤❰❰ ❮‑

"I finally tracked you down," Jon said, anger in his voice. He shot Max a sharp look. "Who's this?"

"This is Max Harrison," Emma answered. "He's an inspector with the SFPD. We're working on a case together."

With her explanation, Jon immediately dismissed Max, turning back to Emma. "I need to speak to you."

"We have nothing left to say."

Jon looked back at Max. "Do you mind? This is a private conversation."

"You're the one who interrupted a private conversation," Max said. "You heard Emma. She has nothing to say, so move along."

While Emma appreciated the defense, she was also annoyed by it. She could take care of herself.

"We're done, Jon. I'm going on with my life, and you need to do the same," she said.

"How can you turn your back on everything we had? We were going to get married."

"You never actually asked me to marry you," she reminded him.

"It was understood."

"A lot of things were *understood*," she said. "Fidelity, for one. You cheated on me, and no matter how many times you say you're sorry, it won't change what happened."

"You're a cold bitch."

At Jon's harsh words, Max said, "That's enough." He took a step forward, but Emma caught his arm.

"I've got this," she told Max. "If that's what you think of me, Jon, then why are you here?"

Jon blew out a breath. "I'm sorry. I shouldn't have said that."

"Can't you see that all we do is hurt each other?"

"It wasn't always this way." His expression went from angry to pleading. "I know I messed up. You were the best thing that ever happened to me."

"No, that's not true," she said, shaking her head. "I wasn't right for you, and you weren't right for me. We didn't work, and you know that. I don't understand why you're suddenly acting like this, but it has to stop. We have to say goodbye and wish each other well."

Jon stared back at her, as if he couldn't believe the finality of her words. "Emma…"

"Goodbye, Jon." She turned and walked down the street, hoping Jon wouldn't follow her. When she got to the corner, only Max was by her side. She glanced over her shoulder. Jon was gone.

"Where are you parked?" she asked.

"Right over there."

"Let's take your car."

"You must be shaken up if you're willing to let me drive," he said, as they crossed the street.

"I'm okay. I'm sorry you had to be a part of that."

"What did you see in that guy?"

She gave him a weak smile. "He has some good qualities.

I can't remember what they are right now."

"Do you think he's going to accept your goodbye?"

"I can't imagine why he wouldn't. It's not like he's short on dates. He's got plenty of women who would love to be Mrs. Jon Wickmore the third."

"That title is way too pretentious for you." He paused. "If he contacts you again, Emma, let me know."

"Why?"

"He could be dangerous."

"He's not dangerous, Max. He's just obstinate. You don't need to worry about it."

"I've seen this kind of thing go down more than once, and annoying can turn to dangerous."

"Are you referring to your brother's case?"

He looked surprised by the question. "Actually, I wasn't, but now that you mention it, there are some similarities."

"It's completely different, and don't forget I have five brothers. I'm a tough girl and a cold bitch, according to Jon. I can handle myself. Trust me."

Max opened the door of the gray sedan he drove on the job, and she slipped into the front seat. As they headed toward St. Andrew's, she told herself that Max's worry was misplaced. She knew Jon. He was acting like a spoiled child who'd had his favorite toy taken away. He'd get over it. Jon was not dangerous.

Max was overreacting. She could understand it, because in his job he saw the worst in people. In her job, that was also sometimes true. But she still liked to believe that deep down most people were more good than bad.

⟶⟫⟪⟵

"It looks like they're getting the classrooms back in

shape," Emma commented, as Max parked in front of the kindergarten playground.

"That was fast," Max remarked, his gaze narrowing at the sight of a familiar figure coming out of the classroom with a paint tray and a roller in his hand. "Isn't that your friend from the bar?"

"Tony," she said, surprise in her voice. "I wonder what he's doing here."

"Looks like he's painting. Is that his job?"

"Sometimes. Tony has a lot of jobs. He bartends, does labor for my Uncle Kevin's construction firm, paints, and coaches a kids' soccer team. He doesn't like the nine-to-five life."

"Is he another one of your ex-boyfriends?" he asked, feeling jealous at the thought.

Emma waved a dismissive hand. "Don't be silly. Tony is like a brother to me."

"He didn't act that way at the bar the other night."

"He flirts, because it's in his DNA; he's not serious."

"After seeing you with Jon and this guy, I'm beginning to think your intelligence does not extend to the men in your life."

She straightened in her seat and shot him a dark look. "What does that mean?"

"You underestimate how much men want you. Jon— Tony…"

"You?" she finished.

His gut clenched. "I wasn't going there," he said quickly.

"And yet we're there, Max." She let those words sit, then added, "And you're making assumptions based on very little information. I know Jon and Tony. You don't."

"Just sharing an observation."

"Next time, wait to be asked."

He decided his best answer was no answer, so he got out of the car.

As Emma stepped onto the sidewalk, Tony saw her and came over to the fence, a big grin on his face.

"Emma, what are you doing here?"

"I was going to ask you the same question."

"Joey McCarthy needed some help painting the classrooms, so I took the job. He wants to get the kids back in as soon as possible. They're all doubled up right now."

"It's good you had some time."

"It's good he needed more help. I could use the money. The football season is killing me. My teams keep going down, Emma."

"Then maybe you should stop betting," she retorted.

"I tell myself that every time I lose, but then I win, and I get all excited. But it's not that big of a deal. Just fifty bucks here and there. I don't want you to think I'm a gambler or anything."

"I've known you most of my life, Tony. I already knew you were a gambler."

"And a great guy," he said with a charming smile. "A guy you still owe dinner. I'm waiting for your call."

"I'm a little busy right now."

Tony's expression turned serious. "I couldn't believe it when I woke up yesterday and saw that Brady's was completely destroyed. We were just there that night."

"What time did you leave?" Max asked, interjecting himself into the conversation since Emma seemed more interested in chatting up Tony. He flashed his badge. "I'm Max Harrison with the SFPD."

"Tony Moretti. I saw you at the bar. You two were together." Tony glanced at Emma. "Is he your new—"

"No," she said quickly. "He's not anything. We're

working together on the arson investigation."

"And the homicide," Max added.

Tony shook his head in bewilderment. "That was another shock. I mean, Sister Margaret? Who would want to kill a nun? This city is going crazy."

"Did you know Sister Margaret?" Max asked.

"Too well," Tony said. "She was always calling me out for something, but she wasn't so bad. Sometimes I could make her laugh. I used to bet the other kids that I could get a smile out of her. I won more times than not."

"Did you take that challenge on in detention?" Emma asked. "Aiden said you and Jarod and him spent a lot of time there after school."

Tony nodded, a sheepish grin on his face. "That's true. And sometimes Aiden was the ringleader. Don't let him tell you he was following Jarod and me. He had his own ideas."

"Trust me, I know," Emma said. "And Aiden would be the first to admit that." She glanced over at Max, then back at Tony. "When we were kids, do you remember someone setting fire to the dumpster?"

Tony licked his lips, his expression not quite so open now, Max thought.

"Yeah, I remember that," Tony said. "That was the highlight of my eighth-grade year. I was sitting in the classroom right next to the dumpster. We were taking a math test, and all of a sudden one of the girls started yelling, *Fire!* We spent the rest of the afternoon on the playground watching the firefighters."

As Tony talked about the fire, his energy level increased. Max couldn't help wondering if the guy wouldn't have enjoyed watching Brady's burn to the ground even more than watching a small fire smolder in a dumpster.

"Do you know who set that fire?" Max asked.

"I'm pretty sure it was Christian Brady. He was always fascinated by fire. That's why he went into firefighting. Whoa," Tony said suddenly, as he put two thoughts together. "That's weird. Brady set a fire. Now Brady's bar burns down. Spooky."

Max wondered if Tony's dumb-as-a-rock act was real or just a great pretense.

"Do you think Christian burned down his dad's place?" Tony asked.

Emma shook her head. "There's no evidence that would suggest that."

"Yeah, you're right. He works there, so why would he want to burn down his own bar? Doesn't make sense."

Tired of the conversation, Max said, "I'm going to speak to Mrs. Harbough. Are you coming, Emma?"

"Of course," she said.

"Don't forget that dinner you owe me, Emma."

"I'm sure you'll remind me, Tony."

"So you didn't have a thing with that guy before, but now you're going to dinner with him?" Max couldn't help asking as they walked down the sidewalk toward the front of the school.

"I owe him dinner because he helped me move out of Jon's apartment."

"And you still think he doesn't like you?"

"Does it matter? For someone who wants to keep things professional, you're awfully interested in my personal life."

"Your personal life seems to be showing up everywhere we go."

"I'm popular. What can I say? I'm sure if we were in Los Angeles, we'd be running into your old girlfriends and maybe a few wannabes."

"Well, we're not in L.A., so you don't have to worry

about that."

"Is there a serious ex-girlfriend in your life, Max?"

"No."

"What about a not-so-serious ex-girlfriend?"

"No."

She gave him an irritated look. "There you go with the man of mystery act again. Can't you ever give more than a one-word answer?"

"Yes." He laughed at her disgruntled expression. "But right now we have an interview to do. Can we stay on task?"

"Absolutely."

He held open the front door, relieved that he didn't have time to get into his past with Emma. She was already way too involved in his present. "After you."

Walking back into her old elementary school, Emma felt a wave of memories. Inside the front door were two glass cases filled with trophies, plaques and other awards, some of which she'd helped the school to win, and along the main hallway were class photographs dating back fifty years. There was a lot of history in this school, and she was reminded of how close a fire had come to destroying everything inside, not just damaging two classrooms.

She'd talked to the principal, Gloria Monty, right after the fire at St. Andrew's, and had also interviewed staff members. Max had done interviews with the same people in regards to Sister Margaret. But neither one of them had come up with any leads as a result of those conversations. "I hope this visit doesn't turn out to be as pointless as my last one," she muttered.

Max nodded. "Yeah, I haven't been in the principal's

office this much since I was a kid."

"I can't really picture you getting into trouble. You seem very controlled and thoughtful about your actions."

"I had my moments of rebellion."

"I doubt there were many."

He conceded her point with a nod. "I couldn't afford to bring any more drama into my house. My mom was an angry, unhappy mess before the divorce and pretty much the same after. For most of my childhood, *she* was the drama. When I was at school, I wanted to be normal, boring." He paused. "How's that for a more-than-one-word answer?"

"Better." Max didn't drop many clues about himself, but the few she'd gathered did help her understand him better. She was beginning to realize why he exercised so much control over every aspect of his life. It was a result of his chaotic childhood and the way he'd learned to control his environment and stay sane. Still, she thought it must be exhausting to never let loose. She had a feeling all those feelings and emotions inside of him were going to explode one day.

"Here we are," he said, pausing outside the door to the office. "I have to admit Mrs. Harbough and I don't have much rapport. She's a stern, stoic woman, and I've only seen her vulnerable twice: once when she realized Margaret was gone, and yesterday when I came by here to tell her she was dead."

"She always scared the crap out of me," Emma said. "But she knows more about this school than anyone, so let's do it."

Max opened the door and she stepped into the office. Mrs. Harbough sat behind the counter and was working on her computer. In the office behind her, through a half-open door, Emma could see the principal having a meeting with a teacher.

Ruth Harbough didn't look happy to see them. She

stopped what she was doing and got to her feet. "Inspector Harrison. Inspector Callaway. What can I do for you?"

It felt strange to be called Inspector Callaway by a woman who'd known her since she was five years old. On the other hand, Emma appreciated the respect.

"We need to ask you a few more questions," Max said. "Is there somewhere private we can talk?"

"This will have to do. I can't leave my desk right now, and classes will be out in five minutes. Have you made any progress in the investigation?"

"Some," he said. "Did Sister Margaret have any ties to Lake Tahoe? Did she go there to visit friends? Was it one of your vacation spots?"

Ruth looked taken aback by the questions. "Lake Tahoe? We used to go up there in the summers. We were there last August for a few days."

"Do you have a place up there?"

"No. One of the parents let us use their cabin."

"Who was that?" Emma interjected, her pulse speeding up.

Ruth stared back at them for a moment, as if trying to figure out the reason for their question, and then said, "Carol Parkins."

"Do you know if the Parkinses lent their house to other families in the school?" Max asked.

"All the time. They donate a week in the auction every year, and they allow friends to stay there. But Margaret did not go to Lake Tahoe without telling anyone," Ruth said firmly. "If she was there, it was against her will. She was a dedicated teacher. She wouldn't leave her class without a substitute." Ruth's mouth began to tremble. "I can't believe she's dead, that someone killed her and left her body to burn in a fire in a bar. She didn't even drink. She wouldn't have wanted to die there." Ruth started shaking her head. "It's just terrible."

"You should sit down," Emma said quickly, walking around the counter to help Ruth back into her chair. She was shocked to see such a strong woman look suddenly so fragile. Maybe there was another side to Ruth Harbough, too. "We're very sorry about Sister Margaret, and we are going to do everything we can to find out who killed her."

Ruth blinked back tears. "Thank you." She drew in a breath for strength. "Margaret wouldn't want me to fall apart. She was a very strong woman. I think about who took her, and I have to believe that for the time she was alive, she made their life very difficult."

Emma gave her a compassionate smile. "I think you're right." She paused. "Does the school record detention attendance, and are those records kept for a long period of time?"

"We don't have detention anymore. That disappeared about ten years ago," Mrs. Harbough said. "At one time we did keep those records, but they're long gone."

"What about vandalism or fires here at the school?" Emma asked.

"There have been a few incidents over the years, nothing recently."

"Would you mind checking back through your records and giving me the names of any individuals who were involved?"

"I can do that. It may take me awhile. The last ten years are in the computer, but before that records were kept in cardboard boxes, and most of those are stored in the basement of the church."

"I'm particularly interested in anything involving fire," Emma said.

"May I ask why you're looking so far back into the past?"

The bell rang, and Emma was saved from a long answer. "We're just checking everything we can think of," she said.

Mrs. Harbough rose. "I have to deal with the children now."

"When is the funeral for Sister Margaret?" Emma asked.

"Saturday at eleven," Ruth replied. "There will be a rosary on Friday night."

The office door opened, and several kids entered. The sight of those blue plaid uniforms took Emma right back to childhood. "I can't believe they're still wearing the same uniforms as I did," she said to Max as they left the office.

"Feeling nostalgic?" he asked with a smile.

"It was a simpler time," she admitted. "There was nothing but possibilities ahead. Now, not so many."

Surprise flashed in his eyes. "Cynicism from you? No way."

"What? I can be cynical."

"No, I don't think so. You have an innate sense of optimism."

"You don't know me very well."

He smiled. "I know that you don't like to be categorized."

"Well, that's true," she admitted.

"Why would you take optimism as an insult?"

"Because it makes me sound like I don't see reality, and I do."

"That wasn't what I meant." His steps slowed and then he stopped walking. He gazed into her eyes. "The job takes me to some really dark places. I forget that not everyone has taken the same trip."

"My job sometimes goes down that same nasty road." She paused and smiled. "But you're right. I am generally optimistic, and I do tend to see the good in people, which can be a detriment. I guess that's why I got defensive."

She pushed open the door to the school, and they stepped outside. There was a cluster of parents waiting on the sidewalk for their kids, and Emma saw a lot of eyes turn in their direction. Rumors had to be running rampant at the school today, and she imagined a lot of nerves were on edge with Sister Margaret's death. She couldn't imagine how she would have reacted when she was a child if one of her teachers had suddenly died under suspicious circumstances.

As they walked toward the car, she saw Tony now standing by the white van parked directly behind Max's sedan. He gave them a nod. "How did it go? Did you find out anything?"

She shrugged. "Not really."

"I've been thinking about who might not like Sister Margaret," Tony said. And it suddenly came to me—Mrs. Harbough."

"Why would you say that?" She glanced at Max but saw nothing but disdain in his eyes. He was obviously not going to take anything Tony had to say seriously. "Mrs. Harbough is quite distraught over Sister Margaret's death. They were roommates."

"Well, I heard they were more than *roommates*," Tony said with a gleam in his eyes.

"Do you have any facts to support that?" Max asked sharply.

"No, but the rumor has been going around town for a while. I thought I should mention it."

"Thanks, Tony," she said quickly, sensing that she needed to put some distance between Tony and Max. "We'll look into that angle."

Max rolled his eyes and walked over to the car.

"That old broad in there has some secrets," Tony said to

Emma before she left. "I know I'm not as smart as you are, Emma, but I spent a lot of time in the office waiting to see the principal, and I heard some very interesting conversations between Mrs. Harbough and other people."

"That was a long time ago, Tony."

"People don't change."

"I'll talk to you later. And I won't forget about dinner," she said cutting him off before he could remind her. "As soon as I get this case wrapped up."

Max was waiting for her in the car. As she fastened her seatbelt, she saw Max looking in the rearview mirror at the van parked behind them.

"What are you thinking?" she asked.

"Just wondering how many chemicals or accelerants might be in the back of that van."

"Now you want to make Tony the arsonist?" she asked. "He's painting the classroom. And that's not even his van. It belongs to his boss."

"There's something about that guy I don't like. He's too…"

"Handsome? Sexy?" she offered.

He shot her a dark look. "Seriously? You like that type?"

"Most women see Tony that way. He has quite a reputation in the neighborhood."

Max shook his head. "I don't get it."

She could see why Max didn't get Tony's charm, because Max was a more serious kind of guy, and she didn't think Tony had been serious a day in his life. "I know you'd like to discredit anything Tony has to say, but what do you think of his suggestion that Sister Margaret and Ruth Harbough were lovers?"

"I asked Mrs. Harbough that question when Margaret first disappeared."

"Are you kidding me?" she asked in astonishment. "I cannot believe you got that question out of your mouth."

"I had to consider the possibility there had been some sort of domestic quarrel. Mrs. Harbough told me that they were platonic friends, and that she was horrified I would ask the question. She said both she and Margaret were extremely religious women, and that type of relationship would go against everything they believed in. She was very disappointed in me for assuming that two women couldn't share an apartment as friends."

"It would seem unlikely that they'd be anything else," Emma said. "Mrs. Harbough was married at some point."

"While she was in her early twenties. I checked. She has a son, Jeffrey, who went to live with his father when he was twelve years old."

"That's weird," she said. "How old is the son now? I wonder why I've never heard of him."

"He's thirty-four now."

"So five years older than me," she murmured. "Maybe I wasn't paying attention, but I don't remember ever seeing him around the school."

"He spent most of his time with his father in San Jose."

"You did do your research," she said. "I'm impressed."

"Did you think I'd been sitting on my hands the last ten days?"

"Hard to say since you rarely share what you've been doing," she retorted.

"At any rate, Mrs. Harbough is way down on my list of suspects," he said.

"I didn't realize we had a list of suspects," she said dryly. "But just for the purpose of discussion, why are you ruling her out?"

"Because Margaret's death is tied to the fires, and I don't

see Mrs. Harbough as our arsonist. Do you?"

"I can't say definitively no, but she doesn't fit the profile. And she's a small woman. Margaret had at least fifty pounds on her. I don't know how Ruth could have kidnapped her, hidden her away or left her body at the bar. Although she could have had help, so I can't rule her out. And even though she said she isn't a lesbian, how could we prove it?" She groaned and pressed her fingers to her temples. "My head is starting to hurt."

"I know what you mean. I've been going around the same circles for days."

Her phone buzzed and she pulled it out of her purse.

"Ex-boyfriend again?" Max asked.

"No, it's a realtor friend of mine. I've been trying to get in to see an apartment the last few days, and she said it's available now if I can get there in the next twenty minutes." She glanced over at Max. "How do you feel about a side trip to the Marina?"

"Why are you looking at an apartment?"

"Since I broke up with Jon, I've been living with my parents, and I need to move on."

"Gotcha."

"If I go all the way back to work and get my car, I probably won't make it in time." She gave him a pleading smile.

"Fine, I'll take you."

"I'll owe you one."

He grinned. "And I will collect."

Ten

—➤➤◄◄◄─

The apartment Emma wanted to look at was in a Victorian building in the Marina District. The Marina was at the north end of the city and very close to the Golden Gate Bridge, which connected the North Bay to San Francisco. It was one of the more desirable neighborhoods in the city, and it took several trips around the block to find a parking space.

"You must make more than I do if you can afford this," Max said.

"The building is under rent control, so the apartment is a steal. My friend, who's a realtor, is trying to get me in before it gets listed as a rental."

"I hope your apartment comes with a garage," he said as he squeezed the sedan into a narrow spot.

"It does. I would go crazy looking for parking every night," she said as they got out of the car.

He followed her up the stairs to the third floor. The apartment door was open, and they stepped inside. The living room was completely empty, but the hardwood floors glistened in the sunlight. Everything was clean and freshly painted, and Max felt an oddly immediate sense of welcome. Even completely empty, this place had far more charm than the apartment he lived in.

An attractive redhead greeted Emma with a big smile, and the two embraced. Emma was definitely a friendly, popular woman. He'd never spent a lot of time cultivating friendships. He'd had a few close friends when he was young and in school, but he'd left most of those behind when he'd gone to college. When he'd decided to become a cop, he'd put all his time and energy into making that happen.

Emma motioned him over. "I want to introduce you to my good friend, Alicia Connors," she said. "This is Max Harrison. He's an inspector with the SFPD."

Alicia gave him a friendly smile. She was a pretty woman with her red hair, brown eyes and light dusting of freckles on her nose. She wore a slim-fitting black dress under a black jacket, and her high heels made her a few inches taller than Emma.

"It's nice to meet you," Alicia said, extending her hand.

"You, too," he said, shaking her hand.

Alicia turned to Emma. "Sorry to drag you away from work, but I'm so glad you could make it. This apartment is amazing. If I didn't have a lease, I'd move in here myself. But if you want it, you're going to have to decide today. The owner is putting it up for lease tomorrow. He's doing me a favor by letting me show it to you today. I told him you would be an awesome tenant, and he said he'd met your dad once and liked him very much."

"The Jack Callaway magic strikes again," Emma said lightly.

Max thought there was a bit of a strain in her voice, and he wondered if Jack's shadow was sometimes a little too long for Emma. She liked her achievements to be her own. She had a lot of pride. He hoped she wouldn't let it get in the way. The apartment was better than any he'd seen when he'd been looking for a place to live.

Emma straightened her shoulders and lifted her chin, as if she'd just come to that decision. "I can move fast," she said. "Let's check it out."

"Good. Now I know you're not much of a cook, but let me show you the kitchen."

As the women moved into the adjacent kitchen, Max walked to the window and gazed out at the amazing view. He could see the Marina greens, a large grassy area that edged the bay and sat adjacent to the San Francisco Yacht Club. In the distance was the Golden Gate Bridge and Alcatraz Island with its famous prison.

The sight of that prison reminded him that he needed to check in with Spencer. He hoped Spencer's second day of freedom would be better than the first.

Emma came to his side. "What a view! It's so beautiful. Look at the water and the boats."

"It's very cool," he said. But as he glanced at her face, he didn't think the view could hold a candle to Emma. Her blonde hair shimmered in the sunlight, and her blue eyes sparkled with happiness. Desire ran through him. His gut clenched with a feeling of hunger, but it wasn't food he needed—it was Emma.

She was so pretty, her eyes framed by long, black lashes, her skin a pretty pink, her soft lips parted in wonder. Something inside of him shifted. His heart was beating too fast and out of rhythm. His breath seemed caught in his chest, and there was a knot growing in his throat. He wanted to put his arm around her. He wanted to pull her close and soak up some of her happiness with one long kiss. He wanted her light to wash over him and pull him out of the darkness that had surrounded him for so long.

But what he didn't want was to be the one to pull her out

of the light. He didn't know how to be as happy and as free-spirited as she was. He was practical and cynical, and while she saw the good in people, he saw the bad.

"I'm going to check out the bedroom," Emma said, oblivious to his wandering thoughts. "Are you coming?"

"I'll be there in a second."

As she walked away, he let out the breath he'd been holding and told himself to get a grip. Following her into what would be her bedroom was probably not the wisest idea, but he couldn't seem to stop himself.

Like the living room, the bedroom was large, spacious and very bright. The windows in this room showed a different side of the city, the tall, towering skyscrapers of downtown San Francisco. There was a walk-in closet and an oversized bathroom that Emma and Alicia were currently exploring. He could hear Emma exalting the size of the tub, and his thoughts instantly pictured her in a big tub filled with soapy bubbles swirling around her breasts—breasts that he hadn't seen yet but that he could imagine were as soft and pretty and pink as the rest of her.

Damn! He dragged his gaze away from the bathroom door and tried to think about something else. But as he looked around the empty bedroom, his mind decorated the room with a king-sized bed and big, fluffy pillows, because instinctively he knew that Emma was a pillow kind of girl. He could see dark wood nightstands and maybe on the wall a big screen television.

Emma might not want the television, but if she wasn't alone, if say, someone like him was in bed with her...

He blew out a breath. He was losing his mind.

This was going to be Emma's place, not his. They weren't going to spend time here together.

And if they were sharing a bed, he sure as hell wouldn't

be watching television. He'd be exploring every inch of her body with his hands and his mouth.

Heat shot through him. *Shit!* He was getting turned on by an empty apartment. What the hell was wrong with him?

He obviously needed to find a woman and roll around in the sheets for a few hours. And that woman wouldn't be Emma. She *couldn't* be Emma.

Emma was a long-term, commitment-kind-of-woman, and he was not interested in tying himself to anyone for life. He'd seen love destroy every person in his family. He didn't intend to be another casualty.

"What do you think?" Emma asked.

He started at the sound of her voice. He realized both Emma and Alicia were waiting for an answer to some question. "What?"

"The apartment? Do you love it?" Emma asked.

"It's great."

"I think so, too. It doesn't feel like an apartment; it feels like a home. And I love all the light. I hate dark, shadowy rooms."

And dark, shadowy rooms were where he felt most comfortable.

"I'm going to take it," Emma said. "The rent is more than I wanted to pay, but what the heck? I'm starting a new chapter in my life, and I want it to be amazing, so I should have an amazing place."

"You won't find a better price for this size apartment in this location," Alicia reminded her.

"I'll do it," Emma said. "Where do I sign?"

"I have the application. Why don't we go into the kitchen and you can use the counter to fill it out?"

"Do you mind waiting a few more minutes, Max?" Emma asked as they walked into the hall.

"Not at all, but I need to make some calls. I'll meet you at the car."

"Okay. I'll be quick, I promise."

"Take your time." He could use a breather from Emma. He needed to refocus his priorities and stop picturing himself having sex with her. She was his colleague, not his lover, and he couldn't forget that.

><<><<>

"So tell me about Max," Alicia said as Emma filled out the paperwork.

"He's a detective. We're working together on a case. That's all," she said firmly.

Alicia laughed and gave her a knowing smile. "Are you trying to convince me or yourself?"

"Maybe both of us," she admitted.

"Really?"

"I like him. I'm attracted to him, but..."

"But what? What's the problem? Is he married? Is he with someone else?"

"No, but we drive each other crazy. We argue all the time. I'm an optimist. He's a pessimist. We're both stubborn and competitive, and we each like to win. I don't want a relationship that's a battle zone."

"It could be fun. He's hot, Emma."

"Believe me, I've noticed."

"And he has noticed you. He couldn't keep his eyes off of you. I think he was picturing you both doing some very naughty things in this apartment."

Emma blushed. "Stop. He was thinking no such thing." Despite her denial, her body tingled at the thought of Max and her doing naughty things in the apartment. While living in her parents' house had been a welcome refuge for a few months, she was ready to be on her own again.

She cleared her throat and focused on the paperwork. "What do you think my chances are of getting this place?"

"Very good. As long as your credit checks out, you should be good."

"That shouldn't be a problem," Emma said.

"I hope to have an answer tomorrow morning. How soon do you want to move in?"

"As soon as possible." She was excited at the thought of decorating her own place. "I have some furniture in storage. Not a lot, but it's a start."

"Do you think one of your brothers will help you move?"

"I hope so. There's usually someone around."

"How's Drew doing? I haven't seen him in a while."

"He's fine, although we did have a weird conversation the other day. Drew thought he saw a woman who's supposed to be dead. He was freaked out about it. Which was odd, because Drew never gets freaked out about stuff." She paused, tilting her head as she considered the very curious look in Alicia's eyes. "Wait. Do you *like* Drew?"

"We've gone out a few times," Alicia admitted.

"You never told me that. When did that happen?"

"A few weeks ago. I was going to tell you, but it ended as quickly as it started. We went out twice, and then Drew stopped calling. I don't know what happened. Then we ran into each other and had an awkward conversation, and he said he had some stuff to sort through, but it was nothing personal."

"I'm sure it felt personal." Emma gave Alicia a sympathetic smile. She'd seen her brothers break more than a few hearts over the years, but for the most part they'd stayed away from her friends. "Maybe the stuff he has to sort through has to do with this woman he saw."

Alicia nodded. "He seemed very distracted. I wish he would have just told me what was going on."

"Drew doesn't talk much," Emma said. "He was in the Navy for eight years, and he has never shared that part of his life with me. Even now, I get very little information from him. I'm sorry if he hurt you, Alicia."

"He didn't hurt me. Like I said, we only went out a couple of times. I just think he's a good guy."

"He is a good guy. Maybe he'll call you again when he gets things sorted out in his head."

"Well, I won't hold my breath," Alicia said dryly. "I've been blown off before, and I've never seen anyone come back. But it's fine. Don't worry about it."

Emma didn't believe her. "We should get drinks or dinner one night. Or maybe I'll have you over here for dinner," she said with a smile as she handed over the application. "And I won't cook. We'll get take-out and catch up."

"Sounds like a plan. I'll call you tomorrow as soon as I hear. I feel very good about your chances, Emma."

"I do, too," she said, glancing around the room. "This place already feels like home, and I am so ready to start my life over again."

They walked down the stairs together. Alicia pointed out the door to the laundry room and showed her the garage, and then they said goodbye.

"Thanks for waiting," Emma said as she got into Max's car.

"No problem." He set down his phone and started the car.

"Where do you live, Max? I don't think I know that."

"In an apartment in Hayes Valley near Golden Gate Park. It's nothing special, definitely not as charming as the one you just looked at. The rent is good, and it's not far from work."

"Did you spend a lot of time looking for a place?"

He shook his head. "It was the first place I saw. The job came through, and I needed a place to sleep, so I didn't put a lot of thought into it. I wasn't sure at the time how long I'd be staying anyway."

"Are you sure now?" she asked.

"No. I moved back for my mom and for Spencer. Once Spencer is on his feet, I'll have to rethink my situation."

"I can't imagine why you'd choose L.A. over San Francisco. This is a great city. And you have the same job here that you had in L.A. Your family is close by. Why would you leave?" She paused. "Are you missing your friends?"

"There are a few people I miss," he conceded.

"Female people?"

He shot her a quick look. "Are we back to that question?"

"You didn't answer it before. I'm curious. You're not bad looking. You must have had a girlfriend at some point.

"Not bad looking, huh?" he echoed with a grin. "You're really good for my ego."

"You know what you look like," she retorted. "So what's the story?"

"There have been women in my life, but no relationship that lasted more than a few months. I've always worked a lot, so there wasn't much time for anything else."

"Was it really lack of time that kept you from a serious relationship?" she challenged. "Or do you prefer not to let anyone get too close?"

"You think you have me all figured out, don't you?"

"Actually, I don't have you figured out at all, and it bugs me," she admitted.

He laughed. "You are honest, Callaway, I'll give you that."

"You call me Callaway when you want to put distance

between us."

"What do you want me to say, Emma?" he asked, enunciating her name.

"I don't know. It's hard to get you past cryptic."

"I thought the mystery added to my charm."

"You do have some charm when you choose to use it, which isn't often around me," she pointed out.

"Because we have a professional relationship."

The reminder didn't ring true anymore. They'd moved past purely professional awhile ago, but she let his words slide. "Was it difficult for you to be a cop and have a brother who was in prison?" It was a question that had been on her mind since she'd first read about Spencer's crime.

"In the beginning, there was some talk, but after the trial it went away. My friends and fellow officers in Los Angeles didn't know Spencer. It was easy for them to forget about him."

"Probably easier if you didn't talk about him, either," she put in. "And you didn't, did you?"

"There was nothing to say."

"Did you tell your girlfriends about him?"

"Once or twice. It didn't go well. Dating the brother of a murderer wasn't very appealing. They had to wonder at some point if I was like my brother. Bad genes can run in families."

She thought about his words. "Did you ever wonder that?"

He shot her a quick look before gazing back at the road. Then he said, "No."

"Are you sure?"

"All I wondered was how love could make people so crazy. I watched the emotion destroy every single person in my family."

"There must have been a flip side, a happy beginning..."

"And a terrible ending," he said darkly.

"So you've never been in love?"

"Never have and doubt I ever will." He glanced over at her. "And don't take that as a challenge or a call to action."

She smiled, knowing that a part of her had reacted in exactly that way. Max was starting to read her a little too well. "Why would I take it as a challenge? We're just colleagues, aren't we?"

"Yes," he said. "That's all we can ever be."

Another challenge.

Fortunately or unfortunately—their conversation was over. Max pulled up in front of her office building.

"Here you go," he said.

"We'll talk later?"

"Yeah, let me know if you find any new leads."

"You, too." She shut the door and watched him drive away, feeling oddly lonely. She'd been with him since lunchtime, and for half of that time he'd annoyed her, so why did she feel like she was already missing him?

Shaking her head, she went into the building and upstairs to her office.

She spent the next hour going over her notes. Then she got on the computer. Max had already run a check on Ruth Harbough, but what about the son, Jeffrey?

She found a Jeffrey Harbough living in San Jose. He was the right age and according to Max, Jeffrey had moved to San Jose to live with his father when he was twelve. She wondered about that. Why would Ruth have let her only son live solely with his father? Had there been behavioral issues? Or had Ruth wanted more privacy—maybe so she could have a romantic relationship with a woman?

She felt guilty even thinking that. Ruth had sworn to Max that her relationship with Margaret was platonic. There was no reason not to believe her, although it might be interesting to speak to Jeffrey. In fact, she should get Max to go with her. Max had seen a man looking into the windows of Brady's Bar. If it had been Jeffrey, Max might recognize him.

She was about to pick up her phone to call Max when a knock at her half-open door brought her head up. She was surprised to see her older sister Nicole standing in the doorway.

Nicole appeared to have come from work. Her long blond hair was pulled back in a ponytail, and she wore a cream-colored sheath dress under a black blazer that matched her black pumps. Nicole was a part-time teacher at a private college in the city, but in the past few years she'd dropped her schedule down to only two days a week so that she would have plenty of time to work with her five-year-old son Brandon on his developmental skills.

As Nicole entered her office, Emma noticed the weariness in her sister's blue eyes, which wasn't unusual. Nicole was always tired. Fighting to find a cure for her child's autism, dealing with a husband whose job took him away from the house for days at a time and maintaining a job kept Nicole extremely busy. But today there was more than just exhaustion in her sister's gaze; there was pain.

Emma got to her feet. "What's wrong? Is it Brandon?"

"It's not Brandon; it's Ryan. He moved out this afternoon."

"What?" she asked in shock. Ryan and Nicole had been having problems; that was no secret. Brandon's diagnosis had torn their family apart, but she couldn't believe their marriage was over. They'd been in love since they were teenagers. She didn't want to believe that the kind of love they had could end.

"Don't make me say it again," Nicole said, sinking down

into the chair in front of Emma's desk. "I haven't told anyone else yet. Mom is watching Brandon right now. I had to go to a meeting at school, and I should have gone right home to relieve her, but somehow I found myself driving over here." Her eyes filled with moisture and shame. "They're going to be so disappointed in me, Em, especially Jack. Callaways don't fail."

"They'll understand," she said, although she doubted Jack would want Nicole to give up. Her stepfather didn't quit on anything or anyone, and he expected his kids to put up the same fight. "Mom will definitely understand," she amended. "She divorced our dad. She knows that some relationships don't work."

"Our father was an asshole. Ryan is not." Her voice broke, and her lips trembled as she said, "I thought Ryan was the love of my life. Is it me? Am I the one to blame? I know Ryan thinks so. Do you, Emma?"

Emma didn't know what to say. Nicole's life had gotten so complicated and so difficult. She couldn't begin to judge. "Why don't we go somewhere and talk this out?"

"Do you have time?"

"For you—always. What time is Mom expecting you home?"

"Not for another hour. I cut my meeting short. I lied and said I wasn't feeling well."

"I don't think that was really a lie." Nicole had been a warrior mom the last few years, fighting with every ounce of strength that she had, but right now she didn't see that fierce determination anywhere.

Emma grabbed her bag from under her desk and stood up. "Let's go."

"Where?"

"Wherever they serve really big drinks."

Eleven

He'd never considered himself a family man, Max thought, as he pulled up in front of his mother's house on Tuesday night. His sense of family had been ripped apart when his father left. For years, his mother had been too depressed to really participate in her sons' lives, so he and Spencer had learned how to fend for themselves.

When Spencer went away to school and it was just Max and his mother in the house, the rooms had seemed incredibly quiet and still. He could barely remember what they'd talked about those few years, but their relationship had never had any depth. When he was in high school, his mom was working full-time, so they only saw each other a few hours each night. And as he recalled, they'd spent most of those few hours talking about Spencer. Spencer had been very good at keeping in touch, and his mother loved telling him all about Spencer's exploits. When it had come his turn to leave, she'd barely blinked. She'd just kissed him on the cheek, wished him well, and told him she'd see him at Christmas. But she hadn't seen him that Christmas, because Spencer couldn't come home, and she'd gone to visit him instead. That had been the final straw.

For the last decade he'd spent most holidays either alone or with friends, and he'd been okay with that. There was a freedom to being single. He'd never had to answer to anyone. He had complete control over every aspect of his life.

But sometimes he got a little lonely. Sometimes, he got that hollow feeling in the pit of his stomach that made him yearn for something he couldn't even define. Was that *something* family? Was it love?

That was a scary thought. Shaking his head, he pulled the key out of the ignition and stepped out of the car. When he entered his mother's house, the quiet gave him a bad feeling.

"Mom?" he called.

She didn't answer. He made his way down the hall and into the kitchen.

His mother was seated at the table, a cup of tea by her elbow, a newspaper in front of her, but when she turned her gaze to his, he saw the tears in her eyes.

"What's wrong?" He took the chair next to hers. "Where's Spencer?"

"I don't know. He wasn't here when I got home from work. I gave him a cell phone to use, but he's not answering my calls."

Max didn't like the sound of that. "When did you last see him?"

"This morning. I was going to take the day off, so we could spend time together, but Spencer insisted I go to work. He didn't want me hovering, asking him questions he didn't want to answer. He said he didn't need another jailer." She paused with a sniff, her eyes sad and confused. "Why would he say such a thing to me? I was trying to help him, Max."

Apparently, Spencer's second day of freedom wasn't

going any better than his first.

"He's adjusting to life on the outside. It can't be easy for him," Max said, making excuses for his brother, because he knew that's what his mother wanted to hear.

"I thought we'd go back to the way it was. I guess that was stupid."

"More like optimistic." He wished he could make her feel better. But he'd never had that much effect on his mother's emotions. Spencer could make her laugh or cry or be deliriously happy, but Max had never been able to find that connection with her.

"You're being—nice," she said, suspicion in her voice. "Why?"

"Because you're upset."

"I didn't think you cared about my feelings. It's not like we've spent much time together the last several years."

"We both know why that is."

She nodded. "Yes, I blamed you for not getting Spencer out. My boy was in pain, and I was desperate to help him. I would have done the same for you, Max."

He somehow doubted that.

"At any rate, I want to help Spencer now, but he's changed. I thought he'd be happy to be free. But he's angry about all the time he lost. He can't see the positive. He can only dwell on the negative."

"He's missed a lot. I don't think he realized how much until he got out of the insular world of the prison. Now he can see what he's been missing, and it hurts more. It's going to take him awhile to get his feet under him again."

"I understand that. I don't know what it's like to be in prison, but I do know how it feels when your world is suddenly turned upside down. I felt like that when your father left. It took me years to accept that he wasn't coming back, that our marriage was finished.

She didn't have to tell him that. He'd had a front row seat to her anger. Instead of telling him bedtime stories, she'd railed for hours against his *no-good* father.

Glancing at his watch, Max realized it was after six and already dark outside. He was starting to wonder where Spencer was, too.

"I'm getting worried," his mother said, meeting his gaze. "You don't think Spencer has taken off, do you?"

"With no money and no car, probably not. Maybe he's job hunting."

"I suppose," she said doubtfully. "You don't think that he would…"

Her voice trailed away, but she didn't need to finish the question. He knew exactly what she was concerned about. "I don't know. I hope he knows better than to track Stephanie now. I'll take a look around the neighborhood. Maybe he's just walking around."

Relief filled her eyes as he stood up. "I think that's a good idea."

"I'm sure he hasn't gone far."

"I hope not. I'll get dinner started." She smiled. "I feel better now. You've always had a way of calming everyone down, Max. I'm really glad you're home."

—➤➤◄◄—

As Max left the house, he paused to zip up his jacket. There was a chill bite in the air, and the fog sweeping in off the ocean sent a fine, misty spray against his face. The cold felt good. It was invigorating, re-energizing, and he needed the mental kick to clear his head. He was used to concentrating on his job without having to deal with family issues. He was also used to doing his job without having to deal with a distraction like Emma.

Sure, he'd worked with partners over the years. He still did. That was unavoidable, but no one had ever unsettled him the way Emma did.

He'd been shocked at how his mind had wandered when they'd been looking at her new apartment. He hadn't had those kinds of daydreams in a very long time. It was because she was off-limits, because he couldn't have her. He wasn't supposed to touch her, so that's all he wanted to do.

He wasn't used to saying no to himself or to a woman, but when it came to Emma, that's exactly what he needed to do. Emma didn't just distract him from his work, she also made him think about things that he'd put out of his mind years ago, things like living with a woman, getting married, having kids, being part of a family, having in-laws.

And Emma was a Callaway—talk about pressure. They would want only the best kind of man for Emma, someone who would be absolutely and totally committed to her forever.

Just thinking about *forever* made him sweat.

So don't think about it, he ordered himself. Don't think about *her*.

He picked up his pace and crossed the street, heading down to the beach. Both he and Spencer had liked to escape to the sea, and while it was too cold to surf, the sound of the crashing waves might still have drawn Spencer to the shore.

There was a kids' playground across the street from the beach, and the streetlight revealed a male figure sitting on a low brick wall gazing out at the sea.

Spencer!

Relief fled through him. He'd hoped Spencer would be nearby and not across town trying to see Stephanie.

He walked across the playground and sat down on the wall next to him.

Spencer glanced his way, not looking at all surprised to see him. "Did she send you out to look for me?"

"I volunteered. Mom is worried about you."

"Really? I had no idea. She only left five voice messages and four texts," he said sarcastically.

"So you do have the phone she gave you."

Spencer let out a sigh. "I know I'm being an asshole. I was going to call her back but then I listened to her first message, and she started crying in the middle of it. She cried last night when I said goodnight and this morning when I asked for cereal. Did she always cry this much?"

"Yes. Don't you remember all the fights she and Dad had—all the emotional breakdowns before and after the divorce? She was a mess. She cried over everything."

"That was a long time ago."

"True, but she's always been emotional. She cried at your eighth-grade graduation, the day you got your driver's license, the morning you left for college." Max shook his head. "Actually, when you went away to college, she cried for about three months straight." He paused. "In case you don't know—she adores you. When Dad left, she turned to you for support, and you stepped up. You took care of her, and once you started doing that, you became her savior."

"Some savior I turned out to be."

"Your arrest and conviction did not lessen her opinion of you. When you went to jail, she felt lost again, but she kept her sanity and her focus by concentrating on getting you out of prison. Now that you're free, she wants you to be happy, and she's going to work as hard as she can to make that happen. She wants the two of you to be as close as you used to be."

Spencer shook his head. "I'm not the same man. I can't go back to being who I was. I don't even remember who I was. I'm not trying to hurt her, but I feel distant and shaky, like I'm off balance or on a boat, and I can't get my legs under me. I need some space, and she doesn't want to give it to me."

"She doesn't want to lose you again."

"Then she should stop trying to drive me away," he said in exasperation.

"I hear you, but it's going to take time. She still can't believe you're really free."

"I can't believe it, either. I never thought I'd serve my entire sentence. Every day I believed that some miracle would occur, that someone would see the injustice and free me." He let out a long breath. "But that didn't happen."

"I wish I could have found a way to make that happen," he said quietly. "I know you don't believe that I tried, but I did. I couldn't find enough evidence to change anyone's mind."

Spencer glanced over at him. "Including your own. Wasn't that really the problem, Max? You didn't believe my side of the story. If you'd been on the jury, you would have found me guilty, too."

"That's not true, Spencer. I do believe that Stephanie was being stalked and that you thought she was in danger," he said. "I also believe that Kurt Halstead came to her apartment that night because he was harassing her, and that you fought to protect her. I also don't believe that you intended to kill him."

Surprise filled his brother's eyes. "You never said all that before."

"Yes, I did," he said forcefully. "You just didn't hear me. You were too caught up in your anger and frustration, and I get that. I would have been furious, too. But I wasn't the one you should have turned on. The person who sent you to prison is the person you were trying to protect—Stephanie." As Spencer opened his mouth to defend his ex-girlfriend, Max cut him off. "I know you have a million excuses for why she did what she did, but I don't believe them. In my opinion, she's the reason you went to jail. There are two sides to every story, but in the end, Stephanie supported Kurt's side, not yours."

"She was scared."

"Then she should have told the jury that she was scared, that the Halstead family was pressuring her, that she feared she would lose her job, that she was as terrified of them as she was of their son."

Spencer stared back at him. "Stephanie was scared of Halstead. But after I fought him, after I killed him, she was scared of me."

"Are you saying that she sent you to prison because she was scared of you?" He hadn't heard that before.

"I think that was part of why she got so tentative on the stand. Her friends were telling her to stay away from me. I heard her sister say that I had a hair-trigger temper, and she was lucky I hadn't killed her. As if I could kill her. I loved her!" His voice roughened with emotion. "I never imagined I could feel such an intense love for a woman, like I could give up everything for her, throw myself in front of a speeding train for her, spend hours wanting to watch her sleep. From the first minute we met, Stephanie took over my heart and my soul. I couldn't think about anyone but her. The work that I loved wasn't important anymore. I would rush home to see her, to hold her, to touch her." He drew in a long, shaky breath. "God, I feel like it was just yesterday."

Spencer turned to Max. "Have you ever felt that kind of love, Max? Have you ever thought you'd die if you couldn't touch someone, see their smile or hear their laugh? Have you ever wanted someone so badly that you'd put your own life on the line for them?"

Images of Emma flashed through his head, startling him with their bright, vivid intensity. And a part of him thought if he could feel that way about any woman, it would be her. But he didn't want to be like Spencer. He didn't want to become a fool or a slave for love.

Spencer gave a helpless shake of his head. "Damn. I sound like Dad, don't I? Right before he left, he told me he had to do it. He had to divorce mom, because he hadn't realized what love could be until he met Dana. He couldn't let Dana go."

"But he could let us go," Max reminded him. There might be winners in love, but there are also losers."

"I didn't understand how he could leave Mom until I met Stephanie."

"Oh, come on," he said impatiently. "Love doesn't excuse being a jerk to everyone else. He cheated on Mom. He cheated on Dana. The man cannot be with one woman. He has to live his life on a series of highs. He can't handle the in-between times or the down days. He has to be in love. He has to be happy. Forget about the rest of us. What do we matter?" He blew out a breath. His rant had been building for a while, and Spencer was probably the only person who could truly understand what he was talking about.

"I didn't say I forgave him," Spencer said. "But I understand a little better how love can make you crazy. One day you will, too."

"I don't think so."

"Don't be so sure. When you fall in love, Max, you're going to fall hard. It's the Harrison way."

"It's not *my* way," he said firmly. "Let's go home," he

said.

Spencer slowly rose. "All right."

"By the way," Max said as they started to walk. "I might know of a possible job. How do you feel about working a cash register in a deli?"

"Sounds perfect for a man with an MBA."

Max heard the sarcasm but simply smiled and slapped his brother on the back. "That's the spirit."

Twelve

"Do you know how long it's been since I drank more than one glass of wine?" Nicole asked. "Three years."

"That's a long time," Emma said. "Have some pretzels."

"The last time was the day the doctor told me that Brandon was autistic, that he was probably never going to be normal, and that I would have to find a way to live with it."

"Asshole," Emma muttered.

"The next doctor said the same thing in a nicer way, but the point was still the same."

"But you didn't give up then, and you're not giving up now. You'll fight for Brandon with every breath that you take."

"I will," Nicole confirmed.

"What about Ryan? Why won't you fight for him?"

"I don't have anything left for Ryan," she said wearily. "I know it's wrong, but Brandon is the most important person right now. There's only a small window of time where we can make positive change. Ryan will still be Ryan in two or three or five years, but Brandon could be completely different, if I do the right things now. I don't know why Ryan can't understand that."

Emma admired Nicole's faith. It had been three years, and Brandon hadn't changed all that much despite Nicole's intense efforts. He was still withdrawn. He didn't speak to anyone, except maybe Nicole, and only then in one-word sentences. He was locked in a world inside of his head, and no one could get to him. While she respected Nicole as a mother, she worried that her stubborn, relentless focus on Brandon would cost her sister her marriage.

"You think I'm a bitch, don't you?" Nicole asked.

Emma smiled. "Hey, I was already called that once today, so if you are, don't feel bad. Apparently, it runs in the family."

"Who called you a bitch?" Nicole asked, her gaze narrowing.

"Jon. He came to see me, to ask me to come back to him."

"What? Why? I thought that was over."

"It is over, but apparently he's having second thoughts. I don't understand why he's suddenly obsessed with getting me back. He didn't give me this much attention when we lived together."

"Jon didn't appreciate what he had until he lost it. You were way too good for him."

"Jon does hate to lose." Emma paused. "Our encounter was awkward and embarrassing. Jon tracked me down outside my office, and we had to have this conversation in front of a man I'm working with."

"Who?" Nicole asked curiously.

"This detective," she said vaguely.

Nicole gazed at her thoughtfully. "Are you talking about that man that we saw at the restaurant a few weeks back? The one you said you didn't like?"

"Yeah, that's the one—Max Harrison. He's investigating Sister Margaret's death, so our cases are tied up together. He's actually not as bad as I thought."

"So you do like him?"

"I'm trying not to," she admitted, knowing that she was pretty much failing at that.

"Why are you trying not to? You're single. It sounds like he is, too."

"I made such a mess of my last relationship."

"Jon wasn't right for you. Maybe this guy is."

"I doubt it. And Max and I have to work together on occasion, so it's not like I could avoid him if things got messed up." She shook her head. "No, getting involved with him is a bad idea. And I need to say away from bad ideas, even if they are ruggedly handsome and sexy as hell."

Nicole smiled. "That bad, huh?"

She nodded. "My mouth literally waters when I see him. It's terrible."

"It sounds like fun." Nicole paused as the waitress set down a full basket of snack mix. "Wow, we went through the first bowl fast."

Emma smiled and grabbed a handful of pretzels. "So, where exactly has Ryan gone?"

"He rented a furnished apartment by the airport."

"That sounds like a temporary situation."

"I don't know, Em."

"You're just tired, Nic. And Ryan is, too. But it's going to be okay. You'll work things out."

"I don't know about that. Falling in love is easy, Emma, but staying in love is hard."

—➤➤◄◄—

Max got up at six-thirty on Wednesday morning, dressed in sweats, and headed to the nearest drive-thru coffee house. At seven he pulled up to his mom's house and got out of the car. His mom was just coming down the stairs when he walked into the house. She looked shocked to see him.

"What's wrong?" she asked. "Why are you here so early?"

"Nothing is wrong. Where's Spencer?"

"I assume he's still asleep. Why?"

"Do you still have our surfboards?"

She blinked in confusion. "I think they're still in the garage. Why?"

He headed down the hall.

"Are you going surfing?" she asked, following him through the kitchen.

"That depends on whether or not you still have the surfboards." He opened the door leading into the garage and walked down the steps. The surfboards were hanging on the garage wall, right where he'd last seen them about fifteen years ago. With any luck, the wet suits would also still be in the plastic bin on the shelf. They were. He smiled. So far the day was starting out right.

"I'm so happy you never throw anything away," he said.

His mother still looked confused. "What are you up to, Max?"

"I think Spencer could use a reminder of who he used to be."

A smile suddenly spread across her face, pleasure replacing the worry in her eyes. "Oh, Max, that's a great idea. Do you think he'll go surfing with you?"

"Oh, he's going," Max said purposefully.

"It's cold outside. The water will be freezing."

"That's why we have the wet suits," he said, pulling them out. They appeared to be in good condition, and neither he nor Spencer had put on weight since they'd last worn them. If anything, Spencer was thinner. They should fit. "I'm going to wake Spencer up."

"Don't let him say no," she urged.

He smiled at her, realizing how long it had been since they'd been on the same side of a situation. "I won't."

"Do you want breakfast?"

"We'll eat later," he said, hoping as he went up the stairs that he would be able to convince Spencer to go with him. He'd thought about their conversation the night before and knew that his brother needed an entry point back into his life. And why not surfing? That would take him back to a time when he'd been idealistic and able to dream. He needed to be reminded of what hope felt like.

Spencer was sleeping in his old bedroom. Max knocked on the door and then pushed it open, not waiting for an answer.

At his entrance, his brother bolted to a sitting position, his body going on high alert. "What's going on?" Spencer demanded.

"Sorry." He quickly realized that Spencer had probably slept with one eye open the last seven years. "It's time to get up. We're going surfing."

Spencer's jaw dropped. "Are you crazy? I haven't been surfing since I was twenty years old. And I don't think you have, either."

"It will come back to us."

Spencer flopped back in the bed. "I don't think so. It's cold."

"The wet suits are in good condition. We'll be fine."

"You're out of your mind. We'd more likely drown than catch a wave."

"The waves are not very big this morning. I drove by the beach on my way here. We can handle it. We used to be good."

"We used to be a lot of things."

"I'm not taking no for an answer," he said. "So get up, and get dressed."

"You think I'm taking orders from you?"

Seeing Spencer's stubborn expression, he tried another tack. "You loved the ocean, Spence. I think that's why you went there last night. Surfing was your passion. Remember what you used to tell me—there's nothing like the ocean in the early morning to remind you of all the possibilities. I think you need that reminder today."

Indecision played through Spencer's eyes.

"At least come with me," Max said.

"You're getting in the water?"

"I am," he said. "I was hoping you'd be beside me, but if you want to wuss out—"

"I'm coming," Spencer said, as he got out of bed.

Max smiled. "Good. I'll meet you downstairs in ten minutes."

While he was waiting for Spencer, Max strapped the surfboards to the rack of his SUV and threw the wet suits into the back of the car. He was already cold and was having many second thoughts about his brilliant idea, but he was too far into it to back out now.

A few minutes later they were on their way to the beach. They parked on a side street near the Great Highway and put on their wet suits by the side of the car.

"I feel like we're teenagers again," Spencer said.

He felt exactly the same way, and oddly enough it felt good.

After they got their wetsuits on, they carried their surfboards down to the beach. The sun was climbing into a bright blue sky, and there wasn't a cloud in sight. But the temperature was cold, and the sand was icy beneath his feet.

The water was going to be freezing.

Spencer paused just before the reach of the tide. "It's going to be bad."

"Yeah, heart-stopping," he agreed.

"I don't know if I can do this," Spencer said, his expression doubtful. "The ocean feels so much bigger than it used to."

Max could understand his trepidation. Spencer's world had been very small the last seven years. The sea must feel incredibly vast. But maybe that's what he needed. Hell, maybe that's what they both needed.

Max had been so focused in on the details of his life that he hadn't stopped to take a look at the bigger picture in a very long time.

"The first time you took me surfing, you told me not to be afraid," he reminded Spencer. "You said you'd be right there with me." He met Spencer's gaze. "And today we'll be together again. One of us goes down, the other has his back."

Spencer didn't reply right away, and Max knew that his brother was probably thinking that Max hadn't had his back for a long time. Thankfully, Spencer just nodded and said, "Okay, let's do it. You first."

He waded into the water and as he predicted, his heart skipped a beat at the first icy swirl around his ankles, but he kept going until he was waist deep. He glanced over his shoulder, watching Spencer follow him into the water.

Then Max stretched out on his board and began to paddle. It was tricky getting past the first breaking wave, but it wasn't a big one, and as they got out farther, the ocean became calmer. He sat up on his board, as Spencer paddled in behind him.

Spencer sat up as well. He looked at the beach they'd left behind and then at Max.

"I cannot believe I'm out here again," he said, a sparkle in his eyes. "The sun beating down, the water swirling around us, the wind in our hair. Damn! I forgot how good this felt."

"And we haven't even ridden a wave yet."

"Not much happening today," Spencer commented, looking around.

He shrugged. "It's a good day for two rusty surfers."

"Why did you stop surfing?" Spencer asked.

"I don't remember."

"Come on. There had to be a reason you didn't take your surfboard with you to college. There are plenty of waves in Southern California."

"At the time, I was focused on school and figuring out what I wanted to do."

"That couldn't have taken long. You always wanted to be a cop."

"I had thought about it for a long time," he admitted.

"Because of Hank Crowley. You admired him. He was like your second dad."

"He was more of a father to me than my real dad was. He's a good man. He taught me the importance of trying to do the right thing." Max paused. "He did try to help you, Spencer. He went through the files. He talked to the investigators. He followed some leads himself."

"I don't want to talk about my case anymore," Spencer said, surprising him with his answer. "You still haven't answered my question."

"I stopped surfing when you moved out. It was something we did together. I didn't even consider taking the board to L.A." He gave his brother a thoughtful look. "When did you stop surfing?"

"Early twenties, I think. I remember surfing the morning of my college graduation. That was the last time. The board came home with me. I guess I put it in the garage, and I never went back for it. It was on to grad school and then a job. The stock markets open early on the West Coast. There was no time to hit the beach before breakfast." He let out a sigh. "That was a different life."

"Do you miss the job?"

Spencer shook his head. "I miss my lifestyle. I made some good money for a while. But the job was a crushing amount of work with tons of pressure. I couldn't have kept up the pace forever."

"What do you think you'll do now?"

"I don't know." He paused, then added, "Where's that deli you were talking about earlier?"

"It's the Second Street Deli and it's on Second Street. The owner's name is Gus. His sister, who runs the register, is going on maternity leave, and he needs someone part-time for a couple of months."

"And you think he'd hire me—an ex-con?"

"According to a friend of mine, Gus is an ex-con. He has turned his life around and would probably be amenable to helping someone else get a fresh start. It's not up to your skill or ability level, but it might give you something to do while you're figuring things out."

"Who's this friend of yours?" Spencer asked.

"Emma Callaway. She's a fire investigator. We're working on a case together that also involves a homicide. We happened to have lunch at the deli yesterday."

Spencer gave him a thoughtful look. "And you told Emma I needed a job?"

"Yes."

"You obviously also told her about my record."

Max nodded. "I did tell her a little. She looked up the rest on her own. She's a very curious person, and she likes to get in the middle of everything, which can be really annoying."

Spencer's gaze narrowed. "She's not just a colleague. You're interested in her."

"Far more than I should be," he admitted.

"Why? What's the problem? Is she with someone?"

"No, but we work together."

"Not all the time."

"Enough that it would complicate things."

"I don't think this is about your job. You're afraid of love and relationships and commitment."

"Maybe I am. I've seen the downside of love. And the upside isn't worth what comes later. I'm happy with my life the way it is. No one has ever made me want to think differently."

"Until this woman."

"You're making a big assumption."

"And so far you haven't been able to tell me I'm wrong."

"Emma could drive a man crazy."

Spencer smiled. "You might enjoy the ride."

"And then what?"

"You can't predict the future, Max. I certainly didn't know I'd end up here."

"I may not be able to predict the future, but I think that swell is going to turn into a nice wave," he said, tipping his head to the right. "Are you ready?"

"Probably not, but I'll give it a shot."

"I'll see you on the beach."

As the wave came, Max got to his feet and managed to stay upright all the way to shore. When he came off the board, he saw Spencer coming in behind him. His brother stumbled into the water with a splash, but there was joy on his face.

"That was a rush," he said, wiping the water out of his

eyes. "Man, that felt good. I feel alive again."

"You're back," Max said, meeting Spencer's gaze.

"Yeah, I'm back. Let's do that again. You can tell me more about Emma."

"I've told you more than enough."

"What does she look like?"

"Blonde, blue eyes, gorgeous smile, great curves."

"Sounds perfect."

"But she is one independent woman. She is stubborn and does not take no for an answer, and she is insanely competitive."

Spencer laughed. "Someone you can't control. That's going to be fun."

"No one can control her. She's very determined, and she likes to win. But she also has a really big heart." He paused, his tone turning somber. "I don't want to break that heart."

"That's why you're staying away from her?"

"I don't want forever, Spencer, and she's a forever kind of girl."

"Are you sure about that?"

"I know what kind of woman she is."

"I wasn't talking about her; I was talking about you."

Thirteen

Emma started Wednesday morning off on a happy note when she received a call from Alicia telling her that the apartment was hers. If Emma could meet her that night at eight o'clock with a deposit check, Alicia would be able to give her the keys at the same time. Things were suddenly moving very fast, but Emma was ready for the change. She decided to tell her parents over breakfast.

As usual, her mom and dad were having coffee and reading the morning newspaper, the way they'd done every day of their lives. They didn't talk much to each other in the mornings, but the silence between them was always filled with love.

Her mom looked up when she entered the room. "Good morning, Emma."

"Morning. I have some big news." She sat down at the table.

Her father lowered the newspaper and gave her an expectant look. "What's that?"

"I'm moving out. I got an apartment in the Marina. I can pick up the keys tonight and if all goes well, I can start moving in this weekend."

Jack nodded approvingly. "Figured you'd be ready to move out soon."

"Well, I'm a little too old to be living with my parents, but I am going to miss you both. You were so great when I had to come home again, and I really appreciate that."

"You can always come home, Emma," her mom said with a smile. "And we'll miss you, too. Are you going to have a roommate, or is this place only for you?"

"It's just for me."

"I hope you won't be lonely."

"I know where I can always find people."

"How's the investigation coming?" Jack asked.

"It's slow," she admitted, wishing she could give a different answer. Her father liked results, and because he was so close to Harry Brady, he also had a personal stake in the case.

"I was hoping, sad as it is to say, that Sister Margaret's body might have provided some clues," Jack said heavily. "You're working closely with the police department?"

She didn't want to tell him how close. "Yes."

"Good. Hank Crowley tells me that Max Harrison is a top-notch investigator. He closed a lot of impossible-to-solve cases in Los Angeles. Hopefully, he can do the same here."

"I'm sure he's good, but so am I." She was a little irritated by her father's implied assumption that she needed Max to solve the case.

Jack smiled. "You get defensive very quickly."

"Because I always have to prove myself," she snapped back.

"Sometimes that need keeps you sharp."

"But you don't have to prove yourself to us," Lynda interjected, sending Jack a sharp look. "Does she?"

"Of course not," he replied. "You're a smart woman, Emma. You wouldn't be where you are now if you weren't."

"Exactly," she said, happy that he recognized that fact.

As she finished speaking, the house phone rang. It always startled Emma when someone called on the landline. Her mother got up to take the call.

"Hello?" Frowning, she said, "He's right here." She handed the phone to Jack. "It's your father. He seems upset."

Emma sent her mother a questioning look, but Lynda simply shrugged, then sat back down. They waited, listening to her father's side of the conversation.

"Why would you want to put her so far away? It will be more difficult for the family to visit her," Jack asked, irritation in his voice. "We need to talk about this, Dad." He listened for another minute. "Why the rush?" Another moment passed. "I'll come and meet you. I'll be there in an hour."

As he hung up the phone, Lynda immediately said, "What was that about?"

"Dad wants to put Mom into an assisted living facility in Monterey."

"That's two hours from here," Emma interjected. "There are a ton of facilities in this area. Why would he want to have her so far away?"

Her father's expression turned grim. "I don't understand what he's thinking. He said something about the fact that she always liked Carmel, and she wanted to be by the sea. I need to sit down with him. Sometimes I don't think he makes any more sense than she does. I'll see you both later." He leaned down and kissed Lynda, then walked out of the room.

The familiar goodbye kiss made Emma smile. "You two are so sweet," she said. "It amazes me that you have kept your love so strong for all these years. It's clear Jack adores you. He kisses you when he leaves and when he comes home. You're the first person he wants to see, the first person he wants to talk to. It's very cool."

Lynda smiled. "That's how a good marriage works. One day you'll have that kind of relationship, too."

"I don't know about that," she said doubtfully. "Finding the right person seems like a big long shot. I thought Jon was right for a little while, but I was wrong about him."

"Sometimes, the first love isn't the right love." Shadows filled her mother's eyes. "You said that your new apartment is in the Marina?"

"Yes," Emma said, suddenly realizing that her apartment was only a mile from where her mom and biological father had lived and where she and Nicole had been born. Her parents had started their lives with such hope, but seven years later the marriage was over. After the divorce her mom had brought them to this house. Her grandmother had lived here at the time, but the house was too big for her, and she'd encouraged Lynda to live there while she got a smaller apartment across town. They'd been here ever since. "I hope you won't have bad memories when you come to visit me," she said.

"Oh, of course not. Don't be silly. That was a lifetime ago."

"Yet, when you think of that time, I still see pain in your eyes."

"I don't regret marrying your father, because I had you and Nicole, and you are my two greatest joys in life. But I am sorry that I didn't pick a man who would be a good husband and father. David didn't know how to be either one. He just wanted to have fun, work hard—play hard. That was his motto. Unfortunately, having a family didn't really fit in with those goals. I was probably stupid to hang on as long as I did, but I didn't want to deprive you and your sister of having a father."

"We got a better dad when you married Jack, so it turned

out all right in the end."

"Do you ever think about David?" her mom queried.

She was surprised by the question. They hadn't spoken of her real father in a very long time. "Hardly ever," she said. "And if I do think of him, it's not usually in a good way."

"David did love you, Emma. He just didn't know how to show it."

"Don't make excuses for him," she said quickly. "You did that enough when I was young. He is who he is, and neither of us can change that."

"I wish I hadn't had to put you through a divorce. It was hard on me, but it was probably even worse for you and Nicole."

Her mother's words reminded her of Nicole's faltering marriage. She wanted to talk to her mom about it, but it was not her place to speak for her sister.

"You made it easier for us when you married Jack," Emma said. "I was happy to get a new father, although the four brothers took a while to grow on me."

Lynda smiled. "Those boys adored you."

"They hated me. I always wanted to play with them, and they loved to say *no girls allowed*."

"That didn't stop you."

She grinned. "You're right. It only made me try harder. I was so good at the games they had to let me play. Nicole thought I was crazy. She didn't even want to play with them."

"You both have your own personalities."

"That's true. I only hope that I don't take after my biological father when it comes to love. He was a big failure."

"You are not your father. Bloodlines don't make you who you are."

"That's not what Jack says."

"Well, Jack gets a little carried away sometimes with his

Callaway traditions."

"I like the traditions. I even like that he and Grandpa have set the bar high for all of us. It gives us something to strive for."

"I'm sure that's the intent."

"Speaking of Grandpa, why do you think he suddenly wants to move Grandma so far away from the family?"

"I can't imagine a reason," Lynda said, bewilderment in her eyes. "Even if she's in an assisted living facility, she'll need our help. It doesn't make sense to me, but your grandfather has been acting oddly the past year. He's so distraught about losing the woman he's loved for the last fifty years that he's not thinking straight. He wants to make her happy, but she needs to be in a place where we can help him keep her comfortable."

Emma thought about her mother's words for a moment, wondering if she should raise the question that had been pressing on her mind for a few weeks. "The other night at Jack's party Grandma started talking about a bad, bad day. Do you remember?"

"Yes, I remember, but that was just her Alzheimer's talking. She doesn't know where she is half the time."

"So you don't think there was some terrible day in her life?"

"I'm sure I would have heard about it before now."

"True. But this isn't the first time that Grandma has mentioned a secret. She brought it up a few weeks ago with Aiden and me. And just like the other night, Grandpa cut her off."

"Patrick is protective of Eleanor, but he doesn't shut her up."

"Doesn't he?" she pressed.

Her mom frowned. "Well, he does get a little impatient

sometimes with her, but that's natural. It's an incredibly difficult situation. He's literally watching his wife lose her mind, and he feels helpless. Your grandfather doesn't do well in situations he can't control."

She could understand that. She might not be a Callaway by blood, but she shared the need to control her life. "I'm sure it's terrible. I feel bad watching her struggle to find a word or capture a memory, and I'm sure what he experiences is a hundred times worse. But I get the feeling there's something weird going on, that maybe there is some secret they're protecting.

"You and your feelings," Lynda said in exasperation. "Don't you have enough mysteries to solve at work, Emma?"

"Aren't you a little curious, Mom?"

"No, I'm not, because I've been married to Jack for almost twenty-five years, and if he thought your grandfather had a secret, he'd be the first to say so and the first to dig into it."

Unless Jack already knew what the secret was and was willing to keep it from his wife...

She doubted her mother would appreciate her theory, so she simply got to her feet and said, "I should go."

"All right," her mother replied, her expression somewhat distracted. Maybe she wasn't as certain about Jack's transparent life as she'd said she was.

Not that Emma wanted there to be some big, dark secret. As her mom said, she ran into enough of those in her work life. She wanted her family to stay the way it was—happy, chaotic, a little crazy, but oh, so wonderful.

She turned to leave, then paused, one last question on her mind. "How did you know that Jack was the one?" she asked. "You must have been a little worried about making another mistake, considering your first marriage ended in divorce. So how did you know that Jack was the right choice?"

"I just knew. From the first minute I met him, I had this feeling that this man was going to be important to me. I was nervous. I didn't want to screw things up again, especially since I had two little girls to worry about as well. But I got excited just thinking about Jack. When he'd pick me up for a date, my heart would start beating a mile a minute. I thought he could take over my whole world if I let him, and that was terrifying, but it was also incredibly exhilarating. So I did what I needed to do."

"What was that?"

"I let him take over my world," she said with a smile.

"That's pretty risky—giving someone that much control over your life."

"That's what love is all about, Emma. There are no guarantees, no promise that there won't be mistakes or even failure. You have to take a leap of faith."

"I think I'd rather just skip the whole thing."

Her mother laughed. "Seriously? You don't intend to fall in love? You—my risk-taking, fearless, thrill-seeking daughter—you're going to miss out on the greatest adventure of all?"

"I don't see it that way."

"Well, it's not going to be up to you."

"Of course, it's up to me. Who else would it be up to?"

"They call it *falling* in love for a reason, Emma. You don't plan it. It just happens, usually when you least expect it. And sometimes at the most inconvenient time."

Memories of being in Max's arms flashed through her head—his mouth on hers, his chest hard against her breasts, his hands holding her still for a full-out assault on her senses. She'd been glad for his grip on her then, because that kiss had made her feel like she was flying—or maybe falling, but Max had held her up.

Her mother tilted her head, her gaze narrowing. "Emma? What's going on in that head of yours? Why all the questions about love?"

"No reason," she said, schooling her expression. "I better get to work. In that part of my life, I know what I'm doing. At least most of the time."

The conversation with her mother played through Emma's head as she drove downtown. She was surprised that the woman who had always taught her to be independent would advocate letting a man take over her world. Especially since her mother's first choice of a man hadn't worked out. But even after her divorce, Lynda had not soured on love, which had made her open to finding Jack.

But Emma wasn't sure she wanted to put herself out there again, not that she'd really put herself out there with Jon. She'd held back a lot from him, mostly because he hadn't asked her for more. Jon was not a deep person. He didn't talk about his feelings or emotions, and he hadn't been particularly interested in hers. In the end, that emotional distance had worked against them. Their relationship had been much more on the surface than probably either of them had realized until it was over.

Max was very different from Jon. He was deep and complicated, layers upon layers, a man of serious thoughts and buried emotions. It might take a lifetime to work through them all.

And Max would definitely take over a woman's world. He already seemed to be consuming a good portion of hers. Even when they weren't together, she was thinking about him. She kept reliving their kiss on the beach, wondering if it was as good as she remembered, and wondering if it might ever happen again.

With a sigh, she pulled into her parking spot at work and went into her office determined to put Max out of her mind. After meeting with her boss to update him on the investigation, she returned to her desk and spent the next few hours working the pieces of the puzzle she had, trying to find some way to make them fit together.

She knew there was another fire coming. The arsonist wasn't done. With each new fire, he'd no doubt experienced a rush of adrenaline, a thrill, and an addictive need to feel that rush again. He was probably selecting his next target. She wanted to anticipate his move, but she didn't have enough clues. Two schools, then a bar—his next hit could be anywhere. The pattern had been broken when he'd moved from a school to a restaurant.

Frustrated, Emma left the office around two o'clock to get a sandwich at the deli. She called Max on her way, but his phone went to voicemail. She'd already left him a message earlier. She was beginning to wonder what he was up to and why he wasn't calling her back. They were supposed to be working together.

When she walked into the Second Street Deli a few moments later, she was surprised to see a man standing behind the cash register. Mary stood nearby, watching him ring up an order.

"I see you found some help," she said to Gus as she ordered a veggie wrap.

"He said you sent him," Gus replied in his usual gruff voice.

"What?"

She glanced over at the man again and a surprising thought took hold. He looked very familiar. Was this Max's brother? Had Max actually followed up on her suggestion?

"That's Spencer Harrison?" she asked.

"You don't know him?" Gus queried, his gaze narrowing.

"I know his brother, Max. He was in here yesterday with me. He's a cop with the SFPD. I mentioned that you needed someone to help out while Mary was on maternity leave and that his brother might want to apply for the job."

Gus nodded. "He seems smart enough, and he could start right away, so I'm giving him a shot. We'll see how it works out. I can't be too choosy. Mary is going to drop that kid any second."

"I hope it works out," she said.

"So do I."

She moved down the counter, grabbed a drink out of the case, and then stepped up to the register. Mary had disappeared into the back. Spencer was waiting to take her money. Spencer was taller and thinner than Max, and his brown hair was two shades darker. Instead of Max's green eyes, Spencer's were hazel, but they were just as penetrating, just as wary. Apparently, suspicion ran in the family.

"Hello," she said. "Are you Spencer?"

He raised an eyebrow as his gaze narrowed on her face. "Are you Emma?"

"How did you know that?"

"Max told me a friend of his recommended this job and that his friend was a beautiful, blue-eyed blond. For once he wasn't exaggerating."

His words surprised and flattered her. "Oh. Well, I see Max told you about the job opening."

"Yeah, and apparently there weren't a lot of applicants," he drawled, as he rang up her order. "So I got to start right away."

She handed him a twenty. He quickly made change and

handed it back to her, as if he'd been running the register for years.

"I'm glad you applied," she said. "Max wasn't sure you'd be interested."

"Beggars can't be choosers. Max told me that you know my history, so..." He ended the sentence with a shrug.

"Right. He told me a little. I looked up the rest online. I'm a curious kind of person."

"That can get you into trouble."

"Don't I know it."

Mary came out of the back room with her bag over her shoulder. She looked much happier than she had the day before. "Thanks for the referral, Emma. Spencer is a lifesaver. He's already up to speed, which means I get to go home and put my feet up. Yay!"

"I'm so glad," she said as Mary walked around the counter. "You need to rest."

"I do, because in a few days I doubt I'll be getting much sleep at all. I feel so much less pressure now that Spencer has started. I don't have to worry about leaving Gus in the lurch." She gave Spencer a grateful smile. "If you need anything and Gus can't help you, just give me a call."

Spencer nodded. "Don't worry about it. We'll be fine."

As Mary left, Emma turned her attention back to Spencer. He was looking at her in a way that made her feel a little uncomfortable. Obviously, Max had talked to his brother about her, which seemed somewhat out of character. But perhaps he was more talkative when it came to his family.

She was rarely at a loss for words, but she didn't know what to say to Spencer. He was a stranger, and yet she knew quite a bit about him. She glanced down the counter. Gus had disappeared into the back room. Apparently, he was looking for something for her sandwich, as there were no other customers in the store.

"I hear you and Max are working together," Spencer said, breaking the increasingly awkward silence.

"Yes," she said with relief. "I've actually been trying to get a hold of him today. Have you seen him?"

"Not since this morning. You know that you have him tied up in knots, don't you?"

"What do you mean?"

"You know what I mean," he said with a pointed gleam in his eyes.

She did know, but she couldn't bring herself to admit to it. "I think you're the one he's most concerned with right now," she said. "He wants to help you get back on your feet. You should let him help you."

"Why do you think I'm working here?"

Had he taken the job to please his brother? Or was it easier to pretend that was the reason? For a man with advanced degrees, working in a deli was a big step down. But with his record, he was lucky to have a job, any job.

Gus brought her sandwich to the counter. "Sorry for the wait. I wanted to give you some fresh mushrooms. I got a new order in earlier today. And you deserve the best."

"I appreciate that, thanks. Good luck, Spencer."

"You, too."

She paused. "Why would I need luck?"

He smiled for the first time. "Because you're working with Max. My little brother was never one to share."

"Funny. That's what he said about you."

He tipped his head. "Family trait, I guess."

"Well, Max and I are going to work out just fine."

"I think you might," he said, a gleam in his eyes.

"There's nothing going on between us."

"Oh, there's something going on, and I must admit I'm

intrigued. Then again, I have a lot of time on my hands these days."

"Well, I'll see you around."

"I'm sure."

As she left the deli, she couldn't help wondering what else Max had told his brother about her.

Fourteen

—⟫⟫⟪⟪⟪—

Max stepped into his boss's office and shut the door. Hank Crowley was on the phone but waved him toward the seat in front of his desk.

In his late fifties, Hank was a short, stocky man with a receding hairline, and since he'd been promoted to Captain and spent a lot of time at his desk, he'd also acquired a few extra pounds around the middle.

Hank was coming up on his twenty-fifth anniversary as a police officer and had had a career that Max admired greatly. But then he'd been a fan of Hank Crowley since he was a lonely, unhappy ten-year-old whose father had taken off. Hank had been his Little League coach, and during that season Max had also become close friends with Hank's oldest son Tom.

Over the next few years, Hank had become a surrogate father to him. Growing up in Hank's house, listening to his stories, had made Max want to become a police officer. It was ironic that he'd chosen that path whereas Hank's son Tom and his other son Joel had wanted nothing to do with the profession.

Hank hung up the phone and gave him a nod. "Thanks

for coming in. I wanted to check in on how the investigation is going."

"It's going," Max said, without much enthusiasm. He'd spent the entire day spinning his wheels. "I've gone down a few roads that turned out to be dead ends."

"I understand there's a possible Tahoe connection."

"Based on the forensic evidence, there's a possibility Sister Margaret was in the Lake Tahoe area, but I haven't yet found any corroborating eyewitnesses or any other evidence besides the dirt and plant matter left on her clothes to put her at that location." He paused. "Half of the St. Andrew's school population spends time in Lake Tahoe as do many people in the Bay Area. Sister Margaret was there in August with her roommate, Ruth Harbough. And you know Mrs. Harbough is an upstanding citizen, never even had a parking ticket."

"She's a rule follower," Hank agreed. "A stern woman. When she first came to me to tell me Margaret was missing, it was the first time I saw vulnerability in her. She was terrified, and she doesn't get scared easily. That's why I asked you to get involved instead of letting Missing Persons handle it."

"I wish I could say my involvement has been helpful, but I'm a long way from having a suspect. My gut tells me Margaret knew her kidnapper. But she knew a lot of people, so that doesn't get me too far."

"What about the arson investigation? No clues?"

"Not yet. Emma is working that angle, but arsonists can be difficult to find, especially when they know what they're doing."

Hank gave him a speculative look. "How are you working with Emma Callaway?"

"All right. She'd prefer to handle the case on her own."

"As would you," Hank said with a knowing smile.

"That's true, but I recognize the value of our departments

working together."

"Good. Emma is a smart woman, and she doesn't quit. I've known her father Jack for years, and even though she's not his kid by blood, she has a lot of his intensity and competitiveness."

"I've noticed," he said dryly.

Hank grinned. "She's gotten under your skin."

"I think she gets under everyone's skin. Emma likes to be in the middle of everything, but I can handle her."

"Can you?"

"Yes, I can. You don't need to worry. I've got everything under control. Is that it?"

"Not so fast. Before you go, tell me what's happening with Spencer."

Max was relieved to have the conversation redirected toward his brother. He didn't want to discuss Emma with Hank.

"When Spencer first got out, he was really angry, but we've had a few conversations, and he's mellowed a bit. He still has a lot of bitter resentment festering inside. I hope he can find a way to let it go. On the positive side, he got a part-time job at the Second Street Deli, so he has something to do during the day besides think about his screwed-up life."

"That's great. I know Gus. He'll be good for Spencer. He'll be able to show him that he can turn his life around."

"I hope so."

"And how is your mom?"

"She's over the moon that Spencer's home, but it's not quite the happy reunion she pictured. She wants to hover and take care of him, and he doesn't want that at all."

"It's good you're here. I know you never saw yourself as an important member of the family, but Spencer and Susan are too much alike. They make each other crazy. You're the buffer."

"I don't know about that, but I'm glad I took up your suggestion and came home. My mother has no idea that you were the one who influenced my decision. She might like you better if she did."

Hank laughed. "I always knew why Susan didn't like me. She was jealous. She hated that you wanted to be at our house instead of hers."

"Only when she noticed I wasn't at home, which wasn't all that often," he said dryly. "Her life was really all about Spencer after my dad left."

"I'm sure she noticed more than you realized. Being a parent, I know how difficult it is to make everyone feel like they're loved in exactly the same amount. Speaking of that, Tommy is coming home for Christmas. I get to see my grandson for the first time."

"It's hard to believe that Tom is a husband and a father."

"That tends to happen to all of us at some point."

"Maybe not all of us," he put in.

Hank gave him a knowing look. "That's what I used to say, until I met Vicky. Before her I was all about being a single guy. Couldn't imagine why I'd want to settle down with one woman when I could meet someone new every other weekend. Then Vicky came along, and boy did she see right through all my bullshit. I was done. I wanted her more than I wanted to be single, and it was the best decision I ever made. Look what I got out of it—a gorgeous wife and three fantastic kids." He paused. "I'm glad you came home, Max. I know in your mind that this is only a temporary move. But I hope you'll consider making it permanent. Everyone here is impressed with your work. You're an excellent addition to the department."

"Thanks. I don't know what my plans are yet. I thought I

was done with this city, and to be honest I thought I was done with my family. We'll see how things go."

"Just promise me you'll think about staying."

"Right now I'm thinking mostly about solving a murder."

Later that day, Max wasn't thinking about murder, but about making a three-point shot from the outside corner. After a long day of work, he'd joined his fellow cops for a Wednesday night basketball game against one of the firefighting teams that included two of Emma's brothers, Burke and Aiden. He hadn't met Aiden before, but Aiden turned out to be just as good an athlete as Burke. He didn't play with as much finesse, but he had a great drive down the court and Max had been pressed to keep up with him.

One thing both Burke and Aiden had in common was a desire to win. Apparently Emma wasn't the only Callaway with a competitive spirit.

As Emma's face flashed through his brain, he stumbled and his opponent stole the ball from him. Damn!

Bad time to think about Emma.

He ran down the court again, hoping to rebound after his mistake. He was usually good at compartmentalizing his life. He'd learned to do that early in life, keep the emotions away from work. But lately everything and everyone in his life seemed to be mixing together bringing chaos, and he didn't like chaos. He liked organization and control.

He grabbed the ball back and headed down the court again. He faked a pass, and then drove toward the basket. The ball hit the backboard and swooshed through the net. One of his fellow cops gave him a high five. He ran back down on the court. He had his game face back on. Nothing but basketball, he told himself.

Then she walked through the door of the gym.

What the hell was Emma doing here?

He tried not to look at her, but out of the corner of his eye, he could see her stepping onto the bleachers. She greeted a couple of women and then moved down the bench to give another woman a hug. Of course, she'd know everyone in the stands. She knew everyone in this town. And everywhere he went, she seemed to turn up.

He blew out a breath and ran down the court again. He received a pass and poised to throw. Then he heard Emma's laugh, and his shot went wide. His teammate sent him a surprised look. There was nothing he could say to apologize for how badly he was suddenly playing. Fortunately, it was the fourth quarter. He needed to keep it together for ten more minutes.

"I didn't expect to see you here, Sara," Emma said. Then she glanced at the court and realized Aiden was playing on the fire team.

"Burke recruited Aiden," Sara said.

"That's interesting." Her brothers were suddenly getting along better than they ever had, or else Burke had been desperate for a player and hadn't wanted to forfeit.

"Aiden was surprised to be asked," Sara said. "He didn't say so, but I think he was touched that Burke asked him to play. They haven't been close in a very long time, but that seems to be changing."

"I hope so. The two of them have had some legendary fights."

"What are you doing here, Emma, or do I even need to

ask?" Sara tipped her head toward the court. "Isn't that the hot cop?"

Emma watched Max sprint across the court, dribbling the ball around his opponents, then making a quick fake to the right followed by a drive to the left. His shot swooshed through the net. "That's him," she said, mesmerized by his athleticism.

It was silly. She felt like a teenager wanting the high school star athlete to look over and notice her. Max didn't look in her direction at all. He was completely focused on the game.

She'd seen that intent look on his face before, and she idly wondered what it would feel like to have him gaze at her with that same level of intensity. Just the idea made her more than a little uncomfortable, reminding her again of the conversation with her mom when she had said—*I knew he could take over my world if I let him...*

Emma wasn't interested in letting Max take over any part of her world. Well, maybe one part, she secretly admitted. She wouldn't mind letting him take her to bed. She had a feeling the earth would move more than a few times.

That thought brought with it a wave of heat. "It's hot in here." She ran her hand through her hair, lifting the sweaty strands off the back of her neck.

"It is," Sara muttered, waving a hand in front of her face.

Emma laughed as Sara's fascinated gaze followed Aiden up and down the court. "Well, aren't we fifteen again?"

Sara sent her a startled look. "What?"

"We used to lust after the basketball players in high school, remember?"

"The only one I ever lusted after was Aiden," Sara said.

"I love you like a sister, but I really can't hear any more about your lust for my brother."

Sara laughed. "Fine. Let's talk about you then. What are you going to do about him?"

"I don't know. He does get to me," she said quietly, not wanting anyone else to hear, but she and Sara were separated from the other women by several feet. "We've been trying to keep things professional, but every time we see each other there's a tension between us."

"Maybe you should stop fighting your feelings and just enjoy," Sara suggested.

"I'm tempted," she admitted. If Max could rock her world with a look, what could he do with the rest of his body? "But it's complicated."

"Which is exactly the way you like it. You always push the envelope, test the boundaries, so why are you holding back with Max?"

It was a good question, and one she couldn't really answer.

"Are you afraid of getting hurt?" Sara asked. "Because aren't you the girl who always told me no pain, no gain?"

"That was when I wanted you to run another mile with me."

"Okay, bad example. But you've always been about risk. You run into burning buildings. You challenge yourself every day. I've always admired that about you, Emma."

"This is different. When I run into a burning building, I know what to do. I've been trained."

"That's true. There's no training for love."

"We're not talking about love—just lust. I don't know. Let's not talk about it anymore. Tell me what's new with you?"

"Not much. Dad is coming home on Monday. Kitchen remodel is moving along."

"And you and Aiden?"

"Having a really good time," Sara said with a wide smile. "We're going to the wine country this weekend."

"That sounds like fun."

"Apparently, one of Aiden's friends bought into a winery."

"Anyone I know?"

"I don't think so. His name is Travis Montgomery. I think he was a smokejumper."

"Maybe Aiden will want to become a winemaker in his next career."

"Right now he's only interested in drinking some good wine," Sara said. "We're putting off the career decisions for a few weeks. We've both been working so hard that it's nice to have some time to relax, be with family, friends."

"And each other."

"That, too. In some ways, I feel like I've known Aiden forever, and in other ways I'm continually discovering new things about him."

"Like the fact that he can be a slob?" Emma put in.

Sara laughed. "Spoken like a true sister."

Emma paused. "Looks like the game is over. I need to speak to Max."

"So you did come to see him."

"For professional reasons," she said, even though that was only half true. She did want to touch base on the investigation, but she also just wanted to talk to him.

They walked across the court together.

"Very impressive," Sara said, giving Aiden a kiss.

"You were my good luck charm," Aiden said.

Emma rolled her eyes. "You guys are sickening."

"I agree," Burke said, shaking his head in disgust.

Aiden just laughed. "You two are jealous."

Emma glanced at Max. "You've met Aiden, I see."

"Yeah, he introduced himself with an elbow to my gut," Max said dryly.

"You were in my lane," Aiden said.

"My lane," Max corrected.

"It was, until you tripped," Burke put in. "You were way off your game tonight, Harrison."

"I was distracted," Max said, scowling in her direction.

"Well, isn't there a lot of testosterone in this gym," she said, feeling a little charge of pleasure that she might have been the reason for Max's distraction. Not that she wanted to say anything in front of her brothers.

"We're going to take off," Aiden said. "Nice to meet you, Harrison."

"You, too," Max said.

"I'll walk out with you," Burke added.

As they left Max turned to Emma. "What do you need?"

His tone was not particularly inviting, but she was getting used to his changing moods. "A conversation. We're supposed to be sharing notes. You didn't return my call."

"I had nothing to report, and if you did, you would have left me a message."

"I'd still like to run down my notes with you. Can we talk?"

"All right, but not here. I need to take a shower."

"How far away is your apartment?"

He hesitated, obviously not thrilled about her seeing his place, which only made her want to see it more.

"It's about five minutes away," he said.

"We'll go there. You can change, and then we'll talk."

"I could meet you somewhere in a half hour."

"I'm fine with waiting for you to shower. Besides, I want to see your apartment."

"Why?"

"Because I do. Because I'm curious."

He smiled. "And as soon as I'm in the shower, you're going to snoop around. I have to warn you, you'll be disappointed."

"I'll take that risk."

Fifteen

As Max had predicted, Emma was extremely disappointed in his sparsely furnished apartment. She'd hoped to find a few more clues to his personality in his living space, but it was clear that he hadn't really moved in. There were no pictures on the bare white walls. The furniture in the small living room was basic male—brown leather couch and matching recliner, big screen television, a box of books against the wall that looked like they'd been thrown in there when he moved. A few other boxes were on the floor by a plastic table that seemed to be serving as a dining room table.

His kitchen revealed the fact that he really liked cereal and oranges. His refrigerator had six beers, some eggs, milk, and several cartons of take-out Chinese food. Everything was neat, though. No dirty dishes in the sink, no overflowing trash can. Max obviously didn't like clutter.

She returned to the living room and noticed a large glass statue on a side table. As she drew closer, she realized it was a trophy featuring a surfer riding a wave. The placard read *Second Place, Mavericks*. Max had obviously been pretty good. She wondered if his brother had taken first place.

Underneath that table was another open box. She squatted down and flipped through a bunch of pictures, some framed some loose. Many shots were of the sea and several included action surfing shots. She recognized a much younger Max in one of the shots, and the tall thin guy next to him looked a lot like Spencer.

Despite the evidence, it was difficult to see Max as a surfer. She'd really like to see that laid-back part of his personality.

But as she took another look around the apartment, she wondered how much time she'd have to get to know Max. He hadn't made much of an attempt to move in. He hadn't hung pictures, bought bookshelves, or invested in tables of the non-plastic variety.

Was San Francisco a temporary stop for him? Once Spencer was settled, would Max return to Los Angeles?

That might be good. He'd been a thorn in her side for three months. She should probably be happy. Instead, she felt oddly unhappy. They were becoming friends, and if either of them let go of their control for one second, they'd probably be more than friends. The attraction between them had been smoldering for days. It wouldn't take much of a spark to set it on fire. Maybe that's why Max had been avoiding her. And if she had any sense, she'd be doing the same.

On the other hand, if Max wasn't sticking around, maybe she shouldn't be so worried about getting involved with a colleague. He might not be a coworker for long. She straightened as Max came out of the bedroom.

"Find anything interesting, Emma?"

He'd changed into jeans and a pullover shirt. His hair was damp from his shower, and his cheeks looked like they'd just seen a razor. Her stomach clenched, and she was suddenly very aware that they were alone in his apartment, and the bedroom was really, really close.

The silence between them changed, became charged, and she knew she needed to say something, because Max's eyes had darkened, and if he took one step closer, she might not be able to stop herself from jumping into his arms.

"Emma?"

"What?" she asked blankly.

He walked forward, stopping a few inches away from her, and it took all of her will power not to back up. "You shouldn't have come here."

"I know."

Her nerves tightened as his gaze moved from her eyes to her lips. He was so close she could feel his breath on her cheek.

"So beautiful," he murmured, his fingers running down her skin. "This was a really bad idea."

Her heart skipped a beat even as her brain started screaming *caution*. "What—what are you doing?"

"Thinking about kissing you."

"We shouldn't," she said halfheartedly. "Should we?"

At her query, desire flared in his eyes. "That is not the right question."

"I know, but you look really, really good." She took a deep breath. "And you smell even better. What are you wearing?"

"Soap," he said, gazing into her eyes. "I told you I wouldn't kiss you again unless you asked. And I know you're stubborn enough not to ask."

"I can be stubborn—if I want to be."

"Do you want to be?"

"I don't know," she murmured, torn between her body and her brain, her emotions and her sense of logic.

"I can't promise anything, Emma. You have to know that upfront. I don't have relationships. I don't fall in love. But I like you. And I want you."

His husky words shook her to the core. She'd never had a

man speak so bluntly, so honestly. He was trying to scare her way, but it wasn't working. She didn't want promises from him. Nor did she want to make any herself.

"We could be together for now, for this minute." She couldn't believe she'd made the suggestion, but she couldn't take it back. She didn't *want* to take it back. She'd always been fascinated by fire, and tonight the heat was coming from Max. She knew she could get burned, but she couldn't back away.

"It's going to take way longer than a minute," he drawled, his gaze roaming across her face and then running down her body in a possessive, territorial sort of way. She told herself she didn't like it when he tried to be in charge, but she found herself wanting him to take charge now.

But he wasn't doing anything except looking at her, and that look was enough to make her breath catch in her chest. Her body tightened, and her nipples tingled beneath her shirt. She'd been battling her desire for weeks, and she didn't want to fight anymore. She didn't want to be smart or logical. She wanted to touch Max, to taste his lips, to run her hands under the shirt clinging to his damp skin. She wanted to inhale his musky scent and lose herself in his arms. She wanted to surrender.

Unfortunately, she couldn't surrender to someone who was just standing there, watching her. He was waiting for her to ask him. But she didn't need to ask.

She knew what she wanted. She wanted him. And what she wanted, she went after.

She moved forward, her gaze on his. She saw the flicker of excitement in his eyes as she put her hands on his arms. His biceps tensed under her touch, and a wave of heat shot through her. She felt a little female thrill at the idea of all that power around her, inside her.

She lifted her face to his and rocked onto her toes so their mouths touched. His mouth was warm and inviting. She nipped at his bottom lip, hearing him groan with pleasure. Then she pressed her leg between his and felt his arousal. She smiled against his mouth and slid her tongue between his parted lips.

She could feel the tension in his body and sensed that he was trying desperately to hang onto his control. But she didn't want him controlled. She wanted him to let loose, to let her past the brick wall that he had built to protect his emotions.

Deepening the kiss, she took her time, tasting the minty mouthwash on his breath, reminding her of the shower he'd taken earlier. She should have joined him in that shower. She would have liked to explore his body, to take her time. Later—she silently promised. Later, they would go slow. But now—now she just wanted to go fast.

Max must have read her mind. His arms came around her body, and he pulled her up hard against his chest. He changed the angle of his head, and he was suddenly the one exploring her mouth. Their tongues tangled together in the push-and-pull dance they'd been doing for months. The simmering sparks were bursting into flames, one after the other.

Max moved his mouth from her lips to her cheek, his tongue trailing along her jawbone, and then tracing the line of her ear, flickering inside the tender shell, setting off more sensitive nerve endings. Jolts of desire ran through her.

She unzipped her jacket and shrugged her arms out of it, throwing it on the floor. Then she slid her hands under Max's thin knit shirt, feeling his abdominal muscles clench beneath her fingers. She loved the feel of his skin, and she wanted more of it.

Pulling away from his kiss, she tugged on the hem of his shirt and helped him pull it up and over his head. Then he did the same for her.

His eyes widened as he saw her barely-there lacy pink bra. She had to wear such manly clothes at work that she went really feminine underneath, and the appreciation in his eyes made her feel even more female.

He lowered his head and placed his lips in the center of her cleavage, then ran his tongue along the edge of her bra, making her anticipate what it would be like to have his mouth on her breasts, his teeth tugging at her nipples.

His hands rested on her hips, his grip just firm enough to keep her right where he wanted her.

"You're torturing me," she said breathlessly.

He flashed her a killer smile as he lifted his head and gazed into her eyes. "I haven't even gotten started yet." His gaze turned serious. "Are we doing this, Emma?"

"Yes," she said without a doubt in her mind. She put her arms around his neck and brought his mouth back down to hers.

One long, deep, wet kiss, and then they broke apart. Max pulled a condom out of his pocket.

"Always prepared," she said, not at all surprised.

"Since the day I met you," he said.

"Really?" she asked in wonder.

He nodded, shoving off his jeans and briefs.

Her mouth watered at the sight of his beautiful body. Max was a rugged, physical man with not an ounce of fat on him. Every muscle had been toned to perfection. Dark hair was scattered across his chest, making a V down to a fairly spectacular erection. She didn't have long to look, because Max was helping her off with her pants, and once she was naked, he walked her backwards across the room.

Her legs hit the couch, and they tumbled together onto the soft leather. Max's body covered hers, and she loved the feel of his weight on her body, his chest crushing her breasts, his hard legs between hers. He kissed her mouth, then moved his lips down her neck and then lower to her breasts.

He took his time, kissing, sucking, teasing each of her nipples into fine, hard points of desire. Her legs moved restlessly under his as the need built within her. Her world was consumed with his touch, his smell, and the desire she felt for him.

"Max, I want you now," she muttered.

He lifted his head. "Patience."

She wanted to hate him for that word, but she couldn't. Because he'd moved down between her legs, his sexy mouth taking her to the next peak. She ran her hands through his hair, as the tension built inside. Max was relentless in his attention, in his intensity, and she was a prisoner of her desire. Her body began to tremble and shake and then finally came the long, shattering waves of release.

She blew out a breath as Max lifted his head and smiled. "Beautiful. You should let go more often."

"Your turn. Let me—"

His finger on her mouth cut off her request. She wanted to do for him what he'd done for her. She wanted to roll him onto his back and make love to him with her mouth. But he sat back on his heels, put on a condom and then moved between her legs. His hands threaded through her hair as he looked into her eyes. "Are you ready for me?"

"I've been ready for weeks."

He entered her body with one hard thrust.

She sighed with pleasure. He filled her so completely. She could feel him deep, deep inside. And as he moved within her, the pressure began to build again.

Once more his assault was patient and thorough as he shifted his angle to hit just the right spot. He moved harder, faster, and then buried his face in her neck, biting down gently as one long, seemingly endless orgasm rolled through them.

Finally, he collapsed on top of her. She ran her hands up and down his back, feeling the tension release in his muscles. They clung together for a long moment. She didn't want to let him go. She didn't want to lose the connection, because as her brain came slowly back to life, she wondered if they would ever be this close again.

He'd said no promises. She'd said the same.

So why did she want them both to make a promise now?

"I'm crushing you," he said as he lifted his head. He slid out of her and rolled on to his side against the back of the couch, putting his arm across her bare belly as they snuggled on the cushions.

She turned on her side to face him. He had his eyes closed now, and she appreciated the opportunity to just look at him, to admire the strong planes of his face, the sweep of his insanely long black lashes, the thick brows that often drew together when he was lost in thought.

Her gaze dropped to his sexy mouth, the one that could tease and torture, cause her great annoyance but even greater pleasure.

"You're staring at me," he said.

"How do you know? Your eyes are closed."

"I can feel you." He opened his eyes. "I always know when you're watching me."

Her heart skipped a beat. She should be completely satiated, but obviously having him once wasn't going to be enough.

"I can feel when you're watching me, too," she returned.

"I know. I like it when the awareness flashes in your pretty blue eyes. I like it even more when you try to cover it up."

"Well, I'm not covering up much now," she said dryly.

He smiled. "You have one hell of a body. Who knew you were hiding such gorgeous curves under that bulky firefighter gear you like to wear?"

His words brought with them a blush of pleasure. "I have to be fit to do my job."

"You're definitely that."

"You're not so bad yourself, Max."

Silence fell between them and grew awkward and uncomfortable the longer it went on. What happened now? Did they make their way into the bedroom? Did they stay where they were and cuddle? Should she grab her clothes and get dressed?

The buzzing of her phone broke through her wandering thoughts. She let the call go to voicemail, not wanting to move out of Max's arms just yet. She had the distinct feeling that as soon as she left his embrace, it would be a long time before she got back. Or maybe she'd never get back. Max was putting his guard up. She could feel it with each passing second.

She wanted to know what he was thinking, but she was afraid to ask a question for which she didn't really want an answer.

He looked at her like he wanted to ask her something, too, but in the end neither one of them spoke.

Her cell phone buzzed again. She looked around for her bag. It was on the coffee table.

"I better check my phone." She turned onto her back so she could grab her phone out of her bag. She saw two missed calls from Alicia. She glanced at her watch and abruptly sat up.

"Oh, no! I'm late." She scrambled off the couch. "I can't

believe it's eight o'clock already."

"What happens at eight o'clock?"

"I'm supposed to meet Alicia at the apartment to pick up my keys."

"You got the apartment?"

"Yes." She grabbed her clothes and ran into the bathroom. After dressing, she splashed water on her face and ran her fingers through her hair. Looking in the mirror, she could see her swollen mouth, her red cheeks, and the tender bite mark on her neck. She really did not want to leave. But she did want to get the keys to her apartment.

When she returned to the living room, Max had on his jeans and was pulling his shirt over his head. She grabbed her phone again and punched in Alicia's number.

When Alicia answered, Emma said, "Sorry I'm late. I can be there in ten minutes."

"I'm late, too," Alicia said. "I'll be there in five. Don't worry about it."

"Great. Thanks." She was relieved she hadn't kept her friend waiting. She looked over at Max. "I'm sorry to run out like this."

"It's not a problem."

"We do still need to talk about the case. That's why I came over here."

He gave her a disbelieving look. "That's why you came to my apartment?"

"I came to your apartment because you wanted to take a shower," she reminded him. "I came to the gym to talk to you."

"Why don't I come with you now?" he suggested. "After you get the keys, we'll get a burger and compare notes."

"Really?" She was surprised by his suggestion. "I was getting a different vibe from you just now."

"What vibe is that?"

"The I-wish-I-hadn't-just-slept-with-her vibe. This is going to get complicated."

He met her gaze. "I don't have regrets, Emma. Do you?"

"No."

"Good. But this is going to get complicated."

"Not tonight it doesn't. Can we agree on that?"

He slowly nodded. "Yeah, we can agree on that."

As they left the apartment, she felt happy that they weren't saying goodbye just yet, although she suspected that day was probably not that far away.

Sixteen

While taking one car to pick up the keys to her apartment was a good idea, Emma was acutely aware that she would have to eventually return to Max's place, and then what? Was what had happened between them a one-time thing, or a one-night thing? Because there was still a lot of night left.

It would probably be smarter to end things now.

Then again, it would have been smarter not to start up anything at all.

But she'd told Max she didn't regret it, and she didn't. In fact, she'd really, really liked being with him. A small sigh escaped her lips at the memory.

Max stopped at a red light and glanced over at her, a question in his eyes. "Are you okay?"

"Yes, I'm fine," she said quickly.

"You're awfully quiet—for you."

She had to admit she wasn't feeling in the mood to talk. "You should be happy about that," she said lightly.

Silence followed her answer, then Max said, "Should we discuss what happened?"

"No. Let's not talk about it. Let's just let it be. We said no promises, no regrets. What else is there to discuss?"

"You're right."

She glanced out the window, trying not to read too much

into the relief she'd heard in his voice. She knew men. She had five brothers, and she'd worked on a firefighting crew for six years. She'd heard a lot of locker room stories, and the last thing most men wanted to do after sex was to talk about it; next on the list were cuddling and sharing feelings.

Max had been lucky to escape all three. She, on the other hand, kind of wished they'd had more time for the cuddling part. She'd liked being in Max's arms; she'd liked it a lot.

They got to her new apartment in no time. Max opted to wait in the car while Emma got out to meet Alicia. Her friend was waiting on the sidewalk with the keys.

"Thank you so much," Emma said, as she handed over her deposit check. "I can't believe I got this place. I owe you big time for finding me such a great deal."

"I'm happy it worked out. The place is all yours. There's no electricity, so you'll have to get that turned on as soon as possible."

"I'll do that tomorrow. I can't wait to move in. This is going to be so great."

Alicia tipped her head to the car. "You're with Max again?"

"I told you, we work together."

"At eight o'clock at night?" Alicia asked with a laugh. "I'm not judging. I'm actually a little jealous. He's gorgeous. Have you taken him home to meet the family?"

"No," she said, no longer bothering to deny what was apparently quite obvious. "It's nothing serious."

"Too bad."

"It's not too bad. It's just right. It's what I want."

"If you say so. Don't forget to invite me to the housewarming."

"I will," she promised, then walked back to the car.

"All set?" Max asked as she got into the passenger seat.

"Yes. I should be able to start moving in this weekend. You know, I might need a little extra muscle."

"Don't you have a bunch of brothers for that?"

"They usually disappear when I need to move something."

"I might be around," he said halfheartedly.

"Then you might be able to help me. Think of all the great exercise you can get carrying boxes up three flights of stairs."

He gave her a smile. "You can put a positive spin on anything."

"I prefer not to dwell on the negative."

"So tell me something—how did you and your ex-boyfriend decide to live together? Was it love at first sight? Did you move in together right away?"

She was taken aback by his questions. Max usually made it a point not to ask her anything personal, and she kind of wished he hadn't changed that philosophy now. Living with Jon had not been her proudest moment.

"I moved in with Jon a few months after we started dating," she said. "It happened in a roundabout sort of way. My roommate was getting married, and her parents owned our condo, so she wanted to live there with her new husband. He was in. I was out. Jon suggested I stay with him until I figured out what I wanted to do, and that's what I did."

"Not the romantic story I expected to hear from you," Max said, giving her a thoughtful look.

"I suppose it was more practical than romantic," she admitted. "We were spending a lot of time together, so why not share expenses?" She frowned. "It was better than I'm making it sound. It was fun in the beginning. But it wasn't long before I realized that things weren't so good. I just didn't want to admit it. I was working a lot, and so was Jon. I regret that I didn't take a stand and choose to leave, that I let things go. That was a mistake, but I can't change it now. I can only move forward and try not to make the same mistakes. What about you, Max? Do you like living alone?"

"Yes. I've had my own apartment for about eight years now. I shared a house with a couple of guys right after college, but there was way too much partying. I was always hungover. I needed to make a change, so I moved out, and I have not missed having a roommate."

"You don't get lonely?"

"I keep busy."

"And you've never been tempted to move a woman into your place?"

He glanced over at her and smiled. "Not for a second."

"Right. No promises, no commitment, no regrets. I get it."

"Where do you want to eat?" he asked.

"I'm starving, so wherever you want to go is fine with me."

"There used to be a good burger place on Divisadero. I forget the name, something about a hat."

"The Mad Hatter," she replied. "Burgers and all kinds of toppings. It's still there, and it's delicious. Good choice. If you take the next left, I'll show you a shortcut."

Max followed Emma's directions, and fifteen minutes later, they entered the restaurant. It was eight-thirty, and the dinner crowd had thinned out. They ordered at the counter, grabbed two beers from the bar and then sat down at a table next to the window. Max hoped their food would come fast, not just because he was hungry, but also because they were now face-to-face again, and one look at Emma's sweet mouth made him remember how good she'd tasted.

A part of him couldn't believe they'd actually had sex. He'd been thinking about making love to her since he'd met her three months earlier, and then tonight—suddenly it was happening. Emma was kissing him, putting her hands on him, urging him on.

Damn! It had been even better than he'd imagined. Emma was one of a kind, smart, beautiful and passionate. She lived her life with joy and generosity. He'd never met anyone like her. She drove him crazy in three dozen different ways, but she also made him feel things he hadn't thought he was capable of feeling.

Emma's cheeks turned pink under his scrutiny, and her tongue darted out to lick her bottom lip. He wanted that tongue, that lip, that mouth. His body hardened, and he told himself to get a grip. He needed to think about something else, but his brain didn't want to cooperate. His mind wanted to play back the memories of Emma's sexy body under his, her soft legs, the curve of her thighs, her breathy cries of passion. He'd loved watching her climax, watching her give in to the desire and the need. She didn't do anything halfway. Whatever she was doing, she gave it her heart and her soul.

And that's what worried him. He didn't want her heart and her soul. That would be too big of a responsibility. He would hurt her. And he didn't want to be the one to take her down.

Emma cleared her throat. "So…"

"So…" he echoed.

"I went to the Second Street Deli for lunch today."

It took a minute for her words to register. "You saw Spencer."

"Yes. And you told him that he should apply for the job,

like I said he should. I knew it was a good idea."

"Spencer didn't have a lot of options. How was he doing?"

"He looked comfortable at the cash register. Mary said he picked it up in no time."

"Spencer had a lot of jobs in high school. I don't think it was his first time collecting money, although I'm sure the systems are different now."

"Apparently not different enough to be a challenge." She paused. "He has a dry, bitter wit about him, doesn't he?"

"Why do you say that? What did you talk about?" he asked, feeling a bit nervous about the fact that Spencer and Emma had been talking. He'd known that would happen if Spencer went to work there; he just hadn't expected it to happen so fast.

"We talked a little about you."

"That must have been boring."

"Do you think you're boring?" she countered.

"What did Spencer tell you?" he asked, ignoring her question.

"Are you afraid he spilled some big secret?"

"No, because I don't have a big secret. And if I did, Spencer would be the last person to know what it was. Until this morning, we hadn't talked longer than a half hour in more than ten years. We'd grown apart long before he went to jail."

"That's sad."

He shrugged. "Not every family is as close as yours."

"I am lucky." She sipped her beer, then said. "What did you tell Spencer about me?"

"Nothing much."

Her gaze challenged his. "He told me that you said I was beautiful."

He frowned. "How did that come up in conversation?

How did you two even start talking to each other?"

"I introduced myself."

"Of course you did," he said with a sigh.

"I'm a friendly person."

"A little too friendly."

"You didn't think that earlier," she said, giving him a mischievous smile.

He grinned back at her. "True. That was the perfect amount of friendly. And yes, I did tell Spencer you were beautiful—along with stubborn, infuriating, and competitive. Did he leave those adjectives out?"

"There you go with the downside again."

"That's me. I'm the glass-half-empty kind of guy. And you're the opposite. You're optimistic and hopeful no matter the odds you're facing."

"That sounds like a compliment," she said slowly, giving him a suspicious look. "But with you, I always feel like there's another shoe about to drop."

"Not this time." He sat back in his seat as a waiter delivered their orders. Emma's thin patty was stacked high with grilled onions, mushrooms, olives, tomatoes and some kind of sauce. It was definitely creative and maybe a bit risky. He'd gone for more meat and fewer toppings, which pretty much described their personalities. He smiled at the thought.

"What's so funny?" she asked as she took a bite of the juicy burger and then immediately reached for her napkin.

"Nothing. How is it?"

"Awesome," she said.

He bit into his quarter-pounder and had to admit the burger was damn good. For a few minutes they just ate. And it was a companionable silence. They finished at exactly the same time, kind of like the way they'd had sex earlier.

As the memory ran through him again, he felt like a

teenager with sex on the brain twenty-four hours a day, only it wasn't random sex—it was sex with Emma. And it was quite possibly the best sex he'd ever had.

They weren't going to be able to go back to the way they were, not with all the sexual tension brimming between them. Their working relationship was going to be compromised. But at the moment he didn't feel much like working anyway, so he'd worry about that later.

"Did Spencer say anything else to you while you were at the deli?" he asked.

"Not really. It was a short conversation. He wasn't super friendly, which reminded me of you."

"Spencer used to be very outgoing. He was a fun-loving kid when we were growing up. He always had a lot of ideas in his head. Not all of them were good, but some of them were." He paused. "Spencer and I went surfing this morning."

"Ah, so you took another one of my suggestions. I am on a roll."

He laughed at her self-satisfied expression. Emma might think he was arrogant, but she was just as confident in her opinions as he was. She simply covered up her attitude with a lot more sexy charm. "Yes, you are on a roll," he admitted.

"How did the surfing go?"

"The waves were not very big, so we managed to ride a few into shore. And in between, we talked for the first time in a long time. Surfing took us back to a time and a place when we were brothers. We needed to remember that relationship. And in a way we needed to remember who we used to be."

"According to the enormous trophy I saw in your apartment, you were a pretty good surfer at one time."

"My mom gave me that a few weeks ago. She was getting Spencer's room ready for him, and she found the trophy. She insisted I take it. I was going to throw it away, but I didn't get around to it."

"That explains why it was one of the few items not in a box. So does this morning's run mean you're going to be a surfer dude again?"

"Possibly. It was fun and freeing to be out on the water. It felt like my world got a lot bigger. I often have my head down, looking at the computer, at evidence, at case files; sometimes I forget to look up."

Her eyes turned thoughtful. "It seems to me like you've been in a metaphorical prison since Spencer went to jail. You couldn't get the charges dropped. You couldn't save him. You couldn't find a way to get him out on appeal, so you were stuck in that prison right along with him."

"I was not in prison. He was," Max said, not sure he liked her take on the situation.

"Let's examine the evidence."

"There is no evidence," he protested.

She ignored him. "Did you make any big changes in the last seven years? Did you move? Did you change jobs? Did you buy a new car?"

"I moved back here."

"Only because Spencer was getting out. What about before that?"

"I didn't move, but I lived in a nice place so that doesn't mean anything. And I liked my job. Why would I change it?"

"And your SUV? It looks at least ten years old."

"It's a good car."

"Let's talk about your relationships."

"Let's not."

"Have you made any new friends since Spencer went to jail?"

"I'm sure I have," he said vaguely.

"But no serious romantic relationships."

He frowned as he stared back at her. "You've made your point."

"I think you've been punishing yourself for not saving your brother. And it's time to stop."

"I didn't think I was doing that," he said slowly, but her words made him think. He had put a lot of things on hold for later—for down the road—for when he had more time. Had he been so caught up in Spencer's problems that he'd stopped living his own life? Or was there more to it than that?

"Maybe it was subconscious," Emma suggested. "Or I could be wrong. It happens rarely, but occasionally…"

"I can't believe you'd admit that you could possibly be wrong."

She shrugged. "I am only human."

"You might have a point, Emma, but I think I put the bars up long before Spencer went to prison."

"What do you mean?"

"My childhood was unpredictable. I never knew what I was going to find when I came home. Would my parents be fighting? Would my mom be crying? Would there be dinner on the table, or would everyone be too upset to notice I was hungry? Or that I was even home?"

Emma's gaze filled with compassion. "That's a terrible way to grow up."

"After my father left, things got better, or at least they got quieter. The fighting stopped, but my mom was depressed for years. Sometimes she didn't get out of bed. She'd work for a few months, then miss too many days, and she'd get fired. Spencer and I both got jobs as soon as we could so that we could bring in some extra money. My father gave my mom the house, but the mortgage payments came along with it, and they were tough to make some months."

He picked up his beer and took another drink, wondering

why he was spilling his guts to Emma. But now that he'd begun, he wanted to finish. "Spencer could joke my mother out of her moods. He could always make her laugh. He was the one who kept her from completely withering away. She really relied on him. When he moved out to go to college, my mom and I didn't know how to connect to each other without Spencer around. When it was my turn to leave to go to school, I was relieved. In fact, I couldn't wait to get out of the house. I was tired of that old life. I wanted to meet new people, be someone different. I never looked back."

"But you are back," she pointed out. "And geography rarely changes a person. You are who you are no matter where you live."

"Maybe, but I was a better version of myself in L.A. I didn't have to worry about her. I just had to take care of myself."

"How did your mother handle being on her own when both you and Spencer were out of the house?"

"It took awhile, but she finally bounced back. She got a job she liked. She made friends. I think she even had a few dates. Over the years I have tried not to ask, but she occasionally forces me to listen."

Emma smiled at his dry tone. "I'd like to meet her."

"You've already met my brother. Let's not get carried away. One Harrison at a time."

She leaned forward, resting her arms on the table. "Thanks for telling me a little about your life. Now I have a better understanding of why you're so guarded, and why you're so independent. You learned how to protect yourself a long time ago, and you've never stopped doing that. That's why you don't let anyone get close to you."

"You were close earlier tonight."

"To your body. But you keep your heart under lock and

key."

"You don't seem in a rush to throw your heart on the line, either," he said pointedly.

"That's true. Right now I'm more interested in having some fun."

"Got any ideas?"

Her eyes sparkled. "I always have ideas."

"Then we should get out of here."

"We still haven't talked about the case," she pointed out.

"If you had any groundbreaking news, you would have already told me. Anything else can wait. Right now, I think we should explore some of your ideas back at my apartment." He held out his hand and pulled her to her feet. "Let's have some fun, Emma."

"Sounds good to me. But this time, I get to be on top."

"You can be anywhere you want to be."

Seventeen

Max's bedroom was as barren as the rest of his apartment. He had a king-size bed and two nightstands, but there was no other furniture in the room, and the open closet door revealed several unopened boxes on the floor. Was San Francisco just a pit stop for him? Would he return to his other life as soon as his brother was back on his feet? She'd told him she was okay with no promises, but was she?

"Second thoughts?" Max asked, reading her mind. "You can go home, Emma."

"I know."

"I don't want to hurt you."

She wondered about that. "Are you sure it's me you're worried about hurting? Maybe it's you. Maybe you're the one who's afraid you'll get hurt. That's why you don't make promises and don't have relationships."

"I think if someone could hurt me, it could very well be you."

"That's not the nicest compliment I've ever gotten, but I appreciate the sentiment."

"I'm not good at the smooth talk. In fact, I'm not really good at talking at all."

"I've noticed."

"This was supposed to be about fun, Emma, so…"

"So let's have some fun," she said, pushing aside her momentary doubt.

He crossed the room, stopping just inches away from her. She caught her breath, anticipation already building.

"I have to say, Max, that you look really good to me right now, so what's going to happen next is not my fault. It's really yours. You're kind of irresistible."

He smiled. "And you think these beautiful lips are completely blameless for what's about to happen next?" He slid his finger along the edge of her upper lip.

The tender caress sent a jolt of electricity through her body. She opened her mouth and sucked in the tip of his finger. Desire filled his eyes.

He pulled his finger out of her mouth and framed her face with his hands. For a long minute he just looked at her as if she were the most beautiful woman in the world. Her breath came short and fast. Her heart thudded against her chest, and her blood ran hot through her veins. She'd never felt a want so keen, so needy, and all he was doing was looking at her.

Fear suddenly gripped her.

Max wasn't going to just take her body, he was also going to take her heart—if she let him. How could she let him? How could she take that risk?

How could she not?

His thumbs caressed her cheeks. Then he lowered his head ever so slowly and kissed her with tenderness and caring that only made her more afraid. She could handle the hot sex. She wanted the physical release. But this emotional pull was almost too much to handle.

"What are we doing?" she murmured.

He shook his head, his gaze never leaving her face. "I don't know. Do you?"

She shook her head, her throat tightening with emotion

as he kissed her again, sending another wave of heat through her body. His hands moved from her face to her shoulders, then down her arms to her hands. His fingers entwined with hers. And then he brought one hand to his mouth and kissed her knuckles. He did the same to the other hand.

They stood together fully dressed, inches apart, holding hands and looking into each other's eyes, and it was quite possibly the most sensual moment she'd ever experienced.

The air crackled with tension and desire. She'd wanted to be in charge, to take the lead, but she couldn't seem to move. It was as if Max had cast some sort of spell over her, and all she could do was cling to him. But she wanted to do more than hold his hand. This might be their only night together. She would make the most of it.

She drew in a breath and pulled her hands away from his. Then she stepped back and pulled her shirt up and over her head. Her bra quickly followed along with her jeans and thong. When she was completely naked, she went to work on Max's clothes, helping him off with his shirt and jeans. And then she pushed him back onto the bed.

For a moment, she let herself look, let herself enjoy the hard planes of his body, the broad chest, lean muscles, narrow hips, and really appealing arousal.

She got onto the bed and straddled his hips.

Max's hands cupped and kneaded her breasts. He didn't seem at all bothered by being on the bottom.

She leaned over and kissed his mouth, then ran her tongue across his jawline. She dropped down to his chest, anointing each spiked nipple with a kiss and then moving lower. She took him into her mouth, licking and sucking, enjoying his groans of pleasure, wanting to give him everything he had given her earlier, and more. She had him at her mercy, and she would have her way with him. She could feel him trying to hold on to his iron clad control, but she wanted him to let go. She would take nothing less. And finally he gave her everything.

Several minutes later, she rolled onto her side and let out a breath. She saw Max's satisfied expression and smiled. "See how good things can be when you let me take charge?"

"You can take charge any time you want—as long as we're in the bedroom."

"Hey, no disclaimers allowed."

He turned onto his side and smiled at her. "Now it's your turn." He pushed her down against the mattress.

"You don't need a minute?" she asked. "Oh, I guess not, she added as he moved on top of her. "Impressive."

"I'll show you impressive," he said, and then he proceeded to do just that.

—➤➤◄◄—

Hours later, Emma woke up and glanced at the clock next to the bed. It was one o'clock in the morning. She knew she should go home. But with her head on Max's chest and his arm around her waist, she felt too comfortable to move.

"Stay," he said sleepily.

"Really?" she asked, unable to keep the doubt from her voice. The morning after this incredible night was going to be hard enough to deal with without adding in waking up together. On the other hand, why not steal a few more hours with Max? It might be all they had.

That thought depressed her. She told herself to get over it. She'd gone into this night with her eyes wide open. She would not regret it.

"If you want to stay," Max added.

She lifted her head to look at him. He opened his eyes,

his gaze questioning.

"Is it okay with you? This is just a one-night thing, so…"

"So it's still night," he reminded her with a sleepy smile.

"That's true. But tomorrow we have to work together."

"I'm not thinking about work right now."

"Me, either. You know, you're really quite something when you let yourself go."

His eyes sparkled as his gaze met hers. "Likewise, Emma." He paused, a knowing gleam in his eyes. "What do you want to ask me?"

"Who said I wanted to ask you anything?"

"I can see it in your eyes."

He was starting to read her a little too well, which was exciting and scary.

The question in her head was not one she wanted to put into words. Max might not answer it the way she wanted. Better not to ask. She put her head down on his chest and snuggled against him. She felt content and protected within his embrace. She was an independent woman and used to taking care of herself, but it felt nice to be with someone who was as strong, if not stronger, than she was.

"Emma," he said.

"Yes."

"You were really good, the best ever."

A tingle ran down her spine, not only because of the compliment, but because he'd read her mind. "I knew it," she said happily.

He laughed. "Go to sleep."

She closed her eyes and let the steady beat of his heart lull her to sleep.

⇒⋙⋘⋖

Max woke up expecting to see Emma in his bed, but she

was gone. He glanced at the clock. It was only seven-thirty, but his apartment was very quiet. He got up, grabbed his robe and used the bathroom, then made his way into the kitchen. The smell of coffee told him Emma hadn't been gone long.

He walked over to the coffeemaker and saw a note scribbled on a coffee filter.

Last night was great. Let's talk about the case later. Em.

He frowned. It was a little strange that Emma had taken off without saying goodbye. That was usually his move.

Shaking his head, he told himself to be happy she'd left. Now he didn't have to make awkward small talk. He could have his coffee, read the paper, and get ready for work, which was exactly what he was going to do.

Unfortunately, thoughts of Emma filled his morning routine. He turned the shower to ice cold but that didn't help much. As he dressed for work, he remembered Emma's hands on him, her fingers touching his hot skin.

Damn! He threw on the rest of his clothes and headed out the door. He needed to focus on his job and stop thinking about Emma. He tried to tell himself that having had sex would lessen the tension between them. They'd given in to their attraction and gotten that out of the way. But that was one big, fat lie. They'd made love three times, and he wanted three hundred more times or three thousand more times. But that would take more than a night, and the idea of a lifetime was far too terrifying to contemplate.

When he got to his office, he was surprised to find Ruth Harbough waiting for him. She was sitting in the waiting room, clutching her big black handbag with both hands and looking very nervous. She got to her feet when she saw him.

"What can I do for you, Mrs. Harbough?" he asked.

"I was hoping you could help me. We're having the service for Margaret tomorrow night, and it will be an open casket. I would like to bury her with the rosary that she always carried. You said it was in her pocket when you found her body."

"That's part of the evidence, I'm afraid," he said slowly.

"There's no way you can release it? It's very important."

"I'm sorry, but I can't. Not at this time."

"Well, another time will be too late, won't it?" she said tartly.

"I am sorry," he repeated. It went against procedure to release the evidence in an ongoing investigation.

"I don't understand. Were there fingerprints on it? Was there blood? How could it possibly be important?"

"I really can't say, but I want to assure you that I'm doing everything I can to find out what happened to Margaret. And I can't jeopardize our case in any way."

Her lips tightened. "All right. I also came to tell you that I reviewed the school files you were asking about the other day. Emma mentioned a fire in the dumpster about fifteen years ago. It was set by Jarod Moretti."

His nerves tightened. "Are you sure?"

"Positive. He was suspended for a week, and there was talk of expulsion, but Jarod had recently lost his mother, and his poor behavior was believed to be due to grief. He hadn't been in trouble before that, so after the suspension he came back to school. There were no other behavioral problems during his time there."

"That's odd," he said. "Because we spoke to Tony Moretti, and he said he thought it was Christian Brady who started that fire."

"It wasn't."

"Wouldn't Tony know if his brother was suspended?"

"As they are twins, I believe so. Perhaps his memory is faulty. Tony was in trouble many times during his years at St.

Andrew's. It would have been easier to believe that he set the fire than his brother Jarod."

"Maybe Jarod covered for him."

"I suppose that's possible. If you'll excuse me now, I need to get to work."

"Thanks for the information," he said.

As Ruth left, he walked to his desk, his mind wrestling with the implications. Had Jarod covered for Tony? Was that why Tony had tried to blame Christian for the fire?

He needed to talk to both Morettis, and he was fairly sure Emma would want to be there when he did.

—➤➤◄◄—

"It was Jarod who set the fire in the dumpster?" Emma repeated, her hand tightening on the phone as she thought about what Max had just told her.

"Yes. I want to talk to both of them, and I assume you do, too. So I'm keeping you in the loop."

"I appreciate that." She felt a little foolish now that her heart had skipped a beat when she'd first seen Max's name pop up on her phone. She'd thought that he was calling to say something personal, maybe talk about how wonderful the night had been, but he was all business, no mention of the time they'd spent together.

She should be happy that he was keeping things professional. One of the reasons she'd left his apartment early had been to avoid any awkward conversation where Max might feel compelled to say something that he didn't mean just to be polite. Or worse, that she might say something that would lead him to believe she wanted more than a one-night stand.

"Emma?"

Max's sharp voice brought her attention back to the conversation at hand. "What?"

"Do you want to go with me?"

"Yes, of course. Let's start with Jarod. I'll call him and see if I can track him down without raising suspicion. I'd rather catch him off guard. Make it sound friendly."

"Agreed. We might as well use your long-term friendship with the Morettis to our advantage."

She frowned at that suggestion. She did not like to *use* her friends. But she had a case to solve and right now the Morettis were the best lead she had.

"I'll get back to you as soon as I reach Jarod," she said.

"All right. That sounds good."

"Good," she echoed, reluctant to end the call.

"Is there something else, Emma?"

"No. I just—" She couldn't find the words to express what she wanted to say, because she didn't know what she wanted to say.

"You didn't have to run out this morning," he said, as the silence between them lengthened. "I would have made you breakfast."

"With what? You had very little in your refrigerator."

"Then I would have taken you out for breakfast."

"I wanted to get an early start on the day."

"That's not why you left. Why don't you tell me the real reason?"

"I thought you were the man who didn't like to talk about sex."

A tense few seconds ticked by and then he said. "I don't want you to be upset in any way."

"I'm not upset. We both agreed it was a one-night thing. I didn't want to complicate things by hanging around this morning. I thought you'd be happy I was gone."

"I would have thought that, too," he said, surprising her with the words. "Call me when you reach the Morettis."

"I will."

As she ended the call, she drew in a breath and slowly let it out. Her pulse was racing a little too fast, something that happened often when Max was around. But she needed to focus on her job. She might not be good at relationships, but in work she could excel, and that's what she intended to do.

Picking up her phone again, she tried Jarod first. His number went to voice mail. She left him a message asking him to call her back. She tried Tony next, but he didn't pick up, either. She really hoped they were both just busy and not screening her calls. She wanted to find the arsonist, but she didn't want that person to be Jarod or Tony. That would hit a little too close to home.

Eighteen

At two, Emma was still waiting for a call back from Jarod. Frustrated with the slow pace of her investigation, she took a break and headed down to the Second Street Deli for a late lunch. There were a few people in front of her in line. Gus worked behind the counter, making sandwiches as fast as he could. Spencer ran the register with the same speed.

They seemed to make a pretty good team, Emma thought, as she watched them communicate in brief, short sentences. They didn't waste time with questions or explanations. They just got their work done. She hoped the job would keep Spencer going for a while. It would certainly ease Max's mind to have his brother focused on rebuilding his life and not reconnecting with the woman who had pretty much ruined his life.

Emma was both impressed and a little bewildered by Spencer's feelings about his ex-girlfriend. Max said his brother wasn't bitter, that he still loved Stephanie, and Emma couldn't imagine why that was. It seemed to her that Stephanie had betrayed Spencer, but apparently he didn't see it that way. It was none of her business, but that didn't stop her from thinking about it.

The two brothers seemed completely different when it came to love. Max didn't want to love anyone or have any kind of relationship that came with expectations. Spencer seemed to love with every particle of his being.

She fell somewhere in the middle of the love spectrum, probably closer to Max's position than Spencer's. But unlike Max, she did want marriage and children. She wanted to have her own little family unit someday. She just wanted to be sure she fell for the right man, a man she could count on, not someone like her biological father, who couldn't handle the pressure of a wife and kids, and not someone like Jon, who'd turned out to be shallow and selfish.

Max was a man who could be counted on. Only problem was, he didn't want someone to count on him. She wondered if he'd ever change his mind.

The line moved and she stepped up to the counter to order.

"The usual?" Gus asked. "Or have you switched to the veggie wrap?"

"I am trying to keep the meat to once a week, so veggies it is. How are things going around here?"

"Good. Better than I expected. Spencer works hard, does what I say. Can't ask for more than that."

"I'm glad. How's Mary?"

"No contractions yet, but she's happy to be home decorating the nursery. You want the sandwich to go?"

"No, I'll eat here today." She moved down to the register

Spencer gave her a brief smile. "Back again?"

"I work a block from here."

"Gus seems to have a steady clientele from the neighborhood."

"Are you getting a drink?"

"Right. I forgot." She stepped over to the refrigerator case to grab an iced tea. As she came back to the register, she saw Spencer staring out the window with an odd look on his face.

She followed his gaze to a woman with dark brown hair who was standing on the sidewalk in front of the deli. She had her hand on a stroller and was pushing it back and forth as she talked on her cell phone.

"I'll be right back," Spencer said, then moved quickly toward the door.

She watched as he approached the woman. He said something, then his expression changed abruptly. He held up a hand as if apologizing and then returned to the deli.

"Sorry," he muttered.

"Who was that?" she asked.

"I thought it was someone I knew. It turns out it wasn't."

"Are you talking about your ex-girlfriend?"

His lips tightened. "Max told you about her."

"A little. She was also in the articles I read about the case." She paused as Gus set her plate on the counter. "Thanks, Gus."

"You're welcome. I have to make a call. It looks like we have a break right now," Gus told Spencer. "Give me a holler if we get more customers."

"You got it, boss," Spencer said. "How are you paying, Emma?"

"Credit card," she said, pulling a card out of her wallet.

He ran it for her, then said, "Do you need a receipt?"

"No, I'm good. I'm sorry if I got too personal. I have a really curious nature, and sometimes a big mouth. Just ignore me. That's what Max usually does."

"You must drive him crazy," Spencer said.

"I think I do," she admitted.

"I did think the woman outside was Stephanie," he said, surprising her with his candor. "She's been on my mind a lot, especially since I got out of prison. Max thinks I'm nuts to want to see her again, but I feel like we need to have a talk—just one more conversation."

"Would that give you some kind of closure?"

He shrugged. "I don't know. Maybe it would make things worse. But I can't seem to let the idea go. She's in the city. I'm in the city. How can I not talk to her one more time?"

"How do you think she would feel about seeing you again?"

He shook his head. "I have absolutely no idea."

"When is the last time you spoke to her?"

"Six and a half years ago—the last time she came to see me. I'd been in prison about five months then. She'd come two other times; that was the third visit. It didn't go well. She looked at me like I was a stranger. There was fear in her eyes. I think it came from the fact that I'd accidentally killed Kurt. But it was just a fight. He fell. He hit his head. I didn't know it would end up that way." He drew in a ragged breath. "After that visit, I wrote to her and told her not to come anymore. I was going to be gone a long time. She should be free to move on with her life. And that's what she did."

She thought about his words for a moment. "If you called it off, if you were the one to say don't come back, then why do you want to see her now?"

"Because I'm free. I'm who I used to be. I'm not wearing handcuffs or a jumpsuit. I'm not eating with plastic forks. I'm the guy she fell in love with, and maybe I want her to see that guy again."

"Max said she's married now."

"I'm not trying to break that up."

"Aren't you, Spencer? What resolution comes out of this meeting?"

He frowned, not too happy with her question. "I don't know."

"You should think about that before you go to see her."

"Have you ever been in love?" he asked her. "I'm not talking about puppy love or a high school crush; I'm talking about deep, passionate, relentless love, the kind of emotion that takes over your life, that kind of feeling that becomes part of the air that you breathe."

She stared at him in amazement. She'd never heard a man talk about love in such a way. Spencer was really different from Max. As she considered his question, Max's image came into her head. It should have been Jon's face she saw. She'd spent a year with Jon, and she'd only spent a night with Max, so why was Max the one sending a tingle down her spine?

"No, I've never felt like that. I tried to talk myself into love once, but it wasn't real."

"Love isn't something you talk yourself into. It's something that runs you over like a runaway train. It's powerful stuff."

"Do you still love Stephanie?"

"I wish I didn't," he said. "But I can't forget what we had together. I know our love was real. Whether it lasted for a minute or a lifetime, it was true."

"That's a beautiful sentiment."

"I read a lot of poetry in jail." He sighed. "Sorry, I'm talking way too much. But you asked and no one has asked me in a long time, because they don't want to hear my answer. They want me to move on."

"You're the only one who can decide when to do that."

The door to the deli opened, and Spencer straightened as a customer walked in. "I better get Gus. Nice talking to you."

"You, too."

She took her plate to a nearby table as Gus came back to fill orders. She gazed idly out the window while she ate, her mind jumping from one subject to another, but always seeming to find its way back to Max. She'd just finished her sandwich when her phone rang. Her pulse jumped. It was Jarod.

"Jarod," she said. "Thanks for calling me back. I need to talk to you about something. Could we meet somewhere?"

"I'm pretty busy today, Emma. What's it about?"

"Family stuff, but it is important. I can meet you somewhere. It will just take a few minutes."

"I'm doing a remodel on the corner of Twentieth and Vicente, if you want to come by the job site."

"Great. I'll see you in about twenty minutes." As soon as the call ended, she punched in Max's number. "I have a meeting set up with Jarod. Are you free now? Can I pick you up?"

"I'll be out front."

"Great. See you in a few." She slid her phone back into her bag and got to her feet. She waved goodbye to Spencer, then dumped her trash in the garbage as she headed out the door.

—➤➤◄◄◄—

Max was waiting on the sidewalk in front of the Hall of Justice when his brother called.

"Spencer, what's up?" he asked, hoping there wasn't already a problem at his job. He just wanted Spencer's life to be drama-free for as long as possible.

"Your friend Emma was just in here," Spencer said.

"Yeah, so?"

"So, while she was eating I happened to notice a guy standing outside the deli who seemed to be watching her."

"What?" he asked in alarm.

"When she left the deli, I saw the guy head down the

street after her, so I went outside. I could see him about ten steps behind her. Then they both turned the corner, and I don't know where they went."

His body tensed as fear ran through him. "Why didn't you go after him?"

"That was my first instinct. However, I did actually learn something from going to prison, and that was to mind my own business. Plus, I didn't think Gus would appreciate me abandoning my post. But Emma seems like a nice woman, and my gut told me I should call you. I'm sure you probably think I'm just imagining things again. Paranoid Spencer, always thinking men are following women."

"I don't think that at all," Max said. "What did the guy look like?"

"He had on jeans and a gray sweatshirt with the hood up. I didn't get a good look at his face, and the hood hid his hair."

The description reminded Max of the man he'd seen at Brady's just before that place had burned to the ground.

"I have to go back to work," Spencer said. "I hope Emma is all right."

"I'll make sure of it. Thanks for calling."

As Max finished the call, he saw Emma's car. He felt a wave of relief. He glanced at the other cars on the street, wondering if someone was still following her.

She stopped to pick him up, and he hopped into the passenger seat, quickly fastening his seat belt. Then he took another look in the side view mirror as she pulled back into traffic.

"Have you noticed any cars following you?" he asked.

She gave him a surprised look. "No, but I wasn't looking. Why?"

"Spencer just called me. He thought someone followed you down the street from the deli."

"Are you serious?" She frowned and glanced in the rearview mirror. "The car behind me has two women in it."

"This was a guy."

"I wonder if it was Jon."

"Has he called you again?"

"No, I haven't heard from him since we spoke the other day."

"This man was wearing a hooded sweatshirt."

"That doesn't sound like Jon. He's never not in a suit during the work week."

"It sounds like the guy I saw outside of Brady's last Sunday night."

"What exactly did Spencer say?" she asked.

"Just what I told you. He said he'd seen the guy outside the deli while you were eating and noticed that he took off as soon as you left. He had a bad feeling about it, so he went outside and saw the guy walking behind you."

"That's weird. I didn't feel like anyone was watching me, but I was thinking about the Morettis and what I wanted to ask Jarod." She paused, her brows knitting together. "There have been a few occasions in the last few days that I have felt like someone was following me. The first time was when I went to Brady's for my dad's party."

He didn't like the sound of that. "Why didn't you tell me that before?"

"I forgot about it until now. And the other times I chalked it up to my overly active imagination. Why would anyone follow me? There's no reason. It's probably just a coincidence that this guy started walking down the street at the same time I did."

"And that he was dressed exactly the same as the guy I saw outside of Brady's? I don't believe in coincidences, Emma."

"Well, there's nothing to be done about it now. We need to speak to Jarod. Are you going to let me do the talking?"

"I'll let you start," he conceded. "After that we'll see."

—➤➤◄◄—

Jarod was hammering up drywall in the entryway of a newly remodeled first-floor flat. He wore jeans and a t-shirt and had a tool belt around his hips. He smiled when he saw Emma, but that smile faded when his gaze reached Max.

"Hi Jarod," she said. "This is Max Harrison. He's an inspector with the SFPD."

"I thought you came to talk to me about your family." Confusion and wariness entered his gaze.

"Actually, it's your family I wanted to speak to you about."

"What has Tony done now?"

"I think he's lying about something that involves you."

Jarod glanced over his shoulder. She could see two workers down the hall. Jarod motioned for them to follow him outside.

As they stepped out of the house, Jarod said, "Okay, what is this about?"

"It's about fire," she replied. "In this case, a fire set in a dumpster at St. Andrew's when you were in the eighth grade. Do you remember?"

His eyes widened in surprise. "That's what you came to ask me? You want to know about a fire from what—fifteen years ago?"

"Nineteen years ago, to be precise. And you haven't answered my question."

"Why are you looking into that old incident? Don't you have enough current fires to worry about?"

"There could be a link between the past and the present. According to the school records, you set the fire in the dumpster, and you were suspended for it. But the other day Tony told me that Christian Brady was the one who did it. Tony didn't mention you at all, which seems strange since he would have noticed you weren't going to school for a week. You walked there together every day."

"Yeah, I set the fire," Jarod admitted. "I was playing around with matches one day, and I tossed one into the dumpster. It was a stupid, impulsive decision, and I regretted it immediately. I was glad it didn't do any damage. So you think I burned down Brady's because I was once an idiot thirteen-year-old?" Anger filled his eyes. "Come on, Emma. I thought you were a good investigator, but you're just making shit up."

"Most arsonists start with small fires at an early age," she said, refusing to let his attitude intimidate her.

"Now I'm an arsonist?" he asked in amazement. "Seriously?"

"I didn't say that, Jarod. But I have a difficult time believing you were the one who set the fire. Tony was always the troublemaker, and you were always the one who tried to keep him out of trouble. Are you sure it wasn't Tony who set the fire and you who took the blame?" she asked, fairly certain that that's what had happened.

"No, it was me, so if you want to make a link between that old fire and these new ones, then the connection is me," he said.

She frowned, wondering why he was so eager to take the fall. "Do you want me to make that connection?"

"Can I stop you?" he countered.

"The truth will come out, Jarod. If you're trying to protect Tony—"

"I answered your question, Emma. That's all I have to say."

She felt frustrated by his antagonistic attitude. In her experience, people who had nothing to hide were a lot more receptive to questions. "You're not telling me something, Jarod. And I am a good investigator. I will figure it out."

"I can't believe you think I'd burn down a bar or kill someone, because isn't that why he's here?" Jarod asked, waving his hand in Max's direction.

"That's exactly why I'm here," Max said, entering the conversation for the first time. "Where did you go after you left Brady's Sunday night?"

"I went home."

"Can anyone verify that?"

"I met my girlfriend there around midnight."

"I'm going to need her name and phone number as well as your address and hers," Max added, pulling out a small spiral notebook and a pen.

Jarod blew out an irritated breath but gave Max the information. "Is that it?" Jarod asked.

Where did your brother Tony go after the party?" Max queried. "You don't live together, right?"

"No, Tony lives at my dad's house. Emma knows his address. I dropped Tony off before I went home. He'd had a few drinks, so he wasn't going anywhere."

"What kind of relationship did you have with Sister Margaret?" Max asked.

"The usual student/teacher relationship. I wouldn't say I loved her, but I haven't had any contact with her in years. I certainly didn't kill her." Jarod ran a hand through his hair, his gaze bewildered. "I can't believe you're coming after me, Emma. I don't have anything to do with this."

"We're not coming after you. We're just asking questions.

And frankly, your uncooperative attitude only raises more suspicion."

"How would you like it if someone was accusing you of murder?" he challenged.

"If you are covering for Tony in any way—"

"I'm not," he said, cutting her off. "You can ask Tony the same questions, and he'll give you the same answers."

"But that's the thing. He didn't give me your name when I questioned him; he gave me Christian's. Why?"

"He probably forgot. It was a long time ago. And Christian was always talking about fire. He wanted to be a firefighter from the time he was ten years old. I'm sure that's why Tony thought of him. But Christian is a great guy, and he would never burn something down. He spends his life fighting fires. Plus, he'd never burn down his father's bar. That doesn't make sense."

"Do you have any idea who might have had a reason to pick Brady's and St. Andrew's as targets?" Max interjected.

"I can't think of anyone," Jarod said. "I just know it wasn't me or my brother. Tony is getting his life together. He's working a lot, and he's being responsible. We're not your guys, Emma. I'm not an arsonist. I just set one stupid fire. And there's no link between that one and the ones happening now. I hope you can believe that. Can I go back to work?"

She saw nothing but sincerity in his eyes, and she found herself wanting to believe him. "Yes, we're done for now. Thanks for talking to me."

As Jarod walked back into the house, Emma turned to Max. "What do you think?"

"I don't think he's our arsonist, but he could be protecting his brother."

"You don't really have any evidence on which to base that opinion, besides the fact that you don't like Tony."

"It's instinct. I don't trust him. I think he's worth checking out a little further." Max paused. "I was impressed by your persistence. You grilled Jarod. Never mind that you grew up with him. However, he didn't help his case by calling into question your investigative skills. That was like waving a red flag in front of a bull."

"You're not seriously comparing me to a bull, are you? Because that's not really what a man says to a woman he recently slept with."

Immediately, Emma wished the words back. She'd been trying to keep things professional, but she'd just turned them personal—very personal. "Forget I said that," she said quickly. She glanced at her watch. "I need to go. I have to meet Aiden at my new apartment. He's going to take some measurements for me. I'd like to have some shelves put up in the closet before I move all my stuff in. I can drop you at your office on the way."

"I'll go with you," Max said. "I want to talk to you about Ruth Harbough's son, Jeffrey."

"What have you learned about him?" she asked, as they got back into her car.

"He has a lot of bitterness towards his mother. He told me that she shipped him off to live with his father when he was twelve because she wanted to have a personal life. For a long time he wouldn't even talk to her. But they reconnected a few years ago and were getting closer. Then Sister Margaret moved in, and suddenly Ruth no longer had time for him."

She gave Max a quick look. "Did Jeffrey think his mother was involved with Margaret romantically?"

"He said he suspected that she was, but she's never admitted it."

"Where are you going with this?" she asked.

"Not sure, but you might find it interesting to know that

Jeffrey is a mechanic at a gas station."

"Which would make it pretty easy for him to get gallons of gas," she murmured. "You like him for a suspect?"

"He fits better with a motive for wanting to see Margaret dead than for setting fires to the schools. Although his mother works at St. Andrew's, and he did say she chose her job over him."

She thought about that for a moment. "I keep going back to the fact that no one actually killed Margaret. She died after what we assume was a kidnapping. I just don't think her disappearance or her death was planned. Do you?"

"No, I don't. But I'm trying to cover all the bases." He paused. "What did you do today?"

"Well, I didn't find any new leads, but I did have an interesting conversation with your brother. It wasn't about you this time. It was about Stephanie. He was ringing up my order, and he suddenly dashed out to the street. He thought he saw her outside. But it wasn't her. When he came back in, he told me about his love for her."

Max shook his head. "Do I want to hear this?"

"Probably not. Your brother is very eloquent when it comes to his feelings."

"That he is," Max agreed. "Am I foolish to think Spencer will ever forget about Stephanie?"

"He said he'd like to have one more conversation with her, so I don't think he's planning to forget about her soon."

"If he tracks her down, it could be bad, Emma. She could call the cops. He could end up in trouble all over again."

She stopped at a red light and looked at his hard profile. She could hear the frustration in his voice. "I understand, Max, and you're right, Spencer should stay away from her, but I don't think he will. You can't control his actions. He's an adult. I know how it is with siblings. We want to protect them, but we can't. They have to make their own mistakes—just as we have to make ours."

He glanced at her. "Do you think last night was a mistake?"

"I don't have regrets, but I'm not sure what you want, Max."

"Do you know what you want?" he countered.

Some very dangerous words hovered on her lips—*I want you.* Somehow, she managed not to speak them.

The car behind her beeped its horn, and she realized the light was green. She really shouldn't be having this conversation while she was driving.

As she drew closer to the Marina, she noticed black smoke billowing into the sky.

"Fire," Max said.

"Yeah," she said, her body tensing.

"It looks like it's close to your place."

Her heart began to race and she pressed down on the gas. Sirens rang through the air. She saw engines racing through the next intersection.

She began to think the unthinkable.

She drove two more blocks, then turned onto her street and slammed on the brakes.

There was a line of fire engines down the block, and a traffic control officer was already waving traffic toward a side street.

Emma pulled in front of a driveway and double parked, then jumped out of the car, silently praying that she was wrong, that it was the building next to hers, but as she came around the first fire engine, she saw the flames shooting out of a third-story apartment.

"Oh, my God!" She turned to Max. "My apartment is on fire."

Nineteen

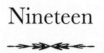

Max was stunned. He couldn't believe what he was seeing. He put his arm around Emma's shoulders and felt tremors of shock running through her. She was used to dealing with fire. That was her job. But this—this was personal. He felt that with every fiber of his being. It was not a coincidence that it was Emma's apartment that was on fire. Someone had known she'd rented it. Someone had wanted to make a point to her.

Anger tore through him. He looked around the gathering crowd, wondering if the perpetrator was out there somewhere, hiding in the shadows, watching them even now.

Emma drew in a breath and lifted her chin. He gazed down at her and saw the light of battle in her eyes. Her momentary paralysis was over. She was ready to fight.

"Let's go," she said, striding forward.

They flashed their badges to get to the center of the action where they found Emma's brother Burke directing the crews on site.

He glanced at Emma, a tense expression in his eyes. "I was just about to call you. How did you know?"

"I was coming to meet Aiden. That's my new apartment, Burke."

Surprise widened his gaze. "No way."

"I picked up the keys yesterday. If you didn't know that,

why were you calling me?" she asked in confusion.

"Because it's definitely arson, and there was a spray-painted message on the front door that might refer to you. Hamilton took a photo of it."

"What did it say?"

"It said—*You're never going to catch me, bitch. I'm better than you.*"

She blew out a ragged breath. "Okay then. He didn't choose this building by accident, but by design." Emma glanced back at Max. "He's taunting me. He left me a calling card."

"Let's hope he left some other clues, too," he said grimly, knowing that the arsonist had probably been tailing Emma all week. It infuriated him to know that they'd been watched the last few days, and he hadn't noticed a damn thing. What the hell kind of detective was he?

"I need to get inside," Emma said.

"Hold on," Burke said. "You're not going in until this is under control."

"The second it is, you tell me," she ordered her brother. "I am going to catch this son of a bitch if it's the last thing I do."

"Well, I don't want it to be the *last* thing you do," Burke retorted. "So get a hold of yourself."

"Don't talk to me like that. I'm not here as your little sister. I'm a fire investigator, and this is what I do."

Burke shook his head and turned his attention to the radio. He moved a few steps away from them as he relayed information to the men on the roof.

"How dare he tell me to calm down?" Emma grumbled. "This is my case. This is my fire."

Max let her rant. He knew her anger was also a cover for her pain. The arsonist had gone after Emma's home, after the place that already meant something to her, if only in a symbolic way. She had been planning to start over here, on her own, independent, free...

His thoughts turned to her ex-boyfriend Jon. The last thing Jon wanted was for Emma to start over. Was it possible they'd been on the wrong track? That the fires had nothing to do with the schools or Sister Margaret or the Morettis?"

"Damn," he muttered.

Emma shot him a sharp look. "What?"

"All the fires are connected to you—your elementary school, your high school, the bar where you helped your father celebrate his promotion, and this apartment. It's you, Emma. You're the common denominator. I said it before, and I let you talk me out of it. But it's you."

Her face turned pale. "I could have become the target after I started working the cases. It's an arsonist against an arson investigator."

She had a point, but his gut told him she was making it too simple.

"I have to get my gear," she said, striding back to the car. "I want to capture what evidence I can before it goes up in flames."

He followed her down the block, feeling a need to stay close to her. She wouldn't appreciate it, but he didn't care.

Emma didn't say anything to him as she grabbed her gear out of the trunk of her car. While she was putting on the thick coveralls, he took another look around the block. There were a lot of shadowy doorways where someone could hide, and a large crowd was gathering at the end of each block.

"You need to be careful, Emma," he said, unable to hold back the warning, even though he knew it wasn't in Emma's DNA to be cautious.

"I know what I'm doing, Max. I have to figure out who

this guy is before he does any more damage."

"And before he hurts you."

She met his gaze. "I don't think this is about hurting me. He loves to watch things burn. His message wasn't a threat. It was a promise to keep going. He was taunting me. He doesn't think I'm good enough to catch him."

Her words struck a nerve. "He doesn't think you're good enough," he echoed. "You might have just come up with a motive."

"Someone who doesn't like me in the job," she said, finishing his thought. "That could be a lot of people."

"Not as big of a pool as we had before."

"Maybe it is another firefighter," she said.

"Or maybe it's your ex-boyfriend. Didn't Jon blame your job for your breakup?"

She frowned. "This doesn't feel like Jon's kind of thing. He doesn't get his hands dirty."

"Maybe he had someone else do his dirty work."

As he finished speaking, Aiden came down the street, his features sharp and worried. "Are you all right, Emma? Burke said the fire was set in your apartment."

"I'm fine. I'll have to find somewhere else to live, but that's not my main concern at the moment." She turned to Max. "I need to get inside and see that message for myself. I'll talk to you both later."

As Emma left, Aiden said, "What message?"

"The arsonist spray-painted a message on Emma's door. *You're never going to catch me, bitch. I'm better than you.*"

"He was talking about Emma?"

"Yeah, I'd say so. What do you know about her ex-boyfriend?"

Aiden's gaze narrowed. "Jon? He talks a lot, usually about himself. I always thought Emma could do better, but she wasn't interested in my opinion."

"I want to talk to Jon, but I don't have a car here. I came with Emma. Any chance you could give me a ride back to my office?"

"Why don't I give you a ride to Jon's office?" Aiden suggested. "I'd like to have a little talk with him myself. In fact, I've been meaning to do that all week. I heard he's been texting her non-stop."

"He was up until a few days ago."

"Maybe he decided to leave his text in spray-paint, where she couldn't ignore it," Aiden said.

"You read my mind."

"I'm parked around the corner," Aiden said as they started walking. "You do know that Emma will not like us talking to Jon without her."

"I know," he said. "But this is my case, too. She's not calling all the shots."

Jon Wickmore had an office on the thirty-second floor of a skyscraper in downtown San Francisco. The front door of the office suite read Wickmore Investments.

"The father," Aiden said, answering Max's unspoken question. "He started the company twenty-five years ago. Jon came in a couple of years back. They're venture capitalists, and they work with big money."

"Can I help you?" the receptionist asked.

"We'd like to see Jon Wickmore," Max said, showing his badge. "Where's his office?"

She stiffened. "May I tell him you're coming?"

"I'd rather surprise him."

"His office is down the hall, second door on the right."

Max strode briskly down the hallway. Adrenaline and anger were running rampant, and he knew he should probably take a breath before he opened Jon's door and put a fist through his face. He'd learned a long time ago not to let his emotions into an investigation, but this one was different, this one was about Emma. He would protect her with everything that he had.

The thought almost stopped him in his tracks. He suddenly realized he'd just echoed Spencer's words. If he didn't want to have the same result, he needed to get a grip.

Taking a deep breath, he rapped sharply on the door, then opened it.

Jon looked up in surprise. That surprise turned to wariness when he recognized both Max and Aiden. He stood up. "What are you doing here? Is something wrong? Has something happened to Emma?"

"Why don't you tell us?" Max said, walking up to the desk.

"I don't know what you're talking about. I haven't seen Emma since we last spoke outside that deli she likes so much. You were there."

"I was there, and I remember how desperate you were to get her back. Have you been here in your office all day?"

"Yes."

"You didn't go out for lunch?"

"I did. I was gone for about an hour. Look, I don't know what's happened, but I would never hurt Emma." Jon turned to Aiden. "You know I love your sister."

"I know you cheated on her," Aiden replied, a harsh note in his voice. "I should kick your ass for that."

"That was a mistake. I've apologized to her."

"And that's supposed to make it all right?"

"What do you want from me?" Jon asked Max, obviously

coming to the conclusion that he was going to get no help from Aiden.

"Where did you go for lunch?"

"A café down the street."

"Can anyone vouch for you?"

"I met a client, Randy Hooper. We talked business for an hour, and then I came back here."

"And you didn't stop by Emma's apartment on the way here?" Max challenged.

"Her apartment?" Jon echoed. "She lives with her parents. Tell him, Aiden."

"She was moving out," Aiden said. "She was trying to get her life back together after you blew it apart."

"I didn't know about an apartment. Is she all right?"

Jon was either a very good actor, or he had no idea what Max was talking about.

"Why have you been sending her harassing texts?" Aiden asked.

"They weren't harassing texts. I just wanted her to give me another chance. Look, there are two sides to every story, and you've only heard one."

"Then tell us yours," Max ordered. "And it better be good, or you're coming down to the station with me to answer questions in a more formal setting."

Alarm flared in Jon's eyes. "I haven't done anything wrong."

"Except desperately trying to get your ex-girlfriend back," Max said. "How far were you willing to go to get her attention?"

"It's not exactly as it seems," Jon said. He paused for a moment and then said. "I'm in the initial stages of putting together a political campaign. Next year I'm going to be running for a supervisor position. In making my plans, I've had many meetings with political strategists, and they all pointed out that Emma was a valuable asset. She's well-connected, and the unions love the Callaways."

"So you wanted to get her back so she could be your political trophy? Do you know Emma at all?" Aiden asked in bewilderment. "The last thing my sister would be is anyone's trophy."

"I do care about Emma," Jon said. "She knows that. And she's always understood my ambitions."

"But you never understood hers, did you?" Max challenged.

Jon didn't answer the question. Instead, he said, "Is she all right?"

"Yeah, she's fine," Max said. "Better off without you. If you bother her again, you're going to be sorry."

"You're threatening me? I could have your badge. Do you know how many connections I have in this city?"

"Just stating a fact," he said evenly.

"He might not be threatening you, but I am," Aiden put in. "You call her one more time, and I will kick your ass."

"Are we done?" Jon asked, ice in his voice.

"Yeah, we're done," Max said.

"Can you believe that piece of shit?" Aiden fumed as they walked to the elevator. "What did Emma ever see in that guy?"

"I have no idea," he said. "She is way out of his league."

"If she knew he was trying to use her for political gain, she'd go nuts." Aiden paused. "Are you going to tell her?"

"I don't know."

"She deserves to know."

"It will hurt her."

"Maybe it will free her to move on," Aiden said. "So do you think he set the fire?"

Max really wanted to say yes, but he couldn't. "No, I don't. Which means we're back to square one."

"What can I do to help?"

"I wish I knew," he replied. But with this new fire, they would have to start over, refocus the investigation. He just hoped that the arsonist had gotten careless in his eagerness to taunt Emma. They could really use a new clue.

➤➤◄◄◄

When Max returned to the scene of the fire, the blaze was out, and Burke allowed him to go inside. The sickening stench of smoke hit him the second he walked into the building and got thicker as he walked up to the third floor. He paused in front of her front door. It had been ripped off its hinges and was propped up on the wall. The painted message looked even more ominous with the red paint dripping down the door, giving the illusion of blood. Max had a feeling the color choice had been deliberate.

As he read the words, he felt angry again and more than a little worried. Emma might not think she was in danger, but he wasn't so sure.

He stepped into the apartment and saw destruction everywhere he looked. The windows were broken, and there was shattered glass on the hardwood floors that had buckled under the heat and the water. The walls were blackened and streaked with ashes. There were several large holes in the roof, and through one of them he could see the first few stars of the night, but even those bright orbs didn't lessen the heavy depressive quality of the scene.

"I'm going to be here awhile," Emma said, coming over to him.

He could see a forensic tech in the bedroom collecting

ashes. "I know. I'll wait for you."

"You don't have to do that."

He looked into her eyes and saw determination but also sadness. She was keeping it together, but there were painful emotions brewing inside. "Are you okay?" He knew she hated the question, but he couldn't help asking it.

"It's different when it's your place," she admitted. "I never realized until now how personal an arson fire can feel. I didn't own this place, but I felt like it was mine. It would have been worse if I'd already moved in. I guess I should be grateful he didn't wait that long to try to get my attention." She gave him a shaky smile.

He smiled back at her. "You do try to find the bright side of things."

"It's not easy tonight."

"You'll get through it."

"I will," she agreed. "I'll do my job, and you'll do yours, and we'll catch the bastard."

"I'll wait for you outside."

"You really should just go home, Max."

"I'm not leaving until you do. And you're coming home with me," he said decisively.

His words brought her back up; he could see it in her eyes. She was going to fight, but he was not going to give in. "That was a statement, not a question, by the way."

She immediately started shaking her head. "Max—"

"Listen to me, Emma. Someone has been following you. Someone knew you rented this apartment. They sent you a message. It won't be the last. Do you want the next message to be at your parents' house?"

His words turned her skin pale. "No, of course not."

"You can't go back there tonight, and you can't stay with friends, because you're a target. And I know you don't want to put anyone in danger. So you'll come home with me. I can protect you."

"I can protect myself."

"And everyone around you?" he challenged.

"You're making this hard," she complained, but he could see the beginning of resignation in her eyes.

"You don't have a choice, Emma. My place is the best option. We'll pick up Chinese food on the way home, and I'll even give you control of the remote for at least an hour."

Her shoulders sagged, releasing a little of the tension she'd been holding. "If you're going to throw in the remote, then you have a deal. I'll be down as soon as I can."

As he left the apartment, the word *home* flew around in his head. For the first time since he'd moved back to San Francisco, he'd actually thought of his barely furnished apartment as home. And that was because of Emma. Maybe it wasn't the apartment that felt like home. Maybe it was Emma.

Twenty

——➤➤◄◄◄——

Emma sat cross-legged on Max's couch, dipping her chopsticks into a carton of chicken and noodles. She'd stopped by her parents' house on the way back from the fire to pick up a change of clothes. Fortunately, neither one of her parents had been home to grill her with questions, so she'd left a note on the refrigerator saying she was staying with friends for a few days and not to worry. They'd hear about the fire at her place from Burke or Aiden, but by then she hoped they'd have a suspect in custody.

She glanced across the room at Max, who had already finished eating and was staring at the laptop computer he'd set up on the coffee table.

"What are you looking at?" she asked.

"My email. I was hoping the Sheriff in Lake Tahoe might have found someone who saw Margaret in the area. But there's nothing yet."

"A lot of those cabins are remote, and if it was night when she was taken into the house, it's possible no one saw her."

"It is a long shot. I checked to see if the Morettis own property in Tahoe; they don't. Neither do the Bradys."

"But any one of their friends could have houses up there. Are you still focused on the Morettis? How do they fit into the fire at my apartment?"

"I don't think Jarod set the fire. We saw him minutes before. Tony could have been involved. He asked us a lot of questions about the investigation the other day. I haven't ruled out Christian Brady. You mentioned that he doesn't like female firefighters, and he was not particularly cooperative when you went to speak to his father. He knows how to set a fire."

She shook her head. "Christian loves his father and that bar. If this were just about my place, I'd put him on the suspect list, because I know he doesn't respect me as a firefighter or an investigator."

"What about his brother? What kind of relationship do you have with him?"

"Robert and I were in the same grade, so I was actually better friends with him than with Christian. Growing up, the Bradys spent a lot of time in our house. Christian and Robert's mother divorced Harry when the boys were really young, so my mom was always inviting them over for meals. Christian and Robert were like brothers. We argued and got annoyed with each other. But in recent years we haven't had much contact." She paused. "Are we taking Jeffrey Harbough off the list?"

"I don't think he's involved. He's too removed from this area. Our suspect has to be from the St. Andrew's neighborhood. And they have to know you."

She hated the idea that one of her friends could be involved. "I don't think they have to be from the neighborhood, but I do agree that they have to know me. They have to have some negative attitude about me. When I go to work tomorrow, I'm going to see if I can get a list of the candidates who applied for my job. If this guy thinks he's better than me, maybe he's upset that I got the job instead of him. I should have thought of that earlier," she added.

"You didn't believe you were the target earlier."

"But you did. You told me that outside of Brady's. You said I was the common denominator, and I blew you off."

"I was just guessing. And I was pissed that everywhere I went, you seemed to be."

"Funny, I had the same feeling about you. And yet our mutual dislike brought us here."

"I wouldn't say I disliked you," he said quietly, his gaze turning more serious. "But I knew you were going to be trouble, Emma. You were going to have an impact on my life."

"Since I'm now your houseguest, I guess you were right. So have we run out of suspects?"

He stared back at her for a long moment, as if he were debating whether or not to tell her something.

"Don't hold back now," she said. "Whatever you want to say, say it."

"You're not going to like it. But I went to see Jon tonight."

Her jaw dropped in surprise. She had not expected those words to come out of his mouth. "My ex-boyfriend? Why would you do that?"

"Because I thought he could be involved. The spray-painted message used the word *bitch*, and we both heard him call you that the other day."

"Jon is not involved. That's ridiculous," she said, getting to her feet. "I can't believe you went there without telling me."

"You were busy looking for evidence. I was looking for suspects."

"How did you even know where to find him?"

"Aiden took me to his office."

"Aiden?" Anger raced through her. "You got my brother involved?"

"He volunteered. We were both worried about you." Max got to his feet. "Jon has been sending you text messages for days. I saw his agitation and desperation when he confronted you outside the deli. He wanted you back, and you refused. It's not that far of a leap to think he'd try to get revenge."

"It's a huge leap to think he'd become an arsonist."

"Is it? He thought you put your job before him. Maybe he wanted to show you that you weren't that good at it."

"So what did he say? Did he confess?"

Max's lips tightened. "He said he didn't do it."

She gave him a long, speculative look, wondering just how that scene had gone down. "What did you say?"

"I told him he better not be lying, and that if he bothered you again, he'd be sorry."

"You threatened Jon? What gave you the right to do that?"

"I'm a cop. I was investigating a crime. And I protect the people I care about. So you're just going to have to get over it, Emma, because I'm not going to let that lying asshole get anywhere near you again."

She stared at him in shock. "I'm just going to have to get over it?" she echoed. "Did you really just say that?"

"Yes," he said flatly.

The air between them sizzled. Every nerve ending in her body was tingling with both anger and arousal. "How I am supposed to get over it?" she challenged.

He took a step forward. "I'll show you." His mouth came down on hers in a hard, demanding, possessive kiss that literally rocked her back on her heels.

All the emotions of the last few hours came together in one explosive moment. Emma couldn't fight it. She didn't want to fight it. She wanted to lose herself in Max, let go of the anger, the fear, and the sense of loss.

So she kissed him back, again and again, until she felt dizzy. They didn't make it to the bedroom. They barely made it to the couch.

Buttons flew in disarray as clothes were removed with rough and urgent hands, and it was no longer about who was in charge. She didn't care if she was on the bottom or the top. She didn't care if it was her kiss or his—her touch or his. She just wanted to be connected to Max in every possible way, to feel the delicious friction of their bodies, to breathe in his scent, and to take him deep inside her.

Their lovemaking was hot, fast and soul-shattering. Whatever barriers had been between them were completely stripped away. Neither one of them was in control. The result was a spectacular blaze of heat and a free-fall into what terrifyingly felt a lot like love.

Hours later, Emma snuggled up against Max in his king-sized bed, wondering how she'd become so addicted to a man so fast. They'd made love twice already, and she wanted more.

"Can't sleep?" Max asked, a husky, tender note in his voice, as he rubbed her back.

"I should be able to. We had quite a workout," she said lightly. "And by the way, I'm still not over it."

He suddenly moved, flipping her onto her back. He smiled at her. "I guess I have some work to do then."

"Stop. I'm exhausted," she said, unable to resist smiling back at him. "No amount of great sex is going to make up for the fact that you went behind my back. And I can't believe you took Aiden with you. He's got as hot a head as your brother. I could easily see him taking a swing at Jon." She paused. "Wait a second. Did either one of you hit Jon?"

"Worried about his pretty face?"

"Worried about whether one or both of you might get arrested for assault."

"Don't be concerned. He's fine. We didn't touch him. I wanted to, but I didn't. I have to admit that for the first time I really understood how my brother felt when he thought Stephanie was being threatened."

"But you didn't let your emotions get the best of you."

"It was a struggle."

"What did you ask Jon?"

"I asked him where he was. I got his alibi. And after speaking with him for a few minutes, I didn't think he did it."

"Of course he didn't. I told you that."

"I wasn't sure you knew him as well as you thought you did."

She sighed. "I'm not proud of that relationship. I feel like a fool for not seeing how shallow Jon was. But part of me didn't want to see his flaws, because then I'd have to admit that I'd made a mistake. And that would be embarrassing. I learned a lot from that relationship, though. So it wasn't worth nothing."

"I think Jon is very good at showing people what they want to see," Max said. "That's probably why he's successful."

She appreciated his words, but there was an odd note in his voice. "Is there something else you need to tell me, Max?"

"You don't want to know, Emma."

"There you go, deciding what I should know. I don't like it when you do that."

"What he told me will hurt you."

"I don't think it will. I'm over Jon. I have been for a long time. His words have no power over me. So tell me, I can take it."

"Jon is running for supervisor next year. He thought the Callaway union connections would help his cause. His political strategists thought you would look good on his arm."

She wasn't really that surprised. In fact, his sudden text messages made a lot more sense now. She'd suspected that Jon had had some ulterior motive for his sudden change of heart. "Okay," she said.

Max raised an eyebrow. "That's it?"

"That's it."

Max brushed her hair away from her face. "He really has no idea what he lost in you, Emma."

"You mean, besides my union connections?"

"Yeah, besides that," he said, giving her a tender kiss. "You're an amazing, strong, smart, beautiful woman. You're way too good for him."

"I like it when you leave out all my negative traits."

"It's hard to remember what they are right now," he said, giving her a teasing smile.

She could feel his hard groin pressing against her hips. "Okay, one more time," she said. Then she pulled his head down and applied her own special kind of pressure.

Max came out of the shower the next morning to see Emma fast asleep in his bed. Since he'd gotten up, she'd taken over the middle of the mattress and was sprawled across the sheets and pillows. Her blond hair was tangled, and her cheeks were pink. He thought she might just be the prettiest woman he'd ever seen. He was thinking about getting back into bed with her when his cell phone rang.

He walked into the living room and retrieved the phone from the pocket of his jeans. His mother was calling at eight o'clock in the morning. That couldn't be good.

"Hello?"

"Spencer is gone," she said dramatically. "I can't find him anywhere, and he's not answering his phone. I checked the beach, and he wasn't there. The surfboard is in the garage."

"He's probably just taking a walk."

"A walk in the wrong neighborhood," she said. "Spencer was on my computer last night, and this morning I saw the search engine window open. Spencer was looking for Stephanie's address, and I think he found it."

His heart sank. "I'll go to her house."

"Do you want me to give you the address he found online?"

"I know where she lives."

"Thank you, Max. I don't want Spencer to get into any more trouble, and where that woman is concerned, he seems to have absolutely no sense."

"I'll call you later."

When he returned to the bedroom, Emma had left the bed, and he could hear the shower going. He finished dressing and went back to the kitchen to start some coffee. As it brewed, he wondered what Spencer had in mind. Stephanie was married with a child. Was Spencer just going to knock on her door? Or was it more likely that he'd wait until her husband left for work?

With a sigh, he grabbed a banana and ate it, then poured two cups of coffee and took one into the bedroom. Emma came out of the bathroom dressed in dark jeans and a black sweater. Her blue eyes sparkled when she saw him. "Is that coffee in your hand?"

"Made it for you," he said, handing her the mug.

"Thanks," she said with a grateful smile. "I heard the phone. Everything okay?"

"I'm not sure. It appears that Spencer has gone to look for Stephanie. I told my mother I'd drive over to Stephanie's house and see if I could find him."

Emma gave him a sympathetic smile. "Brothers can be a pain."

"Yes," he said, sipping his coffee. The last thing he wanted to do was chase down Spencer. And the second to last thing he wanted to do was go to work. He'd rather spend the day with Emma—in bed, out of bed—anywhere, really.

She flushed under his gaze. "You're staring at me again."

"I can't get enough of you."

"Hard to believe after last night." She cleared her throat. "Why don't I go with you to find Spencer? Unless you want to go alone?"

"I'm fine if you want to come with me." Emma could be very persuasive, and he might need her help to talk Spencer into leaving Stephanie alone.

"I'll put on my shoes," she said, setting down her coffee.

"Do you need some breakfast?"

"I'll get something later. Let's go find your brother."

⇒≫≪⇐

Stephanie lived in Noe Valley, a mostly residential neighborhood at the southern end of San Francisco. The houses were small but charming. Max pulled up in front of Stephanie's home. There was no sign of Spencer on the street. He turned off the engine and looked around.

"I don't see him," Emma said.

"I don't either," he replied, a bad feeling in his stomach.

"Let's take a walk."

"Do you want to just knock on her door?" Emma suggested as they got out of the car. "That's probably the most direct approach. I could do it, make something up. She won't know who I am. I can make sure she's okay."

"He wouldn't hurt her. I'm more concerned that she'll hurt him, or her husband will. But you're right. We might as well check the house." He marched across the street and rang the bell. There was no answer. "She's not here. I don't know if that's a good sign or a bad sign."

"Let's take a walk through the neighborhood," Emma said. "I saw some cute cafés and shops on the next street over. Maybe she took her baby out for a walk."

"Good idea."

"This is a nice part of the city," Emma commented. "It's a real family neighborhood," she added, as she playfully jumped through hopscotch squares drawn in chalk on the cement. "I didn't know kids still played hopscotch—an old-fashioned game for our technological age. It's nice to know that some simple pleasures still exist. Not that I would want to give up technology. I'm addicted to email and Internet. I can't go on vacation if there's no Wi-Fi."

"I feel the same way," he admitted. "When I went surfing the other day, I realized just how long it had been since I'd been without my phone. I was just sitting on a board in the ocean at the mercy of a wave for my next ride to shore."

"I used to think you were an impatient person," Emma said. "But I've since learned that you can be very patient."

He smiled at the mischievous look in her eyes. "Well, patience has its rewards. When you pick the right wave to ride, there's no better feeling."

She laughed. "Are you comparing me to a wave?"

"I thought we were talking about surfing, but now I see

where your mind is."

She playfully punched his arm. "My mind was in exactly the same place yours was; don't try to pretend otherwise."

"Guilty," he said, enjoying their conversation, and their walk, and pretty much everything about this moment. He hadn't felt so relaxed, so in tune with another person, in a very long time. He had a mental connection with Emma. They could actually finish each other's sentences. But then they were a lot alike in some ways. They were both driven to achieve, both intensely curious, although he thought Emma might have him beaten in that department, and they were both wary when it came to relationships.

He wasn't sure what they were doing at the moment. He didn't really want to define it or analyze it, because in his experience putting a label on something was a good way to kill it.

As they turned the corner, he saw a children's play park across the street. But on this side of the street, sitting on a bench at the bus stop, was Spencer.

Emma met his gaze. He nodded, knowing that Stephanie had to be in that park, probably with her child and any number of other mothers who would probably be hyper-aware of single men watching a play park with small children.

Spencer looked up as they approached, no apology in his eyes.

"What are you doing here?" Max asked.

"I had to see her." Spencer tipped his head toward the park.

Max saw a slender brunette pushing a little boy on a swing. She didn't seem to be aware that she was the focus of Spencer's attention. "I take it you haven't spoken to her."

Spencer let out a heavy sigh. "That little boy should have been my son. She should be pushing our child on the swing, not some other man's kid. We talked about children a lot. We were going to have three, two girls and a boy."

Emma sat down on the bench next to Spencer and gave him a sympathetic smile. "It's hard to see your role being played by someone else."

Spencer turned to Emma. "That's exactly it. Some other guy has my part. It's not right."

"Let me take you home," Max suggested.

"I don't even know where home is anymore." Spencer gazed at Stephanie again. "My home was supposed to be with her." He drew in a long, ragged breath. "I loved her so much. She was my whole life—my everything. I just wanted to protect her. That's all I was doing that night. I was keeping her safe."

Max's heart tore at the pain in his brother's voice, the anguish of emotions that still hadn't died, even after so many years.

"How did I get to be the bad guy?" Spencer asked. "How did I lose her?"

"Let's get out of here," Max said, knowing that he couldn't possibly begin to answer his brother's questions.

Spencer ignored him.

"She loved me, too, once," Spencer said, gazing back toward the park. "She's actually more beautiful than I remember."

Max wanted to remind his brother that Stephanie was not the saint he'd made her into in his mind, but he doubted Spencer would listen to him.

"You did keep her safe," Emma said quietly. "You did protect her, Spencer. Whether she acknowledges that or not, you know it's true. If you hadn't fought that night, who knows what that man would have done to her."

"Thanks for saying that. Very few people see it that

way." Spencer gave Max a hard look. "And I understand why you couldn't see it that way. Because you've never loved anyone the way I've loved Stephanie. You put your heart away a long time ago. For you there are no messy emotions." Spencer looked back at Emma. "Do you want someone whose heart is locked in a block of ice?"

"Leave her out of this," Max said sharply.

"It's okay. I can speak for myself," Emma said, her tone turning hard. "If you think Max is cold, then you don't know him at all, Spencer. He has deep compassion and a tremendous sense of loyalty. And he cares about you. He moved his whole life here to support you, although you probably haven't given him much thought these last few years. It's been all about you, what you lost, who you loved. What about Max? Do you know anything about his life? Do you even want to know?"

Max was as shocked at Emma's words as Spencer was. She'd nailed their relationship right on the head, and she was the first person who'd ever called Spencer out. He should be pissed off that she was speaking for him, that she was getting into his family business, but at the moment all he could do was admire her courage and her honesty.

"Max is a great person and you're lucky to have him for a brother," she continued. "From where I sit, you don't have too many people who care about you, so maybe you should appreciate those that do." She took a breath and looked at Max. "And yes, I know it's none of my business. I'll save you the trouble of telling me to shut up and go away." She got to her feet. "I'll meet you at the car."

She strode away, her shoulders thrown back, her hair blowing in the breeze. Emma was really something else. He glanced back at his brother.

"You're going to have your hands full with her," Spencer

said.

"Tell me about it." He sat down on the bench next to his brother.

A moment of silence passed between them. "Did you really move back here for me?" Spencer asked.

"And Mom," he said. "I thought you both might need some support."

"I thought it was just a job transfer."

"I don't believe you thought anything at all." Emma had inspired him to be more direct.

Spencer gave him a quick glance. "You're right. I wasn't thinking about you, just about myself, my life."

The words should have hurt, but the admission actually made Max feel better. At least they weren't pretending anymore.

"I know I brought all my problems on myself," Spencer added.

"Stephanie helped," he said. "You need to see her the way she really is and not just the way you want her to be." He waved his hand toward the park. "She's moved on. She fell in love again. She had a child. She's a wife and a mother. She's not your girlfriend anymore. You have to let her go. She let you go a long time ago." He paused. "And you already know that. If you didn't, you'd be at that park talking to her, instead of sitting here on this bench."

"I needed to see her in her real life. She looks happy. I can see that she loves being a mother. She lost her family when she was young. But now she has a new family." He looked at Max. "Life isn't black and white. People are complicated—the good ones and the bad ones. You only saw the bad in Stephanie, but I also saw the good."

"I'm a cop. I see good and bad in people every day of the week. I also see people who get stuck in a pattern that will ultimately destroy them. I don't want to see that happen to you. Let me take you home."

"Mom sent you, didn't she?"

He nodded. "She was worried about you."

"I need to get my own place."

"You will. You're starting over, Spencer. And it's up to you how you want to live your life now. No one else is in charge of it anymore. It's all up you." He stood up. "We both need to go to work."

Spencer rose, sent one last wistful look across the playground, and then followed Max down the street.

"So what's with you and Emma?" Spencer asked. "You're a couple now?"

"I'm not sure what we are."

"Did you spend the night together?"

"That's not your business."

"You're making my life your business. And I'm going to take that non-answer as a yes." Spencer paused. "I like her. She doesn't pull her punches. You ready for that?"

"I don't know," he said honestly. "I've never met anyone who made me want to think about the future."

"Until you met her."

"Until I met her," he echoed. "But the men in our family have a lousy track record when it comes to love."

"You sound like you think you have a choice."

"Everyone has a choice."

"Not when it comes to love, little brother. Trust me. I don't know much, but I do know that."

Twenty-One

After dropping Spencer off at his mother's house, Max drove Emma back to his apartment so she could retrieve her car. Then he followed her down to the Hall of Justice where they had agreed to start the day. Emma wanted to look through the medical examiner's reports, and he wanted to check in with the sheriff's office in Lake Tahoe.

As they waited in the lobby for the elevator, Emma said, "Are you angry with me, Max—for telling Spencer off earlier?"

"It really wasn't your business," he reminded her.

"I didn't like his attitude. He doesn't appreciate what you've done for him." She gave him a thoughtful glance. "Although you two seemed fairly chummy when you got back into the car."

Max nodded, feeling optimistic now that Spencer had seen Stephanie and left her alone. Maybe Spencer really could start to move forward. And Max hoped his relationship with Spencer was also entering a new chapter where they could just be brothers and possibly even friends. "We had a good talk—an honest talk—and that's because of you, Emma. You opened the door and forced us to walk through it." He gave her a reassuring smile. "So, no, I'm not angry. I'm actually grateful."

Relief flooded her gaze, and she let out a breath. "Good. I know that I sometimes speak before thinking things through. I do occasionally try to work on that."

He laughed. "Yeah, let me know how that goes."

She made a face at him. "At least I have some self-awareness."

"At least you have that."

"Spencer is going to be okay, Max," she said as they got onto the elevator.

"I think he will be, too. Sometimes avoiding something is worse than confronting it. I was probably wrong to try to keep him away from Stephanie. It just made him want to see her more."

"In the end, he is the one who decided whether or not to speak to her. He can feel good about his choice, because he's the one who made it," she said.

"I agree," he said. "So back to work?"

She nodded as they got off the elevator and walked down the hall to his office.

Emma sat down next to his desk while he turned on his computer.

"Can I have your case file?" she asked. "I feel like we need to start at the beginning again and look at what we have with the perspective of the most recent fire and the targeted message to me. Sometimes facts look different through a new filter."

He pushed a file across the desk to her. "Here you go."

While she was reading through his interview notes, Max ran through his emails. Nothing new. He needed to check in with the sheriff's office in Lake Tahoe. It might be time to make a trip up there, although he'd like to have an address first or at least a smaller region to investigate.

"We made a lot of the same notes," Emma commented.

"Our minds work the same way—at least some of the time."
She paused and pulled out a photo. "What's this?"

"That's a rosary."

She frowned. "I know what it is, but why is it in the case
file?"

"Sister Margaret had it in her pocket. Forensics tested it.
The only fingerprints on it belonged to Margaret. There were
no hairs, dirt, blood, nothing."

Emma shook her head, confusion in her eyes. "This
rosary would not belong to Sister Margaret."

"Why not? Ruth Harbough said that Margaret never went
anywhere without her rosary." He didn't understand why
Emma was staring at the photo with such an odd look in her
eyes.

"The nuns at St. Andrew's carried a fifteen-decade
rosary, to celebrate the fifteen mysteries. This is a five-decade
rosary, the kind given to every eighth grade student at St.
Andrew's at graduation." She looked up from the photo. "I
need to see the rosary itself."

"It's in the Evidence Room. I can get it."

"That would be great. The rosary I got at my graduation
had a year engraved on the back of the crucifix, two numbers.
If this rosary was in Margaret's pocket, it's possible it
belonged to her kidnapper."

"You just made a big jump."

She met his gaze. "I have a feeling about this, Max.
Where's the forensics report on the rosary?"

"It should be in there, but I'll go get the rosary so you can
take a look at it."

"Thanks."

⟶⟫⟪⟵

While Max went to retrieve the rosary, Emma ran

through the rest of the file. There was a short forensics report on the rosary, outlining what Max had told her previously. But there was a footnote listing the numbers nine-four on the back of the crucifix, with a question of unit or serial number. Her heart jumped. 1994 was the year her brother Aiden had graduated from the eighth grade, and in his grade had been the Moretti twins and Christian Brady. Had they been focusing on the right people all along?

She set down the paper and thought for a moment, her mind racing in a dozen different directions. She was making a leap assuming that the rosary belonged to Margaret's kidnapper. On the other hand, why would Margaret have had it in her pocket?

Okay, there could be another more innocent reason. She could have just had a rosary from that year and had it with her at school when she was taken... No, that didn't make any sense.

So, she had a rosary from the year of three of her suspects, all of whom knew her, at least one of whom didn't like her. Christian?

She pulled out her phone and called her boss, Scott McAvoy.

"Emma," he said, relief in his voice. "Are you all right? I've been concerned about you."

"I'm fine. I'm at the police department now, but I'll be in shortly. I was wondering if you could do me a favor. I need to get a list of applicants for the fire investigator position that I got last year. Or any applicants from the last two years would probably work, too. Is that possible?"

"I should be able to get that list. You think the arsonist is an unhappy firefighter?"

"His message stated that he was better than me, so I'm thinking there's a chance I beat him out for the job, and he's trying to show the world how incompetent I am by burning down buildings around the city." As she said the words, she felt incredibly angry, not just because of the attack on her, but because this revenge-filled person was destroying lives and property.

"You may have to go back further than two years to find someone with a grudge against you. This vendetta could have started when you were a firefighter. A lot of guys grumble about women taking their spots."

"That's true, which brings me to my next question. Before you dig up the complete list, can you see if Christian Brady applied for the position?

"Christian?" he echoed in surprise. "You like Christian for this, even with his father's bar as one of the targets?"

"Maybe it was meant to throw us off. It's just a hunch, Scott. I could be off-base."

"I've always had a lot of respect for your hunches. I'll look at Christian's records."

"Thanks."

"I also wanted to let you know that the brass want a meeting later this morning with you and me. Can you be here in an hour?"

She didn't like the sound of that. "Yes, I can be there."

"Good. I would urge you to be a little more cautious than normal, Emma. You could be in danger."

"It's more likely any building I set foot in could be in danger."

"Are you staying at your parents' house?"

"No, I'm staying with a friend. I'll see you in a while," she said, ending the call before he could ask about her *friend*.

Max returned to his desk and sat down. He took the rosary out of a plastic bag and looked at the crucifix.

"Are the numbers nine and four?" she asked.

"Was that a guess?" he asked with surprise.

"It was in the forensics report. They thought it was a unit or serial number, but '94 is the year the Morettis and Christian Brady graduated from St. Andrew's. Aiden was in that class as well. There may be other suspects in the group. We should run down the entire class list and see where everyone ended up and what they're doing now."

"I'll ask Mrs. Harbough for that."

"I feel like we're about to make a breakthrough, Max."

"I hope so." Frowning, he added, "I wish I'd shown you that rosary earlier—or that I'd shown it to Ruth Harbough. I made an incorrect assumption. That was sloppy work."

Max was very hard on himself. She could relate, because she held herself to the same kind of high standard. "Sometimes seemingly unimportant things become more important when you know the context. I had an advantage. I went to St. Andrew's; you didn't."

"Don't make excuses for me, Emma."

She sighed. "Fine, be pissed off at yourself. But we can't go back in time, so let's focus on the present. Was the rosary left in Sister Margaret's pocket as a clue?"

"Or was it a taunt from the kidnapper?" Max finished. "Because why would our suspect be carrying a rosary from his eighth grade graduation? Who does that?"

She sat back in her seat, frowning at his question. "I don't know. My rosary has been sitting in my jewelry box for years. I certainly don't carry it around with me. What if the kidnapper took Margaret to his home, and she picked it up there?"

"Christian is living with his father, so that's unlikely. Isn't Tony with his dad? Jarod has his own place..." Max shook his head. "I don't think Margaret was taken to anyone's home. We have to find a way to get her to Tahoe."

Emma thought for a long moment, different scenarios playing through her mind, but none of them quite ringing true. "I hate to admit it, but I'm stumped."

"Yeah," he said. "Me, too."

"Let's talk about it later. I have to go to my office. My bosses want a meeting."

"Maybe I should go with you."

She shook her head. "This is my job, Max."

"I just don't want to let you out of my sight."

She was touched. "That's sweet."

"But completely unappreciated," he said with a knowing smile. "I know—you can take care of yourself. I get it. I do respect you, Emma. Just so you know."

"What you just said..." She dropped her voice down to a whisper. "Best foreplay ever."

He laughed. "Respect gets you going, huh?"

"I'd like to kiss you goodbye, but that wouldn't look good."

Max's eyes sparkled. "You know that I'm going to be thinking about that missed opportunity as soon as you leave, don't you?"

"Of course," she said teasingly. "And I kind of like the idea of you thinking about me."

"That's pretty much all I've been doing the last few months," he said.

The familiar pack of butterflies danced through her stomach at the intent look in his eyes. "I'll be thinking about you, too."

—➤➤◄◄—

Emma's meeting with the fire department brass included her father, which did not make her happy. She doubted he would have been involved if she wasn't the fire investigator on the case and now the target of an arsonist. But there was nothing she could do. Fortunately, Jack didn't say much, letting Scott McAvoy run the meeting.

She explained where they were on the joint investigation with the police department, and together the group reviewed her notes on the various fires under investigation. As they wrapped up, Scott told the group that he was compiling a list of people who had applied for fire investigator positions over the last five years, and that it should be ready by the end of the day. Then the meeting was over.

Her father lingered behind in the conference room, waiting for them to be alone before he said, "Nice job, Emma."

"Thank you." She liked seeing the fatherly pride in his eyes. It always felt good to impress Jack.

"Where are you staying?" he asked.

For a split second, she thought about saying she was staying with a girlfriend, but she was twenty-nine years old, and she didn't need to be lying to her father. "I'm staying with Max Harrison. I didn't want to bring the target on my back to the house. It would kill me if anything happened to our home, to Mom or Shayla, Colton, Aiden... I couldn't live with myself."

Her father nodded. "And Max Harrison—he can protect you?"

"I can protect myself," she retorted. "But yes, he's also quite capable. He is a cop after all."

"I know you're tough and independent, Emma. I just don't want you to underestimate your opponent, because that's what this guy has become. Fire is a game to him, and you're the one he has to beat."

"I understand that, and I appreciate the concern." As they

walked to the door, she decided to change the subject. "How are things going with Grandma? Is Grandpa still trying to put her in a home in Monterey?"

Jack paused in the doorway, a tense line to his lips. "Your grandfather is being incredibly stubborn and short-sighted. I'm still hoping to change his mind."

She hated the idea of both her grandparents being so far away when her grandmother might not be able to enjoy her family for too much longer. "It's too soon," she said. "Grandma still has good days. She's going to miss us. She'll be lonely away from everyone."

"I've told him exactly that."

She stared at her dad, feeling a little uneasy about broaching the subject of secrets, but she felt compelled to say something. "Was there some tragedy in the past that I don't know about?" she asked.

He raised an eyebrow at her question. "What do you mean?"

"Grandma mentioned a bad, bad day. And then Grandpa quickly cut her off. It's not the first time she's alluded to some family secret. Do you know what she's talking about?"

"No idea. She could be remembering anything or nothing. Don't worry about it, Emma."

With everyone on the same page but her, she was beginning to think she was putting too much importance on her grandmother's words, but she'd always relied on her instincts, and her gut told her there was something to her grandmother's story. "Well, I hope you can convince Grandpa not to make any big moves yet."

"He's a stubborn man."

"Like all the Callaways."

"You got that right. Take care, Emma. I know you're not a teenager anymore, but you can still call me anytime, day or night, and I will come and get you."

"Thank you," she said.

"Call your mother later and check in with her. She's worrying," Jack added, as he headed out the door.

"I will." After her dad left, she returned to her office. She looked through her emails and tapped her fingers on the desk in restlessness and frustration. She felt like she was on the verge of discovery, but she couldn't quite get all the way there. She'd already spoken to Jarod and to Christian. Maybe it was time to speak to Tony on a more serious note.

She picked up her phone. Tony answered a moment later.

"It's Emma," she said. "Are you busy?"

"I'm working right now, but I'll be done around four o'clock. What's up?"

"I just need to talk to you for a few minutes."

"Is this about the fire at St. Andrew's?"

"Yes. Where can I meet you?"

"Why don't you come to my house at four-thirty? I'm going out to dinner later, but I can give you a half hour."

"Great. See you at four-thirty."

As she ended the call, an odd feeling of fear ran through her. She should have told Tony she'd meet him at a restaurant or some other neutral location, any place besides his house. But that was silly, she told herself. She'd known Tony since she was five years old. He wasn't going to hurt her. They were friends. And she didn't honestly believe he was the arsonist. Although he was a painter, and that spray-painted message could have been another clue. Tony could have been trying to tell her he was right in front of her; she just didn't see him.

Her brows knit together as she frowned. It was both a good and a bad thing to have a big imagination. It opened her mind to the possibilities, but sometimes her imagination blurred reality. Tony had no motive to set fires or try to take her down. Although he had been asking to take her to dinner, and she had been putting him off.

Shaking her head, she got up from her desk and walked down to the lab to speak to the forensic specialists. Maybe if she looked at the science again, she could get back to the facts.

Max stopped by St. Andrew's school after lunch. He showed the rosary to Ruth Harbough, who confirmed that the rosary did not belong to Margaret.

"I don't understand why she would have had this in her pocket," Ruth said. "And where is her rosary, the one she always carried?"

"Probably with the rest of her missing items," he said. "Can you give me a list of students from the graduation class that would have received this rosary?"

"Yes, it will take me a few minutes."

"I'll wait." While she got on the computer, he said, "Did Sister Margaret ever work with any students outside of school hours?"

"She tutored many children," Ruth answered. Looking up, she added, "Do you think a former student kidnapped her?"

"I'm just wondering why she'd have a rosary from that particular year."

"I don't know."

The printer began to hum, and a moment later, Ruth handed him the class list. He ran down the names. Besides Aiden, Jarod and Tony Moretti and Christian Brady, none of the other names meant anything to him. Aiden wasn't a suspect. And he'd already eliminated Jarod in his mind, so that left two. Or there could be someone on this list that Emma would recognize as a suspect. She was the expert on former students.

He looked at Ruth Harbough. "You know every kid in this school, don't you?"

"Yes," she said without hesitation.

"What can you tell me about Christian Brady?"

"He wasn't a good student; he struggled with academics. As for behavioral issues, Christian didn't have many. He was a good kid. He looked out for others, not just his younger brother Robert but also the kids in the class who tended to get picked on. Christian was well-liked and respected for standing up to the bullies. Sometimes those moments landed him in a fight, which is when he ended up in detention. But I remember Margaret telling me that she always had a soft spot for Christian, because she never thought he threw the first punch."

Max filed that away in his brain. "What about Tony Moretti?"

"Tony was a mischievous troublemaker. He didn't like rules, and he was caught in lies many times. That boy spent more time in detention and confession than anyone. But it seems like he has turned his life around. I spoke to him the other day, and he has a job and appears to have more goals than he used to have. He seemed quite excited about the future."

Max wondered if that excitement had come from the adrenaline rush of starting fires all over town.

"What about Jarod?"

"Aside from that one incident with the fire in the dumpster, I don't recall Jarod being in trouble. He was much quieter than Tony and a better student. I always felt a little sad for them. Their mother died when they were in the sixth grade, and their last two years here were rough. Their stepfather tried to be involved, but he was a busy man, and he never seemed to show up for their events."

"Stepfather?" he queried, the word sticking in his head. "I didn't realize they had a stepfather. Where was their real father?"

"He died when they were babies. It was so tragic that they lost both of their parents."

His gut tightened. "Was the stepfather's name Moretti?"

"No. His name was Palermo—Kent Palermo."

"Can you tell me anything about him?"

"No, I'm sorry. I haven't seen him in years." She paused. "Shall I assume from all these questions that you're no closer to finding Margaret's kidnapper?"

Her question had a bit of an edge to it. "We're doing everything we can. I'm not going to stop until we bring her kidnapper to justice."

"Thank you," she said, her eyes blurring with tears. "Margaret was a dear friend. And I have trouble sleeping thinking about her last days and how scared she must have been. Although knowing Margaret, I bet she gave her kidnapper a hard time. She was not a woman to sit back and say nothing or do nothing. Unfortunately, sometimes her honesty got her into trouble."

"Thanks for your time."

When Max got back to the office, he ran the name Kent Palermo through the computer. He didn't know why he couldn't get past the Morettis, but he wasn't going to question his gut. At the moment, instinct was all he had.

A few minutes later, his instinct was rewarded. Kent Palermo owned two houses, one in San Francisco and another in Lake Tahoe. His heart began to pound. He needed to get in touch with Palermo and find out if he'd been in Lake Tahoe over the last two weeks or if he'd lent his cabin out to anyone—maybe one of his sons, or one of their friends.

———————

"Tony," Emma said, as she stepped into the house Tony had lived in as a child. "This place looks a little different. You've redecorated."

"One of my father's ex-girlfriends did it about three years ago. She didn't want to spend time in a man's house," he added with a smile. "At first I thought the fake plants were a little much, but they've grown on me." He paused. "I was going to take a shower before you got here. Excuse the clothes."

"Are you still painting at St. Andrew's?" she asked.

"Just finished up today. The classroom should be ready for the kids by next week."

"That's good."

"Do you want something to drink? I was just going to grab a beer. Do you want one?"

"I'm on the job, but I'll take a water."

"How's the investigation going?" he asked, as they moved down the hall.

"It's a little frustrating at the moment," she admitted.

He handed her a bottle of water and took out a beer for himself. "I heard you talked to Jarod yesterday. He said you asked him a lot of questions about the dumpster fire from years ago. Why are you stuck on that?"

"Because it goes to a pattern of behavior."

He raised an eyebrow. "How so?"

"Arsonists can get their start young. You told me that Christian set that fire, but I know now that Jarod was suspended for it. You had to know that, so why the lie?"

He shook his head. "I didn't lie. Christian did set the fire, but Jarod took the blame."

"That's not what you said the other day."

"I forgot that Jarod had been punished for the fire."

"A five-day suspension is a pretty big penalty to take for someone else," she said, wondering if Tony was really telling her the truth.

He took a swig of his beer, then said, "Jarod owed Christian. Christian had stopped Peter Holt from beating up Jarod. So Jarod paid him back. But it was definitely Christian who set the fire. He loved fire. He was obsessed with becoming a firefighter. You must remember that. How many times did you see Christian hanging onto your dad's every word? I remember when Jack let him get behind the wheel of a fire engine. Christian was over the moon."

She did remember that. Christian had always admired her dad. He'd looked to Jack as his mentor. Would he want to let his mentor down by becoming an arsonist? "How frequently do you see Christian these days?" she asked.

Tony shrugged. "Not that often. I've seen him a few times since he split with his wife and moved back to his dad's house. To be honest, he's kind of a downer these days. He's always complaining about his life, and I just get bored with it. I told him a few weeks ago that he should take a vacation, change his scenery and maybe his perspective. I said he could probably use my dad's Tahoe place if he wanted."

Tahoe?

The word made her stomach clench. "Your dad has a place in Tahoe?"

"Yeah, he bought it a few years ago. He doesn't spend much time there now that he has a new woman in his life. If you ever want to use it, just let me know."

"Thanks," she said, her mind whirling with the implications. Max had checked the Tahoe computer base for any homes owned by the Morettis or the Bradys. But Tony's father's name wasn't Moretti. It was Palermo. Damn! She'd forgotten that very important fact.

"Something wrong?" Tony asked, his gaze narrowing. "You look like you got a million thoughts running through your head."

"Do you know if Christian took you up on your suggestion to go to Tahoe?"

"I don't know. I told him my dad wouldn't be using it for a few weeks, and Jarod has an extra set of keys." A gleam came into his eyes. "You really think Christian did it, don't you?"

"It's beginning to look that way," she admitted.

"What does Tahoe have to do with it?"

"I can't say. But thanks for the info." She set down her water. "I have to go."

"Hey, don't forget you owe me dinner."

"When I tie up this case, you're on," she said.

As soon as she got into her car, her phone rang. It was Scott McAvoy.

"I've got the list of applicants, Emma. I'm emailing them to you now. I recognize a lot of the names, no one I would peg as a potential arsonist. They're all good men."

"No women?"

"You were the only one who applied."

"What about Christian Brady? Is he on the list?"

"Yes," Scott said. "He's on the list."

"Thanks, I'll be in touch." Her heart began to pound. She called Max. It went to voicemail. Frustrated, she left him a message. "I've got a new lead. It's five o'clock, so I'm heading to your apartment. I'll meet you there."

On the drive across town, she considered her next move. They needed to find out exactly what Christian had been doing the last two weeks. She didn't want to believe that a fellow firefighter was setting fires all over the city and taunting her, but then again Christian had never tried to hide his disdain for her. Had his hate grown even stronger when she'd gotten the fire investigator job and he hadn't?

She wished she'd made that connection earlier, but until the fire at her apartment she really hadn't believed that she was the target.

It was disturbing to think that so much destruction had been caused by someone out to get revenge against her. And what about poor Sister Margaret? Had she stumbled upon Christian while he was setting the fire at St. Andrew's? Had he taken her hostage so she couldn't report him?

Despite the animosity Christian had directed toward Emma, she had trouble seeing him as a kidnapper and an arsonist. She'd worked fires with him. He'd saved lives. How did he go from hero to criminal?

She was no closer to an answer when she pulled up in front of Max's apartment building. She walked up the stairs and took out the spare key he'd given her that morning.

As she turned the knob and stepped into the living room, she was stunned to smell smoke, and it was coming from the bedroom. She wondered why the smoke detector wasn't going off. She glanced at the ceiling and saw it had been ripped out of the ceiling.

A part of her wanted to investigate, but another part of her said, don't be stupid. She should get out and call for help.

As she turned toward the door, she felt movement behind her. And then a strong arm came around her neck, and she yanked up against a hard male body and clothes that smelled like gasoline. Panic raced through her.

"You're early," he said. "But that's okay. This time you'll get to see the fire start."

She tried to break his hold. She needed to see who was talking. It kind of sounded like Christian, but not completely.

"This is going to be the last fire you ever see. I couldn't have planned it better—Emma Lou."

Her gut tightened. She knew that voice now. She knew that phrase. Only one person still called her Emma Lou, and it wasn't Christian.

Twenty-Two

——>—⫸⫷—<——

"Robert?" Emma questioned as she struggled to get free. She couldn't believe it was Christian's younger brother who had an iron arm around her neck. "What are you doing?"

"Teaching you a lesson. Showing you that you're not as good as you think you are."

She coughed, her eyes watering from the smoke. "Let me go." She tried to kick at him, but he was stronger than she remembered.

"You're not going anywhere. This is the end, Emma."

"The end of what? Are you crazy? Why are you setting fires?"

"You've always ruined everything—from the time we were little kids. You were always in the way, always taking my spot or Christian's spot."

"What are you talking about? We were friends."

"You never had any idea of the damage you left in your wake. The Emma hurricane would blow through, leaving pain and destruction."

"We have to get out of here, Robert."

"No, it's over," he said, finality in his voice. "I knew it was over as soon as that bitch nun died."

"Why did you kidnap Sister Margaret?"

"She caught me getting ready to set the fire at St. Andrew's. I had no choice but to take her out of there. I had to go back the next day and finish what I'd started."

"Where did you take her?"

"To Jarod's dad's place in Tahoe. I had to listen to her talk for five days. She thought she could make me change my mind. She wanted me to pray about it. She wanted me to ask for forgiveness. She drove me mad. She just wouldn't quit talking. And then she wanted her rosary. She wanted to do penance before she died."

"Why didn't she have her rosary?"

"She lost it when we were hiking through the woods."

"But she didn't have her rosary when she was found; she had Christian's. Was he involved, too?"

"Are you kidding? Christian didn't know anything about it. The bitch wouldn't shut up. She drove me crazy with her begging, so I drove to the house and I got Christian's rosary to take back to her. She prayed on it until she died." His voice changed from harsh to pleading. "I didn't know she was going to die, Emma. I was going to let her go. I was going to disappear, and that would be it. No one would ever find me. But she just passed out and died with her eyes open. It gave me the creeps."

"I know you didn't want to kill her," Emma said. "And you don't want to hurt me, either. We have to get out of here, or we're going to die, too."

"I'm ready to die. There's no way out for me, and it's only fitting I should take you with me. It's actually a better plan than the one I had."

The madness was back in his voice.

"What about your father—your brother? They don't want you to die."

"They probably will when they find out I burned down the bar. I didn't have a choice. I needed to find a place quick to stash her body. Not that the old man didn't deserve it. He cut me out of the bar last year. He said I wasn't reliable. I didn't want to run that bar anyway. I wanted to be a firefighter."

"Then why didn't you become one?" she asked, trying to distract him so she could find a way to escape.

"Because of you, Emma. I went through the academy. I applied for the job, but guess who got the opening—Emma Callaway, female firefighter." His voice dripped with bitterness.

"I didn't know that. I don't remember you going out for firefighting."

"You always overlooked me. I came in second to you in everything when we were in school. Every math contest, every spelling bee, every race at recess, it was you first, me second."

Her lungs were starting to burn. "I'm sorry. I didn't know I was hurting you. Let's go outside."

"We're not going outside, Emma. We're going to die right here."

Fear ran through her at the passion in his voice. He wanted to die, and he wanted her to die, too. "If we're going to die, then tell me why you waited until now to get back at me for beating you out for the firefighter job."

"Because last year you hurt Christian. You destroyed him. He needed the investigator job, but he didn't get it, because you did. The Callaway name strikes again. He started drinking after that. He lost his wife. He had to move home. I couldn't let you get away with it. Christian always took care of me. It was my turn to take care of him."

"You think he's going to be proud of you for this?" she

argued. "He's going to be sad and angry, and your father will be devastated. How can you do this to them just to get back at me?"

"Because you're the reason for everything bad in my life."

"I beat you and your brother out at a couple of jobs, and you want to kill me? You're crazy."

"My mom was crazy. Mad for a man who only turned to her because his wife wasn't paying attention to him."

"I don't know what you're talking about. Your mom left years ago."

"Yeah, but I didn't find out the real reason why until recently. She told me the story of her affair, her love for a man who wanted out of his marriage. And do you know why he wanted out? Because his wife had a new baby girl, blonde, blue-eyed, pretty, and his wife was giving all her attention to her daughter. He couldn't take it anymore. Do you know who I'm talking about Emma?"

"No," she said, refusing to believe what he was saying.

"I'm talking about your mother and father—your real father. He had an affair with my mother. He ruined her. She was in love with him, but he wasn't in love with her. He just wanted to get away from you."

"You're lying."

"I'm not. They slept together for years. When my dad found out, he kicked her to the curb. I grew up without a mother because you were born."

"That wasn't my fault, Robert."

She twisted her head, seeing flames snake up the curtains in the bedroom. Her eyes blurred with painful tears. The fire was building fast. Another minute or two, and it would be too late to get out.

She did not want to die. She had too much to live for.

She had Max. She had love—real love, for the first time in her life. And she was not going to lose it before she'd had a chance to really experience it.

With all the energy she had, she elbowed Robert hard in the gut. His arm loosened slightly around her neck and she took advantage, twisting around, shoving her fist into his nose at the same time she brought her knee to his groin. He howled in pain and let go of her. She ran for the door, but he lunged after her, tackling her to the ground. She punched and kicked, knowing that this fight was for her life and she was not going to lose.

She scrambled to her feet and looked for anything that might be a weapon. She grabbed the heavy glass surfing trophy and smashed it on Robert's head.

He crumpled to the ground.

She tried to flee, but her chest was so tight, she couldn't get in any air. She stumbled to her knees. She wasn't going to make it.

And then the door flew open.

Max ran into the room and pulled her to her feet. Then he swung her into his arms and carried her into the hall and down the stairs.

He set her down on the steps, his expression grim as he gazed at her battered face. "He hurt you."

"I'm okay," she whispered, her throat still burning.

"The fire department is on the way."

"It was Robert."

"I know. I saw him." Max's mouth drew into a tight line. "I'm going back in to get him out, Emma."

"The fire is too hot. Wait for the engines."

"I can't."

She saw purpose and determination in his eyes. "He deserves to die," she said. "But we can't let him. Go, but be careful. I don't want to lose you, Max."

"You're not going to." And with that, he charged back into the building.

A fire engine came around the corner, siren blazing. As the firefighters jumped out, one ran over to help her. "Two men are inside," she told him. "Second floor."

"Got it." He turned to the other firefighters. "Two men on two." Then he turned back to her. "Let's get you some oxygen."

The paramedics led her to the curb and sat her down. They gave her an oxygen mask, and she took welcome breaths of the clean, fresh air. Her gaze never left the front of the building. Finally, she saw Max coming outside, Robert Brady hanging limply over his shoulder. With the help of a firefighter, Max put Robert on a stretcher and then rushed over to her.

"Are you okay?" he asked, his gaze searching her face.

She nodded and pulled the oxygen away from her mouth.

"Don't do that," he said.

"Just let me say something."

"You always have to talk," he said with tenderness in his eyes.

"He looks worse than me, right?"

He grinned. "Now I know you're all right. Yes, it looks like you beat the crap out of him." His smile faded, his gaze serious. "I'm sorry, Emma. I'm sorry you had to go through that alone, that I wasn't there, that I didn't answer my phone."

She put her fingers to his lips. "Hush. It's going to be fine. And this was about me; it wasn't about you. He hated me my entire life."

"Tell me later. Put the oxygen mask back on."

"One more thing."

"What?"

"I love you, Max. You don't have to say anything back. But I just had to tell you that."

His gaze filled with emotion, but before he could say anything, they were interrupted by Burke. Her older brother looked furious and terrified at the same time.

"What the hell happened in there, Emma?" he demanded. "It was Robert Brady?"

She nodded. "Robert wanted us both to die in the fire. I couldn't let that happen. So I used the moves you showed me a long time ago."

"You're going to the hospital to get checked out."

"I don't need to go to the hospital. Robert needs the ambulance, not me."

"I'll drive you to the hospital," Max said.

"Not you, too," she groaned.

"Burke is right. You need to get checked out. Get those cuts fixed up."

She put a hand to her cheek, feeling the swelling. She had no idea what her face looked like, but judging from the expressions of the two men in front of her, she didn't look good.

Max helped her up. "Don't waste any more energy arguing. You can be independent after the doctor says you're okay."

She was actually relieved to have his body supporting her. She felt a little shakier than she'd anticipated.

"Take care of her," Burke told Max.

"I will," Max promised.

Something very male passed between them, but Emma didn't have the strength to say she could take care of herself. The events of the past hour were starting to catch up with her.

"I'm fine, Max," she said, as he helped her into his car.

"I need someone else to tell me that besides you."

Emma was in the Emergency Room for almost an hour. Max paced back and forth in the waiting room wondering if something was really wrong with her, something that some antibiotic ointment and a few stitches wouldn't cure.

While he waited, all he could think about was the fact that he'd almost lost her. She'd fought for her life. She'd knocked out Robert cold, but when he'd entered the apartment, he'd seen her struggling to get up, to make it to the door. And he would never ever forget the fear of that moment. If he'd been two minutes later, she might have succumbed to smoke inhalation.

Damn! His whole body shook at the thought.

He ran a hand through his hair and paced another quarter mile in the waiting room. Finally, a door opened and Emma was wheeled out. She had a bandage on her temple, her right eye was almost swollen shut, and the rest of her sweet face was filled with blue and purple bruises.

He wanted to put his own fist on Robert's face. And seeing her now, he wished he'd left that son of a bitch to die.

"I'm okay," she said gently. "It looks worse than it feels."

"I don't believe that for a second."

"It's true." She gave him a soft smile. "Believe it."

He drew in a much-needed breath and slowly let it out. "I'll take you home."

She nodded. "I guess that would be my parents' house." She gave him a watery smile. "We're both homeless."

He hadn't given his apartment one thought.

"I'm sorry that you lost everything because of me," she said as he helped her stand up.

"I didn't lose anything that mattered to me, Emma."

"I broke your surfing trophy. That's how I knocked Robert out."

He smiled. "Well, it finally came in handy then. Come on, let's get out of here." He put his arm around her shoulders as they walked out of the hospital.

"How is Robert doing?"

"He'll survive. He's been admitted for the night, but he's under arrest and there are two guards at his door. He's not going anywhere except to jail for a very long time."

"Harry and Christian will be devastated."

"They're both with him."

"Did you talk to them?"

"Only briefly. There will be time to get all of our questions answered." He helped her into the car and slid behind the wheel. "Where do your parents live?"

"It's not far. I'll give you directions." She paused. "I'm actually surprised my family didn't show up in the Emergency Room."

"Burke came to the hospital along with his crew. They got another call, so they had to leave, but he did say to tell you that he'd called the family and told them not to come, that you were all right and would be home soon. He said you would owe him for that."

She gave a tired smile. "I do owe him. It's nice to have a minute to catch my breath."

He had a million questions he wanted to ask her, but he needed to give her a chance to recover. Emma was tough, but she was also human and a little bit in shock.

"Robert really hated me," she said a moment later.

"We don't have to do this now."

She ignored him, her tone reflective. "It actually started with my birth."

"What?" he asked in surprise.

"Robert's mother left the family when Robert was about five. No one ever knew why. She just took off. Well, apparently Robert tracked her down recently, and she finally came clean and told him that she'd had an affair with my father. Apparently, my dad was unhappy that my mom was spending so much time with the new baby—with me. So he hooked up with Robert's mom. It lasted for a few years I guess. I don't really know what happened after that. Neither my father nor his mother ended up together, and Robert's mom was not part of Robert's life after she divorced his dad. So I don't know where she went or why she stayed away from her kids. I just know that Robert, in his twisted mind, put me as the source of all his problems."

"That's crazy," he said. "No wonder we couldn't figure out a logical reason for someone targeting you. There wasn't one."

"He has so much hatred for me, Max. The depth of his anger stunned me. He had a long list of things I'd done to him, competitions he'd lost to me. He said he tried out to be a firefighter, but I got the job. I don't even remember that ever happening. And then his hatred of me grew when Christian told him he'd lost the investigator job to me. Apparently, Christian went into a downward spiral after that and his wife left and Robert decided it was time for me to pay for all the trouble I'd caused his family. And he wanted me to know that I wasn't as good as I thought I was." She paused. "He was high on something, too. It seemed like he had superhuman strength when he was holding onto me."

Anger tore through Max at the reminder of how close Emma had been to dying in that fire. But she was safe, he told himself, and he would make sure that Robert went away for a very long time.

"I think Sister Margaret drove Robert crazy," Emma

added. "She tried to talk him into giving up. She wanted to pray for his soul, but somewhere along the way she'd lost her rosary. He got tired of her incessant pleading, so he finally went back to his house, got Christian's rosary and took it to her."

Another piece of the puzzle fell into place.

"Robert said he was going to let her go eventually," Emma said. "He didn't want to kill a nun. I guess something in his Catholic school upbringing stuck. He was just going to disappear. But when she died, he realized it was over. If he got caught, he was going to be charged with more than arson." She paused. "Take a right at the next corner. And then it's the first left after that."

"Are you going to tell your mother about your father's affair?" Max asked.

She sighed. "That's a tough one. I don't really believe in secrets, and neither does my mom, so I will tell her at some point. I know it will hurt her, but I don't want there to be anything between us."

"I think that's a good decision."

Within minutes he was pulling up in front of her parents' house. He knew he should let her go inside on her own, but he couldn't tear himself away from her just yet. "I'll help you into the house."

"Where are you going to stay tonight?"

"I'll figure that out later."

As they got out of the car and walked down the driveway, Emma said, "You're about to see the Callaways in full protection mode. Are you up for it?"

"Bring it on," he said, as he followed her into the house.

Emma had not been joking. Once they walked into the kitchen, Emma was swarmed by family members and peppered with questions about her health, the fire and everything else. He felt very protective of her and wanted to step in and tell everyone to back off, but this was her family, her turf, so he stayed silent.

Fortunately, her mother took charge, insisting that Emma go upstairs to her bedroom where she would bring her some dinner. Everyone else could see her later. Before they left the kitchen, Lynda turned to him and gave him a firm smile.

"You stay, Inspector. Someone will get you dinner."

"That's not necessary."

"It is necessary," she said firmly.

"Don't try to argue," Jack advised. "You won't win."

As Jack and Lynda took Emma upstairs, Aiden said, "I hope you like spaghetti."

"That's great," he said.

"I'll get it for you," a woman said. "I'm Shayla, Emma's youngest sister. We met briefly at my dad's party."

"I remember. Thanks."

"No problem."

"Let's sit down," Aiden suggested, motioning toward the big kitchen table.

As Max took a seat, Aiden introduced him to the rest of the family—Emma's older sister Nicole and two other brothers, Drew and Colton.

"So, is she really okay?" Aiden asked as they sat down.

"She will be."

"Burke said it was Robert Brady. I couldn't believe it. We all grew up together, and now he tries to kill Emma?"

"His thinking was obviously twisted," he said, deciding it would be better to let Emma tell the story, especially since part of it involved her biological father.

"Did Christian know?" Aiden asked.

Max shook his head. "He said no. I talked to him briefly at the hospital, and he seemed as shocked as everyone, including his father."

"Old Harry is going to be beside himself," Drew said, listening in on their conversation. "Robert is the one who burned down his dad's bar, right?"

"Yeah, apparently Harry cut Robert out of the business a few years ago, so I guess the bar didn't mean anything to Robert."

Shayla set a plate in front of him. "Enjoy."

"Thanks." He took a bite of spaghetti and then said, "Here's what I know. Robert kidnapped Sister Margaret because she saw him break into the school. He took her to the Morettis' house in Tahoe and hid her away there. When she died of a heart attack, he panicked. He had to get rid of her body, so he set the fire at the bar and left her body there."

"But why Emma?" Aiden asked.

"She can tell you more about that. They had a conversation before I got there, but Robert blamed her for his brother not getting an investigator position and also for his failure to get hired as a firefighter when Emma and he were competing several years ago."

Aiden's mouth drew into a tight line. "If he wasn't already in the hospital, I'd put my own fist through his face."

He saw the fury in Aiden's eyes and knew exactly how he felt. It had taken all of his self-control and discipline to force himself to pull Robert out of the fire.

"Go ahead and eat," Drew urged. "You've had a long night, too."

"I'm all right," he said. "But this spaghetti is good."

As Drew left, Aiden gave him a thoughtful look. "Are you and Emma together? Is this more than a professional relationship?"

"Yes," he said, without hesitation. "We're together. And I'm not going anywhere."

Aiden nodded, giving him what looked like an approving look. "Okay."

"Okay," he echoed.

Aiden had accepted his decision. Now he just needed to tell Emma. Her words of love had been burning in his brain since she'd said them, and he'd wanted to answer her back, but he hadn't had a chance. He didn't intend to leave until he did.

—➤➤◄◄—

An hour later, Max entered Emma's bedroom. She was fast asleep. He sat down on the foot of the bed. It physically hurt him to look at the bruises on her face. If he could replay the day, he would have found a way to get to her before Robert did.

Emma's mom stepped into the room, her gaze moving from her daughter to him. She smiled. "Are you staying?"

"If you don't mind. And just so you know, I love her."

"I figured as much. Are you a good man?"

"Trying to be."

"I like honesty. So does Emma. She was hurt before. I don't want to see that happen again."

"I would never hurt her."

"She told me that you saved her life today."

"I wish I could have saved her from the beating she took."

"Emma said Robert looked far worse."

He smiled. "Your daughter is very competitive."

"Don't I know it. I suspect you can keep up."

"I think so."

"Stay as long as you like, Max."

After Lynda left, he stretched out across the foot of Emma's double bed and closed his eyes. He felt suddenly exhausted. The stress of the last few days had taken its toll.

At some point, he must have fallen asleep, because the next thing he knew Emma was saying his name.

He sat up, meeting her confused gaze.

"We're in my bedroom," she said.

"Yeah. Sorry, I guess I fell asleep."

She glanced at the clock. "It's one o'clock in the morning."

"You should go back to sleep."

"Why are you still here, Max?"

He scooted forward on the bed so he was sitting right next to her. "Because I couldn't leave until I told you something."

She stared back at him with her pretty, intelligent eyes, and said, "That you're in love with me?"

"Hey, I wanted to say it."

"So say it."

He deliberately hesitated, wanting her to know that he was not saying the words lightly. "I'm in love with you, Emma."

A smile spread across her face. "I knew it."

"You did not."

"I did. I was just afraid it was too good to be true or that I was imagining things."

"You're not imagining anything. I love you, and I'm not leaving San Francisco or you."

"Are you sure this is where you want to be? You had a life in L.A."

"A life I can barely remember now—a life that doesn't

matter at all because you're not in it. I fell for you the first day we met."

"You hated me the first day we met," she reminded him.

"It was a cover. And you pretended you didn't like me either."

"That wasn't pretense. I *didn't* like you. You were so cocky."

"So were you—in a slightly more charming way. I knew you were trouble."

"Likewise." She grinned. "We're two of a kind, aren't we?"

"I think we might be. Does that scare you?"

"No, it's exciting and wonderful. I've finally met the one person who really understands me, who accepts me for who I am, who sees my flaws and my strengths, and doesn't want to change me. You don't want to change me, do you?" she asked, a little uncertainty creeping into her eyes.

"Absolutely not. You're stubborn and sometimes a little too brave for your own good, but you're also smart, generous and extremely hot."

She gave him a playful smile. "You know I've never had sex in this bed. I used to dream about it, but it never happened."

"And it's not going to happen tonight," he told her firmly. "I've already been grilled by your brothers. I'm not going to have sex with you in your parents' house."

"I thought you were brave," she teased.

"You need to rest, Emma."

"Fine. I'll rest. As long as you stay with me."

He stretched out next to her on the bed, and they faced each other. For several long seconds, he just looked at her. "I've never told a woman that I loved her. I couldn't say it unless I really meant it. Unless I was willing to back it up."

Her gaze turned serious. "Really—no one?"

He shook his head. "I saw love destroy my father. He was never happy with the person he was with; he was always in search of this elusive emotion he called love. He told me once it was the greatest high, and he was an addict. He couldn't live without it."

"That doesn't sound like love. That sounds like lust, like the first flame of attraction."

"That's probably why it always burned out. And then there was my brother... I watched Spencer throw his whole life away for Stephanie. I didn't get it at the time. I understand a little better now what he went through. I would have fought Robert for you. I wouldn't have thought twice about it." He paused. "But you took care of him for me. You saved yourself."

"Not really. After I knocked Robert out, I was finished. I wasn't sure I could make it to the door. If you hadn't been there..." Her lower lip began to tremble, and her eyes watered. "Look at me, about to cry when it's all over."

He tenderly wiped a streaking tear off her cheek, knowing that the last thing she wanted to show was weakness. "It's shock. You're entitled. If it had been me, I'd be crying like a baby."

"Liar," she said, his teasing words lightening her mood. "You're a strong man, Max. And that's the kind of person I need and want in my life."

"And you're a strong woman, which is exactly the kind of person I need and want in my life." He leaned over and touched her mouth with his, wanting to show her how he felt, but not wanting to hurt her bruised lips.

"I love you, Max," she whispered again, her heart in her eyes.

"I love you, too, Emma.

"I hope you're ready for the Callaways. You do know that they're going to be interfering in every aspect of our lives?"

He smiled. "I'm more than ready." He slipped his hand under her t-shirt, caressing her warm curves. "You know what I said earlier about no sex..." He kissed her again. "Let me show you how much I love you, Emma."

"Okay. And tomorrow I'll show you." As he slid his hand over her breast, she softly sighed. "So this is love," she murmured. "I never knew what I was missing."

"I'm going to spend the rest of my life showing you," he said, as he kissed her again and again and again.

Epilogue

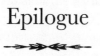

Three months later ...

"We're late," Emma told Max as they hurried down the street to Serafina's Restaurant, where they were going to celebrate her thirtieth birthday with family and friends. "And it's your fault," she reminded him.

He gave her an unrepentant smile. "It was worth it. We had to christen our new apartment."

She smiled back at him. She'd never been this happy in her life. After three fantastically wonderful months of love and romance, they'd decided to move in together. They'd gotten a beautiful ground-floor flat in the lake district of San Francisco. The living room opened onto a deck with a pretty little garden, an oasis of color in the big city.

They didn't have much furniture yet, and they'd already disagreed on how to decorate, but Emma knew the fun was just beginning. Even when she was arguing with Max, she was also loving him, and he felt exactly the same way. They drove each other crazy, but they also brought out the best in each other.

"Look, there's Aiden and Sara," she said, waving at her friend and her brother. "We're not the last ones here."

"Why do I think they were late for the same reason we were?" Max said dryly.

"Happy birthday, Em." Sara gave her a warm hug while Aiden and Max shook hands.

"Thank you. It's a big birthday," Emma said.

Sara nodded. "I know. Mine is coming up soon."

"Well, I think our thirties are going to be pretty spectacular." Emma shot Max a quick glance. "Can I tell them?"

"Tell us what?" Sara asked quickly.

"It's up to you, Emma," Max said.

"Last night Max and I had a little private celebration," Emma said. "And…" She held up her left hand to reveal the sparkling diamond on her third finger. "We're engaged."

Sara grabbed her hand. "It's beautiful." Her face softened, her expression filled with love. They had been friends since they were teenagers, and Sara knew just how much trouble Emma had had finding real love. "I'm so happy for you," Sara said. She looked at Max. "You are a lucky man."

"Believe me, I know," Max said.

"And I'm lucky, too," Emma added. As she stared at her ring, at the hand Sara was holding, she noticed something shiny on Sara's finger.

Sara quickly pulled her hand away, shoving her hands into the pockets of her coat.

"Hold on. What was that on your finger?" Emma demanded. When Sara didn't answer, she turned on her brother. "What do you have to say, Aiden?"

He shrugged. "Nothing. Not a word."

"Sara, come on, show me your hand."

Sara shook her head. "No, it's your night—your birthday, your engagement. Let's go celebrate."

Sara turned to leave, but Emma grabbed her by the arm.

"Wait one second. Did Aiden ask you to marry him?"

Sara hesitated. "Let's talk about this later, Em."

"Let's talk about it now," she said, refusing to budge.

"You're not going to win," Aiden advised Sara. "My little sister is as stubborn as they come. You better tell her."

"He's right," Emma said, looking into her friend's eyes. "So talk."

"Fine. Aiden asked me to marry him," Sara confessed with a guilty smile. "It was last Saturday. We picked out the ring today. I should have taken it off my finger, but I couldn't. We were going to tell everyone tonight. But this is your night. We can tell everyone another day."

"Don't be silly. This is *our* night. And I want to see the ring. How did my brother do?"

"Very well." Sara pulled out her hand to reveal a sparkling square cut diamond.

Emma gave Aiden an approving smile. "Good job, Aiden. This is so wonderful. We're all getting married. I was going to ask you to be in my wedding, Sara."

"I was going to ask you to be my maid of honor, Emma."

Emma glanced around the group. "What do we think—double wedding?"

"That's up to you two," Max said, with Aiden quickly agreeing.

Sara met her gaze. "I can't think of anything better, Emma."

"Let's go tell the family," Aiden said. He opened the restaurant door, and he and Sara slipped inside.

Emma paused and looked at Max. "Are you okay with sharing our day?"

"Absolutely. Just don't ask me to share you."

"Never. I love you, Max."

"I love you, too, Emma. For now and forever."

THE END

Keep reading for an excerpt from

the next book in the Callaway series

FALLING FOR A STRANGER
(Coming June 2015!)

ONE

Ria Hastings was in the mood for trouble. It was a warm tropical night on Isla de los Sueños, a small island off the coast of Costa Rica, known for its white sandy beaches, water sports, deep sea fishing, and rum drinks. On one side of the island, several large estates sat on the rugged hillsides with spectacular views of the ocean. The rest of the town lived near the beach, where three hotels and a dozen restaurants competed for tourist dollars.

Ria wiped a strand of blonde hair off her sweaty forehead. The temperature hovered around eighty degrees at just after midnight, and the beachside bar was packed with tourists. Ria had been tending the bar since seven, and she was ready to call it a night. She'd been hit on four times already, and while she was used to handling men who were a little too drunk or too interested in her, she was tired of wearing a polite smile, but she would do exactly that for another hour. She couldn't risk getting fired, nor could she afford to draw any attention to herself. She'd been blending into the local scene for months. Now was not the night to stand out.

As she wiped down the counter, her gaze caught on a man sitting at the far end of the bar. He'd arrived two hours earlier with a friend—a loud, charming, and now hammered, sunburned blond by the name of Tim. Tim had been doing tequila shots since ten and was now hosting a trio of beautiful girls at a nearby table. The man at the bar seemed to have no interest in joining his friend's party and had been nursing a vodka tonic for the better part of an hour. He also hadn't responded to any of the women who'd slid into the seat next to him, although his gaze had swung in her direction on more than one occasion.

He was an attractive man, athletically built, dressed in khaki shorts and a navy blue knit shirt. His dark brown hair was on the short side, and he had an air of discipline about him. Military, she thought. Just out or on leave, but close enough to his service that his body was still toned and on full alert.

She hadn't missed the fact that his gaze darted to the door almost as often as hers did, as if he were waiting for someone or didn't want to be taken by surprise. Maybe he was military intelligence.

That idea made her frown. The last thing she needed was military intelligence to show up on the island.

She told herself not to let her imagination run wild. A lot of ex-military guys came to the island to decompress and let off steam. Since the location had become a popular destination for bachelor and bachelorette parties, there was usually a good deal of action available for anyone who wanted to find it.

But this man didn't seem interested in escaping reality with alcohol or with women, so what was his story?

Glancing down at her watch, she told herself she had better things to worry about than a random stranger, no matter how sexy he was.

In a few hours, the plan she'd put into motion six months earlier would finally be launched. She'd gone over the details a thousand times in her head, and while she wanted nothing more than to go off by herself somewhere and review everything again, it was more important for her to maintain her usual routine.

The man at the end of the bar caught her eye again. There was something in his dark gaze that beckoned to her, a pull of attraction, desire, feelings that she hadn't allowed herself to feel in a very long time. She couldn't afford to answer his call. She was too close to the end to get sidetracked by a man, especially a man who set her nerves tingling with just one look.

On the other hand...

As two men approached the bar, she moved down the counter toward her fellow bartender, Martin, a twenty-two-year-old ex-Harvard dropout, who had come to the island to find himself. So far, the only thing he'd found was a love for tequila and bikini-clad girls.

"Switch with me," she said.

Martin's gaze moved past her to the men sliding into stools at the other end of the long bar. "Trouble?"

"I'd just prefer not to wait on them."

"Got it," he said.

She walked toward the handsome stranger. At this moment, he seemed the less dangerous choice, or at least, the less *obvious* dangerous choice. It had been a long time since she'd allowed herself to trust anyone.

"Can I get you another drink?" she asked.

His eyes were a deep, dark brown, and there were shadows in his gaze, things he'd seen, things he didn't want to see again, she suspected. But there was also courage and strength in his eyes, a resilient defiance. He might have been knocked down, but she doubted that he'd stayed down.

"Sure, why not?" he replied, with a lightness that was in

contrast to his tense posture.

"I can't think of a reason. Same? Or do you want to change it up a bit? We have an island special you might like."

"What's that?"

"Beso de la sirena, otherwise known as mermaid's kiss."

"Do you see mermaids after you drink it?" he asked, a lighter gleam entering his eyes.

"Some men do."

"It sounds dangerous."

"You look like a man who could handle a little danger."

"And you sound like a woman who knows how to sell a high-priced drink to a tourist." A hint of a smile played around his lips.

So he was smart as well as attractive. "Guilty. So what will it be? Beso de la sirena or another vodka tonic?"

"Vodka, hold the tonic." He pushed his empty glass across the bar.

She made him another drink, then tipped her head towards his friend, who was making out with a busty blonde. "Your friend seems to be ignoring you."

He shrugged. "I can't blame him. They're all very pretty."

"Yet, here you sit by yourself. No one here has caught your interest?" She wiped down the bar with a damp towel. As she spoke, she cast a sideways glance at the two men at the other end of the bar.

They worked as bodyguards for Enrique Valdez, one of the very wealthy men who made his home in the island hills. As much as she didn't want them at her bar, it was good that they'd come in; they would see her doing what she always did. She wouldn't raise any suspicion.

"I didn't say that," the man in front of her said.

"What?"

"You said there was no one here I was interested in, but

that's not true."

Her heart skipped a beat at his direct gaze, and her pulse started beating way too fast. She'd made a point of not getting involved with tourists, or anyone for that matter, but this man was more than a little tempting. She'd been lonely on the island, living a life of pretense. But that pretense was crucial to staying alive. She couldn't let desire get in the way.

"Nice line," she said casually. "I've heard it before—about three dozen times."

He smiled. "I'll bet you have. But I'm the only one who meant it."

"Sure you are."

"What's your name?"

Her body tensed. "You first."

"Drew Callaway."

"Do you want to add a title before your name? Maybe Lieutenant or Captain," she suggested. He had the air of leadership about him.

He tipped his head, a gleam in his eyes. "Lieutenant."

"With the…"

"I'm in between services at the moment. Former Navy pilot, soon to be flying helicopters for the Coast Guard."

Navy pilot certainly explained why he exuded both discipline and recklessness at the same time. It also probably explained where the shadows in his eyes came from.

"What tipped you off?" he asked curiously.

She shrugged. "I'm good at reading people. It comes with the job. Why did you leave the Navy?"

He didn't answer right away, a contemplative expression in his eyes, then said, "My time was up. I needed a change of pace."

"Where were you deployed?"

"All over."

"So you saw action?"

"Too much."

She gave him a thoughtful look. "It doesn't sound like you're making a huge change, moving from one kind of service to another."

"I still get to fly, which is all I ever wanted to do, but hopefully not with as many people shooting at me."

"I can't imagine that."

"No, you can't." He sipped his drink, then set the glass down. "Your turn."

She cleared her throat. She'd been living on the island for six months, and in that time no one had balked at the name that was on her fake passport, a version of her real name. "Ria," she said.

"Pretty. Last name?"

"Not important."

"A woman of mystery."

"A woman who likes her privacy."

"How long have you lived here on the island, Ria?"

"Long enough to know better than to get involved with tourists," she said with a brief smile.

"No exceptions?"

"Not so far. People come, they go. I'm still here." She paused. "What brought you to the island of dreams?"

A smile curved his lips, giving him an entirely different look, one that was even more attractive. She felt a knot grow in her throat.

"I dreamt about a beautiful blonde with big brown eyes," he said. "A full mouth, with soft kissable lips and a killer body." His gaze drifted down to her breasts. "I think I found her."

Her nerves tingled under his scrutiny and she had to fight the urge to cover her breasts, not that much was showing in her bar uniform, a coral-colored red tank top over white shorts. Most of the women in the bar were showing more skin than she was.

"You're quite the flirt," she said lightly.

"Actually, I'm a little out of practice."

"Just getting out of a relationship?" she queried, unable to believe this man would have any trouble getting a date.

"I've been focused on other things. Staying alive, for one."

"I can see how that might be a priority."

"What about you?" he asked. "Are you involved with anyone?"

"No."

"Good."

"Why is that good?" she challenged.

He smiled. "Because I like you, Ria. What time do you get off?"

Her heart jumped at the hungry look in his eyes. "You're very direct."

"I'm leaving tomorrow. I don't have a lot of time."

"Where are you going?"

"San Francisco."

A wistful yearning filled her body. San Francisco was one of her favorite cities. And she'd been away for too long.

"I love San Francisco," she said. "I lived there when I was a child. My grandfather was a fisherman. He'd take me out on the bay every chance he got." She drew in a quick breath, realizing she was talking way too much. "What part of the city do you live in?"

"I grew up in St. Francis Wood, but I'll be living south of Market starting next week. It's the hot area to live in now, right near the new ballpark." He paused. "You didn't answer my question, Ria. What time do you get off?"

She gave him a long look, feeling incredibly tempted. His eyes were so dark and intriguing, his features pure masculine gorgeousness. He had a mouth that looked really kissable, too, and a purposeful attitude that made her think he probably knew what to do with a woman. It had been a long time since she'd lost herself in a man's arms for a few hours. And despite the fact that he was a stranger, she had the strangest feeling that she could trust him not to hurt her. That was a dangerous thought, because she couldn't afford to be wrong.

"Ria?" he pressed.

"Do you think I'm that easy?" she countered.

"Not easy, but I think maybe you're important."

The serious note in his voice shot a shiver down her spine. She told herself not to get carried away. He was just trying to get her into bed. He'd say anything. She couldn't believe a word.

"Why on earth would you say that?"

"I don't know. Ever since I saw you I've wanted to talk to you."

"You didn't ask me what time I got off so you could talk to me."

"Well, that was one of the reasons," he said. "I'm not trying to insult you. If I had more time, I'd ask you out on a date. I'd bring you flowers and take you to an expensive restaurant and buy you a really expensive cut of steak."

"Is that your usual style?"

He gave her a smile. "I don't have a style. And while I would never profess to understand or know what a woman wants, I do have sisters, and they talk and complain a lot, especially when it comes to men and dating."

"How many sisters?"

"Three sisters and four brothers."

"Big family. Where are you in the lineup?"

"Fourth from the top."

"Otherwise known as the middle."

He tipped his head. "Yes. What about you? Big family?"

"No. I'm an only child." It was part of the backstory she'd made up before coming to the island; it was also partly true. "I used to wish I had a big family."

"It's not all it's cracked up to be," he said dryly. "A lot of noise and chaos."

"And love," she suggested, feeling an ache that went deep into her soul.

Her family had always been complicated. Love, betrayal, divorce, death … She supposed that's what made up a life, but it seemed like she'd seen too much of the dark side of love.

"Plenty of love," Drew said. "Sometimes too much. Everyone likes to be in my business."

Despite his complaint, she could see the pride in his eyes when he spoke of his family.

"So, one o'clock, two?" he pressed, raising an eyebrow. "What time are you done here?"

"Two. But I'm not meeting you."

"Why not?"

"I'm not in the mood for a hookup."

"Aren't you? I've been watching you all night, and I'm good at reading people, too, Ria. You're a bundle of nerves. Every time someone walks through the door, you tense. Why is that? Are you in some kind of trouble?"

His words bothered her on two levels, one that he'd read her so well, and, two, that she'd given so much away.

"And I suppose you think I should release some of my tension with you?" she asked, ignoring his other questions.

"I think…" He paused, lowering his voice. "That you are a beautiful woman who knows what she wants and how to get it."

"Who said I wanted you?" she challenged.

"Your beautiful eyes say it."

"You're seeing what you want to see."

"Am I?" He cocked his head to the right as he regarded her thoughtfully. "What's holding you back, Ria?"

"I don't do random hookups. And I have to get up early in the morning. In the daytime I sail boats for Sea Charters."

"So bartender, sailor—what other talents do you have?"

"Wouldn't you like to know?"

"I would like to know," he said with a grin. "Why don't you tell me? Or better yet, show me?"

She shook her head at his charming smile. When she'd first seen him, his expression had been tense, but since they'd started talking, he'd loosened up considerably.

"You're breaking my heart," he said, putting a hand to his chest.

"I doubt that. And there are plenty of women in this bar if you want company."

"I'm only interested in *your* company. You intrigue me."

"I can't imagine why."

"What brought you to this small island in the middle of the sea?"

She thought for a moment, then said the only word that came to mind. "Freedom."

He met her gaze. "Have you found it?"

"I'm close," she said. "When I'm in the middle of the ocean, no land in sight, nothing but blue water and the occasional seagull, I almost feel like I've escaped."

"Escaped what?"

"Nothing I care to share." She drew in a deep breath, trying to calm the tension running through her body, that now had as much to do with her attraction to Drew as with her worries about the next day.

"I understand the desire to escape," he said.

"You do?"

"Yes. I first felt the walls closing in on me when I was a teenager. There were eight kids sharing four bedrooms and two bathrooms. It was always too crowded in my house, kids fighting, crying, yelling, so I'd leave whenever I could. And one day I ended up at the airport. I took a flying lesson, and I was hooked. There is nothing like the land falling away and nothing but blue sky in front of you to make you feel like the world just got bigger." He paused. "We're quite a pair. I need the big blue sky and you need the big blue sea."

She smiled. "Apparently, neither one of us is that good on land."

"Maybe we could be good together," he suggested.

She laughed. "You don't miss an opportunity, do you?"

He finished his drink then got to his feet. "I'm staying in the cottages. Number nine. The door will be open, Ria."

"I'm not coming." She wished her words were a little stronger, a little more forceful.

"Then I'll be disappointed. I turned down the mermaid's kiss, because I want yours."

"Another good line. You're full of them."

"I'm not a player."

"You've given me absolutely no reason to believe that."

"I know," he admitted. "You probably won't believe me, but I haven't done this in a while."

"So, why me?"

"You have a smart mouth, and you're sexy as hell. I'd love to see you with your hair down. I'd love to show you how good we could be together."

His husky tone sent another shiver down her spine. "How do you know we'd be good? You don't know me at all," she said, trying to maintain a strong defense against his charm. "We're strangers."

"For now. But what better way to learn about each other?"

"I'm not looking for trouble."

"There's a light in your eyes that says that's exactly what you're looking for."

She caught her breath, thinking he might actually be right about that.

Drew tipped his head and walked away.

She watched him all the way to the exit. When the door closed behind him, she let out a breath, wondering how she could possibly already miss him.

He was just another guy—only he wasn't, and she couldn't put her finger on why.

Maybe it was the seriousness that lurked just behind his smile. He wasn't like most of the guys who hit on her. Those she could handle. She knew they'd move on to the next woman before she could finish saying *no*. But Drew had left. He'd thrown down his invitation and walked out the door.

He was going to wait for her. He was pretty confident she'd show up, but he was going to be waiting a long time.

She turned her focus back on work. For the next hour, she served drinks, picked up empty glasses, and watched the minutes tick off the clock. Shortly before closing Drew's friend left with two women flanking him on either side. Apparently, he wasn't going to be alone tonight.

At two a.m., she wiped down the bar and closed out the register. She said goodnight to Martin and walked outside, the scent of flowers and sea all around her. She paused for a moment and drew in a deep breath of sweet and salty air. The heat of the night echoed the passionate need burning through her body, a need that had been lit by the sexy smile of a stranger.

She lived in a furnished rental three blocks away from the resort. The cottage where Drew was staying was only a hundred yards away.

Indecision made her hesitate for a long minute. She hadn't been lying when she told Drew she wasn't into hookups, but tonight she was feeling restless and reckless. She wasn't going to sleep anyway. She was too worried about the morning, and the reality of what she was about to do.

In six hours she could be dead.

She wasn't being a pessimist, just a realist.

Maybe she should spend those hours doing something that would make her happy, something that she never ever did. It had been a very long time since she'd thought of anything but the plan, the goal. Nothing else mattered but fulfilling the promise she'd made to her sister. But tonight, Drew had reminded her that she was a woman, and she was lonely and scared, defiant and determined—all at the same time.

It was the worst possible time to get involved with anyone.

On the other hand…

She pulled the band out of her hair and let the long waves flow loosely around her shoulders. Then she walked down the path to the cottages, her nerves tingling and tightening with each step.

She knocked on his door, turned the knob and stepped inside. The cottage was one big room, a small sitting area and a king-sized bed.

Drew sat on the couch. He was reading a book when she walked in. It looked like some sort of mystery novel. It was silly, but the sight of that book pushed her over the edge. She'd always found intelligence to be a turn-on, and this man was smart, maybe too smart. He'd read her pretty accurately so far.

But in a lot of ways, she liked his honesty. He hadn't set the scene with candles. There was no wine or champagne chilling. He wasn't trying to seduce her. He was just waiting...

After a moment he set the book down and stood up, his gaze meeting hers. Then slowly he walked over to her. He made no move to touch her or kiss her. He simply looked at her with his shadowy dark eyes, and she felt an incredible pull. All her nerve endings tingled. There was electricity between them—a dark, dangerous attraction.

"I'm glad you came, Ria. Why did you?"

Such a simple question—such a complicated answer. She settled for the basic truth. "I want you."

The fire in his eyes flared. He put his hands on her waist. "I know the feeling."

"For tonight," she added. "That's all I can give you. I need you to know exactly where I stand."

"All I care about is that you're standing here in front of me. You're beautiful, Ria. And I want you, too."

Her stomach clenched at the desire in his gaze. And then he was done looking. He pulled her in for a kiss.

He tasted as intoxicating as the vodka she'd served him, and he kissed like a man who hadn't had a woman in a long time. She met his demanding mouth with the same sense of urgency and need.

A part of her called for caution, but she couldn't listen to that voice anymore. For a few hours she was going to just be a woman, the woman she used to be, the woman she hoped to be again some day.

They knew nothing about each other, and yet there was a connection between them that went far deeper than the touch of their mouths. Something inside of her recognized something inside of him. What that was, she had no idea.

But she didn't want to analyze or worry. That's all she'd been doing for months. She just wanted to lose herself in Drew, to be a woman with no past, to reach that elusive moment of complete and utter freedom. Because there was a good chance in a few hours, her future would be over, too.

--->≫≪<--

Drew woke up just before dawn to the feel of a warm breeze coming through the open window and the sound of the birds singing in the trees outside. For the first time in a long time he'd slept a dreamless sleep. The nightmares from the past eight years had receded in his mind. There were no explosions, bloody scenes, screams of pain and anguish—no more horror or grief.

Instead, he felt a hazy, happy feeling, as if everything was suddenly right with the world. He was completely relaxed with an ease that came after great sex and a hard, deep sleep. He almost didn't want to wake up, to face the day, to have to think about the decisions he'd made regarding his past and his future. He just wanted to stay in this warm, wonderful place, the place Ria had created.

God! What a woman. So beautiful with her shoulder length silky blonde hair, brown eyes, sunburned nose, and a mouth just made for kissing. She'd brought a light into his life, a beauty that he hadn't seen in a while. She'd been passionate, generous and fun. They hadn't just made love; they'd laughed, and they'd talked, and the sound of her voice had warmed him.

He'd come to the island to relax, to recharge, to find his smile again, and he'd found it in her arms. She'd smelled like orange blossoms, like the flowers surrounding his beachside cottage, and he'd felt like he could breathe in her scent forever, and forever wouldn't be long enough.

That thought jolted him awake. He didn't think of women in terms of forever. Having just himself to worry about was a lot easier than having to worry about anyone else. But that didn't mean he couldn't enjoy the time they had together.

He rolled over on to his side, reaching for the soft curves he'd explored for the better part of the night.

Ria wasn't there.

He sat up abruptly, realizing how quiet the cottage was. The bathroom was empty, and while his clothes were still tossed on the floor, Ria's were gone. There was no sign of her white shorts or pink tank top. No sign of the lacy pink bra and matching thong he'd peeled off her body just a few hours earlier.

He felt a wave of disappointment. He was leaving this afternoon, but he'd thought they'd have a few more hours together. He wanted to know more about her. He wanted to talk to her, at least to say goodbye. What a strange feeling that was. He was used to leaving first, to avoiding morning-after conversations, but this time Ria had beat him to the door, and he didn't like it.

He flopped back against the pillows and stared up at the ceiling. Memories of the night before flashed through his mind. The heat between them had burned all night long. It had been a long time since he'd felt—swept away. He'd always been one to over-think, over-analyze, but last night his body had completely taken over. He hadn't given one thought to what would happen next, until now.

Now, it was obvious nothing would happen. Ria was gone. He should be happy about that. No goodbyes, no messy emotional scenes, no promises to call or keep in touch. It was in actuality the perfect morning after a one-night stand. The only problem was that he didn't want it to be over yet.

He told himself it was better this way. He was starting his new job on Tuesday, a job thousands of miles away from this island. The next phase of his life was about to begin, and he needed to be looking forward instead of backward.

Getting up, he headed to the bathroom and took a long shower, trying to drive Ria out of his head. But as he soaped up, all he could think about was the way she'd touched him, kissed him, smiled at him, and cried out his name as they'd climaxed together.

Damn! He turned the water temperature to cold and stayed under the spray until he was freezing. Then he stepped out of the shower, dried off and got dressed. He threw the rest of his clothes into the duffel bag and glanced around the cottage to make sure he wasn't leaving anything behind.

He couldn't shake the feeling that what he was leaving behind was the one and only woman who'd touched his soul, and he didn't even know her last name.

Was he just going to walk away?

The question ran around and around in his head.

He finally came up with an answer—*no*.

He had a few hours before his plane left. He would find her, talk to her, maybe get her phone number. Walking outside, he paused, realizing he didn't know where she lived, and the bar/restaurant where she worked didn't open until lunchtime.

Then he remembered that she'd told him she was taking out a boat charter in the morning. He felt marginally better realizing that she'd left early to go to work. Someone at the marina would be able to help him find her, or at least tell him when she'd be back.

The dock was only a short walk away. Colorful sailboats

and well-worn fishing boats filled the slips. In the distance was an enormous luxury yacht. He wondered who that belonged to—someone with a lot of money. Probably one of the people who lived in the mountaintop mansions that he'd noticed while bodysurfing the previous day. It would be nice to have enough money to have a home on an island. He didn't see that in his future.

Near the entrance to the pier was a small building with a sign that read Sea Charters.

He entered the building and stepped up to the counter. A young Hispanic man with a nametag that read Juan greeted him with a friendly smile.

"Hola, Señor. How can I help you?" Juan asked.

"I'm looking for a woman. Her name is Ria. Do you know her?"

"Si," Juan said with a nod. "Ria is a beautiful girl, very popular with the customers."

"Do you know when she'll be back?"

Juan glanced down at the large calendar on the counter. "A few hours. I have other guides available if you want to go out."

"No," he said, tapping his fingers restlessly on the counter.

So that was that. Ria was out on the ocean and probably wouldn't be back before he had to catch his plane.

"Do you want me to give her a message for you?" Juan asked, a curious gleam in his eyes.

Drew thought about that for a moment, then shook his head. What the hell was he doing? It was a hookup. That's all. He needed to let it be.

"No, thanks."

As he walked out of the office, a thunderous boom lit up the air, rocking the ground under his feet. He heard a gasp from a group of tourists on the pier. Then the door opened behind him, and Juan rushed out. Together, they looked toward the sea. Over the curve of the nearby hill, they could see smoke racing toward the sky.

"What was that?" Drew asked.

"I don't know," Juan said. He ran down the pier toward the Harbormaster's office, and Drew decided to follow.

A crowd of people gathered outside the office. Rumors were flying, all centering around a boat explosion.

Drew's stomach turned. It was crazy to think the explosion had anything to do with Ria, but he had a really bad feeling in his gut.

"Juan, I've changed my mind," he said. "I need to rent a boat."

The other man looked reluctant. "Better to wait. We should stay out of the way."

"I do search and rescue for the U.S. Coast Guard." He pulled out his wallet and all the cash he had. "I need a boat."

Juan's greed won out. "I'll take you."

It took several minutes for them to launch a boat and maneuver their way through the harbor, as more than a few people had had the same idea and desire to help. It seemed to take forever to get past the breakwater, the reef and then around the island hills.

A good thirty minutes had passed by the time they reached the burning vessel, or what was left of it. It had been completely blown apart, with nothing but fiery debris floating in the water while divers began to search the ocean for survivors.

Drew's chest was so tight he could barely get the words out. "It's not the boat Ria was on, is it?"

Juan's somber gaze said it all. Drew stripped off his shirt.

"What are you doing?" Juan asked.

"I'm going to find her."

"There's nothing left of the boat."

"She could have jumped off before the explosion. How many other people were on the boat?"

Juan shook his head. "I don't know. She made the reservation—probably one or two. I didn't see them board. They left before I got to work."

Drew looked at the debris field and couldn't imagine how anyone could have survived, but he wasn't going to give up without a fight. This is what he did—he saved people. And he was going to save Ria.

He kicked off his shoes and dove into the water. It was a strange feeling to be the one in the water when he was usually the one flying the helicopter that launched rescue swimmers into the sea. For the first time in a long time, he wasn't hovering above the scene, he was right in the thick of it.

For almost two hours, he searched for Ria, but he couldn't find her. He couldn't find anyone.

When a shiny piece of gold floated by him, Drew could no longer deny reality. It was Ria's necklace, the one he'd tugged at with his teeth as it lay in the valley of her breasts. He grabbed it and swam back to the boat. He felt completely exhausted and overwhelmed by unexpected emotion and a terrible certainty.

He stared at the gold heart with the emerald stone and knew that Ria was gone. Beautiful, sexy Ria was dead. He was never going to see her again. One night was all they would ever have.

Falling For A Stranger Releases June 2015!

About The Author

Barbara Freethy is a #1 New York Times Bestselling Author of 42 novels ranging from contemporary romance to romantic suspense and women's fiction. Traditionally published for many years, Barbara opened her own publishing company in 2011 and has since sold over 5 million books! Nineteen of her titles have appeared on the New York Times and USA Today Bestseller Lists.

Known for her emotional and compelling stories of love, family, mystery and romance, Barbara enjoys writing about ordinary people caught up in extraordinary adventures. Barbara's books have won numerous awards. She is a six-time finalist for the RITA for best contemporary romance from Romance Writers of America and a two-time winner for DANIEL'S GIFT and THE WAY BACK HOME.

Barbara has lived all over the state of California and currently resides in Northern California where she draws much of her inspiration from the beautiful bay area.

For a complete listing of books, as well as excerpts and contests, and to connect with Barbara:

Visit Barbara's Website:
www.barbarafreethy.com

Join Barbara on Facebook:
www.facebook.com/barbarafreethybooks

Follow Barbara on Twitter:
www.twitter.com/barbarafreethy